THE POLICE
CHOPPER
WAS SEARCHING
FOR WALKER...

•

He ran low and fast, legs pumping as
though the Cong were cutting a rapid-fire
trail behind him. He crawled into a small
clearing by the road, bringing the butt of
the 30-60 rifle to his shoulder.

*Come on, you fat, nosy bird! Let me
show you a nice little trick only a scum-dog
pig would fall for!* He switched his flashlight
on, then off. The pilot swung the chopper
over to investigate.

Hissing like a cornered cobra, Walker
flung himself to his knees, swung the rifle
skyward, and put a slug right into the
middle of that damnable light.

•

BLAC
MOON

BLACK MOON

BY RON POTTS

POPULAR LIBRARY

An Imprint of Warner Books, Inc.

A Warner Communications Company

POPULAR LIBRARY EDITION

Popular Library® and the fanciful P design are registered
trademarks of Warner Books, Inc.

Cover art by Greg Olanoff
Cover design by Jackie Merri Meyer

Popular Library books are published by
Warner Books, Inc.
666 Fifth Avenue
New York, N.Y. 10103

 A Warner Communications Company

Printed in the United States of America

First Printing: August, 1987

10 9 8 7 6 5 4 3 2 1

To those who've been there.
Especially to Al Zuckerman for his infinite patience and understanding.

Oh, I hope you fall in a punji pit, doo-dah, doo-dah,
I hope you fall in a punji pit, oh, doo-dah day.
They'll send you home in a body bag, doo-dah,
    doo-dah,
They'll send you home in a body bag, oh, doo-dah day.
So why don't we fight all night, why don't we fight
    all day,
They'll send us all home in a body bag, oh, doo-dah
    day.

> —Old American folk song

"You are the iron wall of defense around America. You
have but one purpose...and that is to close with and
destroy the enemy. You have no other purpose."

> —Old Army lecture

A Note to the Reader

Involved in the Vietnam War were certain commando detachments known as "black units." Spooks, the line grunts called them. They wore no unit patches. They wore no dog tags. The only thing they wore were tiger fatigues and some of the most sophisticated firearms ever seen in the history of creation. They took off in the middle of the night in unmarked choppers to go God knows where to do God knows what. Nobody ever referred to CIA as CIA. They took their orders from Air America. They participated in such tricks as Operation Phoenix. They infiltrated denied territory and harassed the enemy in its own bedroom. They asked no quarter and they gave none. And if they bit the bullet, well, tough shit. Because nobody knew who they were. But what would I know?

—Code Name: Commando Snowbird

CHAPTER
ONE

The transport van was brand-new, shiny green, and purring quietly down the winding mountain road, effortlessly swaying around the bigger ruts. It was a lot more comfortable than the older rattletraps, which were so rust-riddled and airy that the prisoners choked from dust and exhaust fumes. A heavy, wire-mesh barrier separated the driver from anyone in the back. The benches along the walls of the cage behind the mesh were padded with black vinyl, not yet torn to hell by vandalizing inmates venting their frustrations. There was even a layer of carpet on the floor.

Big Bill Ridley, the van's operator, was a monstrous pile of excess flesh and fat, and he was possessed of a miserable disposition. These were seeming favorable qualities among prison guards.

"No smokin' back there!" he snarled over his shoulder at the lone prisoner. The screw's hairy forearm rested on the wheel as he steered around a bump in the road. "A damn fool can see there ain't no ashtrays back there. State puts out

1

good money to make it easier on you guys, and all you do is fuck things up!"

The vast mountain forest was brilliant in its autumn glory. A soft breeze made the bright red, yellow, and orange leaves of the giant sawtooth poplar, which were interspersed among the endless miles of evergreens, shimmer like fire. And the sun shining down from a cloudless blue sky enhanced the rich colors. The occupants of the van, however, were so engrossed in their dark moods that they were unable to appreciate the spectacular beauty revealed throughout the rolling hills.

Big Bill's jaw was tight with righteous rage, and his quivering jowls gave him the appearance of an overfed bulldog. He shook a cigarette out of his own pack and lit it with the engraved lighter that his equally obese wife had given him for his last birthday. He sucked smoke deep, then snorted it out through his nose.

Christ, but these uppity punks were getting on his nerves more and more each day. The bastards all ought to be out on the goddamned chain gang where they belonged, instead of sitting around like hogs in hog heaven, bitching about rights this and rights that. No wonder there was so much crime in the country today. Sons of bitches go out and break every law in the book, and all the state ever does is pamper 'em like they weren't but a bunch of naughty brats and lets 'em have anything their thievin' little hearts desire. Like that new prison they built up on Buckley Ridge where Big Bill worked. Hell, those bums lived better up there than his daughter did at the university downstate. They slept on fat bunks and ate better grub than they ever did out on the streets. They could get just about whatever schooling they wanted without it costing them a blessed nickel, yet they still complain. All they ever do is bitch, bitch, bitch. Same story, even if you gave 'em everything but the goddamned key to the gate.

Bill glanced in the rearview mirror. His beefy, whiskey-veined face reddened, and his narrow eyes sparked anger.

Impertinent little fucker! Still smokin'! See, by God, they don't even pay attention to a word you say anymore!

"I said put that goddamn cigarette out, fella, and I mean do it right now!" The screw's harsh voice thundered dully within the confined van. He was unaware that he had accelerated the van beyond the posted speed limit.

The lean, skeletal-visaged man behind the cage caught Big Bill's slitty glare in the mirror and held it. Big Bill had been on the job long enough to know that he did not like the noticeable lack of fear in those deep eyes. In fact, he did not like those eyes at all. There was a disturbing quality to them. It was like they were sad or forlorn, and yet—what else was it—murderous?

Come to think of it, Bill didn't much care for Jim Walker at all. He was somehow different from the other cons, and even though he was slight of frame, not even the bullies or queers ever fucked with him. Unusual in itself. Maybe it was the way he carried himself; it was like even when he was walking around normally, he always seemed to be sneaking up on something. Uncomfortably, it reminded Bill of the time he'd been making his rounds and was strolling down what he thought was an empty corridor when a light finger tapping him on the back had nearly caused him to jump out of his skin. And there stood Walker behind him, smiling like a school kid. "Got a light?" had been the whispery request. Bill wasn't articulate enough to express it, but he thought he sensed a lurking menace beneath that cool, quiet demeanor.

An odd feeling crept up his spine. He wanted to look away, break contact, but he didn't. You must never back down from an inmate, no matter what.

The prisoner finally solved the dilemma, allowing Ridley to focus his attention back on the road before he ran off it. Walker looked away, aware of this simple defeat, recognizing his helplessness against the monster system that had gobbled him up. How are you supposed to play a hand when the pigs had every card in the deck? If they wanted to deal you shit, you got shit. After all, it was their game—and you had to play by their rules simply because there were no other rules. Break a rule and they're going to ream you, that damn simple. How well Walker knew that they might ream you, anyway, whether you broke a rule or not. Even still, there was this thing about a man's honor, a man's pride, a man's human dignity. Sure, the jails were full of scumbags. And it takes an asshole to deal with a jerk. But something was wrong somewhere. Something. Something god-awful wrong. Like that screw's eyes. For a second, just for the briefest flash, they looked—God help me—they looked just like a fuckin' gook's eyes!

The inmate slowly brought his shackled hands up to his lips. He took a long, deep drag from the condemned cigarette, then let it drop on the new carpet where he ground it under his heel.

This sent Big Bill bananas over what was obviously a deliberate desecration of the brand-new official vehicle that he had been placed in charge of. Sloppy bastard should have put it out on the sole of his shoe or something. Shouldn't have had it lit in the first place!

"By God, Walker, you little punk! You just bought ten days in seg for that! And you'll scrub this van inside and out just as soon as we get back! Jeezus! What ails your head, boy? Christ, you don't need X rays, you need a goddamn shrink!"

Bill puffed furiously on his own cigarette, accelerated even more, then finally checked his speed, wondering why he was letting Walker rattle him so. It was because there was something creepy about the guy, that's why. Certifiable nut, that's what he was. Hardly ever said two words to anybody. The quiet ones were the ones you watched—no telling what they were thinking. Big Bill would be glad to get him into that hospital, get his damned X rays done, get him back to the prison, and be done with him. Creepy son of a bitch. Always drawing pictures of dead people and bombs and shit. As far as Ridley was concerned, Walker didn't need to be in jail, he needed to be in the damned loony bin!

Suddenly Bill didn't like the idea of being alone with him.

He wished another guard had come along. A premonition swept over him that he struggled with his undeveloped mind to identify. He even found himself wondering why in the hell they hadn't included X-ray facilities when building the new prison. Then you wouldn't have to run these whining assholes to a civilized hospital every time they sprained an ankle or bumped a knee.

But the screw's bullish machoism quickly dispelled his silly notions. Hell, he could wring that scrawny prick's neck with one hand. Besides, none of the other officers considered Walker a high-security risk, because if he was, he'd still be behind the Big Walls, since Buckley Ridge was medium-security, reserved as a privilege for cons exhibiting good behavior. And Walker was always mild-mannered enough around the block, always doing as he was told. Playing the game like a good little inmate. Maybe that was the trouble . . . playing the game.

> Walker, James, a.k.a. "Crazy Jim." Docket number 8592-A. Aggravated assault with intent to commit robbery. Felony Class A. Guilty as charged.
> Sentenced: five years to the custody of the Department of Corrections followed by two years' probation.
> Special conditions to probation: that the defendant undergo psychiatric treatment.

Something god-awful wrong somewhere. Walker had seen it. He'd been on office cleanup duty when he'd chanced across the inmate transfer papers on the two-to-nine officer's desk. At first he thought it was an hallucination, a dream, like the continuous parade of intrusive war images that had been dancing through his head lately. So he had picked the papers up, examined them, felt them to make sure they were real. Then, horror-struck . . . he realized. The whole scenario had been an elaborate setup. J was coming for him, anyway. Colonel Jarvis. Coming to take him back. And then, for the first time in years his mind had exploded in a blinding rush of animal rage. Images, faces among shattered ruins, come rising and screaming out of the stinking jungle, come to take me back. No! *Tiger cages. Pathet Lao. Montagnard scouts squatting in the compound, their hands tied behind them. Murdered. Sharpened bamboo stakes hammered through their ears. Kill! Kill!*

He had known he was under surveillance for over two weeks. Nobody has to tell a commando when he's being watched. You don't learn that trick, baby, and you don't walk out of it alive. And then came the phone call. Walker's body went rigid, and the slightest tremor swept through him. It was Colonel J, a voice from the grave. J wanted to talk, alone. A safe place, in a crowded bar. No tricks.

Somehow J didn't look so powerful, so impressive, under the dim lights at a far table in a roadside bar. But then he rose and the power returned. But it didn't matter. Because tucked beneath Walker's oversize leather jacket was a MAC-10 submachine pistol, capable of laying out an awesome burst of firepower. At the slightest indication of treachery he would cut J in half. J knew it.

They stood staring at each other for a long time, frozen statues carved in ice. And then they sat, slowly, carefully, and a cloud of tension hung thick enough to slice with a knife.

"What do you want?" Walker asked, his voice barely audible above the din of the jukebox.

J's answer sent a freezing blade of fear through Walker's heart. "The technicians want you back."

"Why?"

"They think you may not be sufficiently deprogrammed. They think you may be unstable."

"Why now, after all these years?"

"You, Mike, and Lou were the last survivors of the team. Mike and Lou fell apart within weeks of each other. Did some terrible things. They had to be hospitalized."

"Where? At the lab?"

"Yes."

Long moments of silence passed, interrupted by noisy patrons and the blaring of the jukebox. The two men stared at each other again, unmoving, jaws clenched. And Walker's right hand lurked dangerously close to his unzipped jacket.

"Have you come to take me back?" The threat of instant death hung behind the answer to that point-blank question.

Yet J showed no fear. He never did. "I was supposed to," he replied simply. "But I can help you . . . if you can help me." No words were ever minced among men of this nature. No beating around the bush. No cat and mouse. They understood each other even before the thoughts were expressed. They had to. There was a time when all their lives had depended on it. And they did it to such a degree as to be almost uncanny. But now there were not many of those lives left. "I need a night stalker. The best."

"Why? And why me?"

"I told you, Mike and Lou lost it and had to be reeled in. That leaves you. You, because there can be no mistakes. It could easily have international repercussions. You understand the mission. As you know, your destination and your target will be revealed to you when the time comes, but it is a city on the coast. We found a safe house, and we found the dead drop. But we don't know what they're dropping. And we don't dare approach the drop for fear they'll move it. Because three days from now a courier is expected to approach with highly significant information. Your mission will be to lay for the courier. Deliver a nonlethal strike—for God's sake don't kill him, just cold-cock him—clean him out, and deliver those items to the designated rendezvous. Not hard for a man of your unique talents."

Walker took a sip from the beer on his table . . . left-handed. "No, not hard. But what country will I be striking against? And how will it benefit me?"

J leaned across the table, and his voice grew harsh. "You are a commando! Why should you care what country, so long as they are enemies! As for your benefits . . . well . . . do this for me and I will make you free. I need a night stalker. You were trained for it. Complete this mission and I will tell the technicians that you can't be found. You can go back to your mountain hideaway with that girl of yours and you will never hear from me again. Ever."

So Walker had done it. He'd lain motionless in the shadows of an alley for hours, waiting for his target to arrive. Finally the courier came by. He'd been dropped in his tracks by a precise blow to the base of his skull, knocking him colder than yesterday's breakfast. But it was while he was rifling the man's pockets that he was suddenly confronted by more than half a dozen yawning gun barrels, with one specific law officer emphatically stating, "Freeze!" What the fuck . . . ? Had the courier been under a stakeout? Why hadn't J mentioned the possibility?

Because it was a motherfuckin' setup, that's why!

Like the 'Nam Dinh conspiracy, when Walker had been sent north, alone, to murder a Russian technical adviser who was teaching the enemy the use of advanced ordnance and such tactics as were not necessary for a somewhat backward people to know. Walker had accomplished his mission, all right. He'd penetrated deep within the enemy compound and had soundlessly knifed the fucker in his sleep. Clean and flawless infiltration. It was during the exfiltration that things went wrong. Why? A simple accident of fate? Or a tip-off? But Walker had fought his way out with the skilled use of himself, his automatics, and his grenades. And it was only when he'd confronted the startled look of amazement on Colonel Jarvis's iron face that he'd fully understood. The unknown assassin had been meant to be a sacrifice in order to appease the death of an important man. A high adviser terminated on the night of a black moon when the kill squads roam the jungle. We couldn't have the enemy screaming, Cheaters! Geneva Convention! now could we?

J had smiled with tightly clenched teeth. So glad to see you made it back, soldier. Walker had smiled with tightly clenched teeth, his body bruised and bleeding from the thrashing he had taken in the bush.

Yes, I'll just bet you are, Colonel. Bet I know something you know.

Maybe so, soldier. But that's all irrelevant now, isn't it? Don't worry, though, there'll be a new mission.

And over ten years later, on the streets of a Maine city, a new mission came. And, like a fool, Walker stepped right into it again.

Segregation. Walker couldn't do seg time. It was hard enough being locked in his cell at night. Every time that heavy steel door slammed shut behind him, it was all he could do to control the unreasonable panic that seized him. Locked alive in a cold steel tomb. And they're all going to die, and nobody is ever going to come and let you out! Then the panic would step aside and the rage would take over. Rage! That they could do such a thing to a fellow American. A man who had fought, who had killed for the precious freedom they were depriving him of.

Rage!

No, he could no more allow himself to be locked in seg than he could let someone bury him alive. Not just because of his claustrophobic horror but because J would find him there in naked helplessness, utter despair. And J would take him back. J, in his treachery, would deliver him to the technicians. The technicians. With their needles, their mind-altering substances, their lab. Nobody leaves this place alive! Poor Mike and Lou.

Walker stared disconsolately at the cuffs on his wrists.

And then came a terrible sensation that he had not felt since the war. Was he really losing it like Mike and Lou? The familiar clacking began at the back of his skull. Soundless clacking, yet he heard it from within. Heavy metallic clacking rising up the back of his head, splitting through his brain, making his mind scream, What would a commando do?

The van wheeled adeptly into the Corinth Community Hospital parking lot. It was full of cars, but Big Bill finally found a space along a distant row, under a big maple tree. He rightly figured people didn't park there because they didn't want bird shit on their hoods. Bill didn't care, seeing's how Walker was going to scrub the van when they got back, anyway. He figured.

The big guard took out his logbook and penned 1345 hours in the appropriate section. Then he removed the microphone from the mobile unit bolted to the dashboard and pressed the transmit button.

"Unit 59 to Unit 30, come 'own." He drawled his words in the tradition of a flaked-out cowboy CBer, even though north-central Maine was not what one would consider southern by any standards. Walker grimaced. The game.

"10-3, Unit 59," the receiver crackled.

"Have arrived at destination. Over and out."

Bill replaced the mike. He took the keys from the van and stuffed them in his right pants pocket, and this was no easy maneuver. The light green uniforms, with the black stripe down the legs, came in only so many sizes, and Bill's fit him tightly. He had to jack his ass up off the seat in order to fit the keys in. And when he did that, the black epaulets on his shoulders threatened to sever themselves from the main material of the shirt, and the buttons across his gut seemed like they would surely pop.

He picked up the manila envelope containing Walker's medical records and got out of the van, shouldering the door hard. Had he taken a quick glance back over his shoulder, he would have seen his caged prisoner hunched tightly, watching him the way a half-starved vulture puts the mean eye on a dying beef.

The panel door slid open and Walker stepped out, pushing his manacled hands before him, squinting hard against the bright and chilly November sun. Hai, fuckers! So this is the hospital, he thought, closely observing the modern, rambling white building. From his lonely, solitary distance he had listened very carefully to prison talk, separating the bullshit from the reality . . . and he had learned that the hospital was considered the best bet for escape . . . and the need for X rays was the best way to get to the hospital.

So he had feigned back pain in order to check it out. Pulled a reconnaissance, or, as the boys in the outfit used to say, a ree-con. But things change. Nothing ever stays the same. Nothing. Now J was coming for him, to take him back to the technicians. Party's over now, pal.

Walker could've taken the rap. He could've done the time standing on his head. Five years? Shit, with the good-time law he would have been out in less than three . . . and it would have been worth it, so long as he came out free. Free forever. But now they wanted to take him back to the lab. Sure. If you want needles with God knows what jacked up your arm day after day, if you want to end your life as an experimental war zombie like Mike and Lou, then let them take you back.

Otherwise, go for the gusto and pick your own way of dying! Which meant that every move now, from here on out, would be absolutely critical. Like J said—no mistakes. J, thrusting his gnarled hand up out of the jungle stench, coming to snatch him back. . . .

Big Bill Ridley loomed like an aerosol-smelling monster in front of the prisoner, fists planted on wide hips, sneering in disgust. Disgust at himself for ever having thought that this puny punk could even hope to offer him any real resistance (but what he didn't know was that Walker always wore loose clothing over his slight frame, effectively concealing sinewy, steel-trap muscles; what he didn't know was that Walker was capable of striking with a velocity sufficient to tear half a man's face off).

"Now you listen up good, Walker, 'cause you're in enough hot water with me already. You give me any shit in there—and I mean any trouble at all—your ass is grass and I'm gonna be the lawn mower. And if you try to run, or if you even look like you're gonna try to run, then I'm gonna shoot. And I'm gonna *shoot to kill*. You got that?"

Code word! Christ, that fat fucker just hit me with a code word! Clack . . . and Walker's mind slipped into overdrive. Shoot to kill! Chemical indoctrination, they called it. Shoot to kill! It will make you *see*, they said. It will make you *feel*, they said. It will make you *move*. And then they would ram the injection up your arm, and it would make your head clack and your mind scream from within, and it would make you *murder!*

"You got that?" The harsh voice barked again, and Walker snapped out of it.

Is this the way it was for Mike and Lou? Walker wondered. Is this how they lost it, because, by Christ, I'm losing it too!

He looked up at Big Bill with a glazed expression and smiled. "Sure, I got that. Besides, you don't have to worry about me. The boys might think I'm a little loose upstairs, but I know better than to try on a man your size, Billy Boy."

The hefty screw grunted. "Good. You can either make it easy on yourself, or you can make it tough. Now let's go." As an afterthought he added, "And if you ever call me Billy Boy again, smartass, I'm gonna slap the shit out of you for attemptin' to assault an officer!"

They walked across the parking lot with Ridley gripping Walker by the elbow, maneuvering him between the rows of cars. They went through the glass doors at the main entrance and entered the carpeted lobby. A lot of people were sitting in the reception lounge, thumbing magazines, trying to act as though there were nothing in the world unusual about a valiant guard escorting a furtive-eyed, weasely-looking criminal among them. Shackled, thank God, the population was safe against him. They didn't want to draw attention to themselves, so they tried not to look. But they were looking, anyway, conjuring visions of cat burglars, murderers, rapists, crazed drug dealers. What did that one do?

They were looking all right. Walker could feel it. His teeth were clenched as he swallowed the bitter bile of his humiliation. They don't even know who I am, he was thinking. Or what I am. Or what I've seen and done. All they see is the naked disgrace of a dirty little white boy being paraded in front of his fellowman, chained like a circus beast, stripped of his human dignity, pushed around by an arrogant, insufferable idiot. Ridley. Fat boy. Sucking it all up like a vacuum cleaner sucks up dirt. Swaggering around like he shit himself. Chest puffed, jaw thrust forward. Yes, sir, folks, no need to fear, John J. Law here. I got the law-breakin' faggot right by the balls. And I *shoot to kill.* . . .

Ridley. Billy boy. You stupid, jerkoff screw. You ignorant lard-ass motherfucker. You never should have said that, Ridley, boy. You never, never should have said that to a commando!

Ridley had a word with the lady at the information desk. Then he took Walker by the elbow and steered him down a long, busy corridor, dodging bustling, white-dressed nurses and orderlies and respectfully stepping aside for wheelchair traffic. The two of them turned left at an intersection and went about halfway down another hallway, stopping at an inset cubicle that had a sign above it reading LAB.

Big Bill gave the manila envelope to a bespectacled, frowning old fat lady behind the typewriter. "X rays," he grunted. He jerked a thumb at his charge. "Claims he's got lower back pain," saying it in such a way as to insinuate the prisoner was lying, and that made Walker's lip curl.

But the grim receptionist was unamused. She asked Walker a few crisp questions, typing his answers with lightning ease. Pure business, she ripped the paper from the roller and handed it, with another paper, to a lady wearing a long lab coat.

The lab technician turned, and Walker's heart jumped as he found himself staring. Her face—soft and delicate beneath flowing blond hair. Like Claudine. Innocent, sensitive Claudine, who would hold him and rock him gently against her soft breast. And she would be unable to hide the pain of her deep understanding. Sometimes she would merely look at him and burst into tears. And he would feel dirty in her presence. Ugly. Defiled. As though he could stand under the shower all day and never come clean. And then sometimes the intrusive images would consume him, war-blasted bodies strewn across the slimiest hellholes in the universe. And the clacking would come up the back of his head and his mind would explode from within and he would scream and smash holes in the walls until his fists were bloody stumps. And Claudine would cry. And cry. And cry.

"Come with me, please," the lab technician said, her manner also portraying plain business, and Walker found himself being urged along. She moved briskly down the hall, then turned right as he followed.

Walker saw a red exit sign way down at the far end and noted that there was little traffic in this corridor. And with a certain amount of disgust he was also aware of Ridley's pronounced swagger. Impressing the ladies, are we, Billy Boy?

They went into the X-ray room, the big machinery squatting impassively in the middle of the floor, patiently waiting to probe invisible radiation through the next victim. Walker's nose twitched at the tang of disinfectant. They could use every cleaning product on the market, but to him, hospitals still smelled like lingering death, and nothing could ever wash it away.

The lab technician, whose name tag said Arlene (*Ay, Claudine!*), brusquely handed Walker a backless johnny-smock. "You'll have to undress down to your shorts," she said. Then she went to the side counter and rummaged through a drawer for the proper ID tags to attach to the X-ray plates.

There was a hard, warning look in Ridley's eyes as he reluctantly fished out the keys to the handcuffs. If he hadn't been so dense, if he hadn't been so thoroughly immersed in fascination with his own self-image, he might have thought it odd, or even *felt* it odd, that Walker was not looking away this time—that Walker was glaring weirdly, unblinkingly, trancelike.

That's because Walker could not do seg time. The cold horror of lying naked in a locked steel tomb. And nobody is ever going to come and let you out! And J will find you there, lost in a nightmare of loneliness and despair. And J will take you back. And the technicians will work on you. And you will never see the sun rise over the mountain again. That wicked lab. They already had your mind, now they want your body. The pigs! The gooks! Shoot to kill. . . .

The cuffs clicked free.

It was like pulling the pin out of a loaded grenade and watching the handle fly off while it was still in your hand. Some dull, buried instinct deep in Ridley's brain warned him

of danger. That sudden flash of animal insight also told him
that it was too late to do anything about it. In the split second that it took Walker to tighten up with a short step backward, Ridley knew with dead certainty that he was fucked.

Walker speed-kicked with mighty force, his face and neck
muscles distorted by the exertion. He kicked Ridley in the
nuts so hard, the guard puked, splattering his vomit all over
his assailant's pant leg. Gasping horribly, the big man buck-
led forward, following a savage elbow smash to the side of
his head, which rattled his teeth, blackened his vision, and
sent him toppling heavily to the floor. There he helplessly
squirmed in more pain than he had ever known.

Walker streaked across the room, a sudden blur of precise
movement. He had hold of the terrified nurse even as Ridley
was falling. Her mouth was open, poised for a scream, but
nothing came out. Walker had her by a handful of blouse
(*Don't kill her!*), and his fist was cocked back, karate-style,
for a power punch that would knock her unconscious, maybe
even break her neck. The blow wasn't necessary, though.
Her eyes rolled back in their sockets and she fainted with a
sigh. Relieved, Walker let her limp body drop. Only for the
briefest second did a softness wash across his violence-tight
face, as he looked down upon the fallen girl, crumpled in
white. Arlene. *Claudine*. So vulnerable. A poor victim of
the tragedy of existence.

He worked quickly but without frantic haste. He was a
commando, and commandos, by God, have their shit together. And this was war—just like in the 'Nam. Hey, hey!
Look out now, motherfuckers!

The first thing he did was to go to the lab sink and wet the
smock the nurse had given him. He cleaned the vomit off his
jeans. He was glad the "progressive" prison allowed you to
wear your personal clothing instead of uniforms. It saved
him the problem of wasting time trying to find something
else to wear. Anyway, he didn't want to attract attention to
himself with puke on his pants. That it belonged to Ridley
made it all the more disgusting.

Ridley lay doubled up, his knees practically touching his

chin. His face had an odd, sweaty sheen, and he was rasping in a peculiar manner, his jaw working like a fish out of water, slime dribbling out of the corner of his mouth. For a moment Walker was afraid he might have killed the man. Even though the karate blows had been delivered with commando force, it had not been his intention to grease the screw.

Walker's main concern right now, though, was that the fat son of a whore was lying on his left side, leaving easy access to the gun and the pocket with the van keys. Having to roll that mountain of blubber over would surely have been a pain in the ying-yang.

The gun was a .38 police special revolver, with a pack of speed-loaders on the belt. It was fully loaded with the exception of the empty chamber upon which the hammer was resting. Walker tucked the gun under his shirt, experiencing a rush of confidence at the hard feel of the cold metal against his belly. We'll see which way the shit flies now, he grimly thought. You want me, do you, Colonel, baby? Well, come right on! If the Lord has any mercy at all, at least one of these slugs will have your name on it!

He was surprised when he pulled out from the pocket a roll of bills, along with the van keys. Prison guards weren't supposed to carry money on their person while on duty. The reason was so that potential escapees like Walker couldn't rob them like he was doing just now. A few hundred bucks there. Dirty bastard was probably on the take, wheeling and dealing contraband with the inmates.

Walker took a last scornful look at the disabled enemy who had previously tormented him. He scooted down to the gasping, squirming Ridley and grabbed him by the hair and yanked his ear close. "Shoot to kill, huh?" he whispered harshly. "That was the worst thing in the world you could have said. Now look at you, you're in bad shape, Billy Boy. Your own fault. Next time you threaten to kill someone, know your enemy, because you stepped right out of your class this time, pal. I just gave you a lesson in what tough shit is. So long, sucker." He let go of the hair with a violent shove, and Ridley's head bounced off the hard, tiled floor, and he kept groaning.

Careful now, Walker crept to the door, opened it, and peered out. The corridor was clear. He eased out, closing the door behind him, sauntering toward the exit light, walking casually, unhurried, reorienting himself with the familiar feel of danger. His back felt like a naked bull's-eye, jacking up his pulse rate, also a familiar sensation. High tension. Curiously he welcomed it back like a lover gone too long. The prospect of a shoot-out filled him with a dark warmth . . . a dark warmth like drowning in his mother's womb. He was a commando. He was not a natural man.

Superintendent Collins, the treacherous bastard. No wonder he never answered Walker's request for a discussion on a parole hearing. Collins must have known the transfer was going to take place, and he never intended to let Walker know until it was too late. Poor, stupid fool. If only he knew what Colonel Jarvis was. But Walker knew. And it was all or nothing now. He'd rather get shot down with his back against the wall than let J reclaim him. So go for the big time, baby. Take it tothe limit. He was staking it all on this one play. He had nothing to lose, and a man with nothing to lose is a clear-cut desperado.

He pushed the release bar on the heavy fire door and stepped outside. The crisp autumn air seemed so much cleaner without Ridley around. Although he was in imminent danger, he felt as though he had been relieved of a great, ugly weight. He breathed deeply, smiled, and looked around to see where he was.

He was at the rear of the hospital where the dumpsters and the loading docks were. No activity back here. The van was parked over to the side, back along three rows of cars. He walked toward it, whistling softly, one hand in his pocket, the other appearing to scratch his belly, close to the gun, fully prepared to use it should any man alive be foolish enough to challenge him. People were coming and going, but no one seemed to be taking any special interest in him. Indeed, why should they? After all, there was no swaggering, lard-ass screw with a weasely criminal to attract their curious stares.

He got in the van, got comfortable in the driver's seat, and inhaled the smell of newness. He put the key in the ignition and fired it up. He laughed. Then he roared, "No smoking back there, motherfuckers!"

As Walker wheeled out onto the main road, easing the van into common traffic, Big Bill Ridley, still kissing the X-ray room floor, went into spasmodic convulsions prior to kicking the bucket. Had he known what it was that had killed him, he might have gone to hell with some of his dignity still intact. Because he would have known just how far out of class he had stepped.

CHAPTER

TWO

The van had barely passed the Corinth city limits sign on the way to the hospital, so the town itself must lie shortly to the south, but Walker didn't want to get caught in any town. He'd be surrounded and roasted to the ground within minutes. So he headed back in the direction of the prison, knowing he was taking an awful chance. He remembered seeing signs directing traffic down tributary roads to I-95, but he didn't want to try that route, either. He was not foolish enough to imagine that he had more than precious little time, and he was sure the area would be sealed off before he could ever make the Interstate. Besides, this bitch rig wouldn't stand a chance in a run against the state troopers on the open highway, and he wasn't armed well enough for a down-and-dirty confrontation. Shit, they'd blow him away like piss in the wind. He had to get off the road, into the woods where a commando belonged. Nobody would ever stop him in the woods. Nobody.

He remembered seeing a logging road shortly up ahead, used, no doubt, by the huge timber-hauling trucks of the

Eastern Pulp and Paper Company. He remembered it because it brought to mind one of his pet peeves concerning the big corporations ripping the forests all to hell. Not just ripping it up, but clear-cutting it, leaving not a twig standing over vast acres. The greedy, money-grubbing bastards. Ripping it all to hell for nothing more than a handful of filthy dollars. Soon the Maine woods would be like Kentucky strip mines, and the slimeballs who flattened it would drift to new horizons, flattening those horizons too. And they always had to tell you something wrong. Something god-awful wrong somewhere. Grease gooks in order to protect rubber plantations. Kill Arabs in order to protect oil fields. Who gives a shit about who gets to be president in the Third World countries—as long as he's willing to do business. That's what it was really all about. They used the good earth, and they used the people on it like suckers at a fish fry. They used Walker like a cheap whore, then threw him in the gutter when his mind began to stink. But now he was back, by God, a stray missile off its trajectory, coming back. He was coming back.

There wasn't much afternoon traffic along Route 15, not unusual in this mountainous region. Other than some isolated lakes visited mostly by hard-core fishermen and hunters, there wasn't much to attract anyone beyond the correctional facility, which was about another fifteen miles up the road.

Walker was lucky. There were no cars on the road to see him when he wheeled off the main drag and disappeared down the logging road. He was in the woods now. He could finally breathe a tremendous sigh of relief. Come now, shitbirds! Come run me down in the kind of country where a commando screams fire! The big forest loomed all around him, big, swaying spruce and fir, choked with underbrush, majestic and wise in its silence, offering him a warm, protective shield against the insanity he had left behind. Safety and refuge against undesirable elements that meant to do him harm. He loved the forest and the forest loved him. He could live in it, wild and free forever. Like a bear. Like a moose. Like a high-bounding deer.

Except it was now hunting season. And they shot to kill. . . .

The rutted dirt road was winding out toward the Moose-head region. Every once in a while Walker caught a glimpse of Mount Katahdin way off in the distance, rising like a giant, angry fist smashing up out of the face of the earth. White-capped, a magnificent deep purple, with lesser ranges trailing down like a long dragon tail. Hell, thanks to the paper companies, these interlinking woodland highways could go for hundreds of miles, skirting the mountains, going way out into the Allagash Wilderness, and even beyond the Canadian border. Walker knew. He'd traveled them before. Before J came and set him up. When he'd run away and left Claudine because he'd thought he was too much of a burden for her. When the woods had been the only sanctuary left to him. When he'd wandered blindly through the remote forests, like a man in a trance, admon-ishing himself for hurting what he loved most and letting the fathomless wilderness soothe his pain, the pain of waking up at night in a cold sweat, tormented by things too horrible to remember. The woods. The jungle. He was only safe in the jungle.

The road was beginning to get awfully rough in places. It was meant for tractor-trailer log-haulers and four-wheel-drives. He'd soon have to start looking for a place to ditch the van, anyway, so it wouldn't get spotted from the air. He figured the alert must be out by now.

He spared the vehicle no mercy. He bounced it full throttle over big rocks, spinning it crazily through wet holes and banging it against trees while skimming around particularly deep ruts. Finally he spotted a passable twitch trail, where the skidder-tractors haul logs up to the head of the road. He gunned the van down it, and soon it was deeply bogged in a swamp. At least it was under a thick stand of evergreens, and since it was painted an accommodating green, it wouldn't be readily found.

He laughed, happy, feeling as free as the chilly breeze that caressed his thin-whiskered face and made his long hair dance. Then he took the tire iron from behind the seat and systematically smashed the shit out of the radio unit, battering it until it was a useless heap of twisted metal, plastic, and wires. "Ten fuckin' four!" he yelled, wild-eyed. He was hurting to blow the whole goddamned van up, but prudence overwhelmed the dangerous impulse. Much as he was intimate with explosions, he knew he didn't need the attention. Besides, it would cost them enough for bodywork if they ever recovered the thing. Another small blow against the corrupt monster machine.

As a gesture of contempt, he drove the tire iron through the radiator before heading back to the logging road. He walked with light, quick steps, pleased with the success of his escape so far. He imagined all kinds of pandemonium back at the hospital.

But the elation was short-lived. Thoughts of J turned his mood dark. Fuck these redneck dipshits. J was the man who had the means to lay your soul to the ground. Either by accident of fate or subconscious drive, Walker was headed north. And north was where Claudine's comfortable little homestead farm was. *No!* He must not see her, no matter how much the longing ached and hurt him. J would come. She would be no match for him. J would tear her apart like a hawk making a feast out of a dove. J, you treacherous, murderous breath of the devil . . . *come for me!*

Then, getting his bearings from the sun, he left the logging road and disappeared into the woods. He waded through brooks and swamps so icy cold that his legs turned numb. Sharp, thick brush and branches tore at his light clothing and scratched his face and arms. He slipped and slid while struggling across heavily wooded ridges, utterly frustrated that the slick soles of his shoes were insufficient in the deep woods. He instinctively knew that if his escape was to remain successful, he would have to find a way to outfit himself. His most immediate fear, though, was the prospect of being mistaken for a deer by an overzealous hunter. After all, the prison didn't provide its inmates with hunter's orange. Not that it would be a good idea to wear it under the circumstances. The irony of that thought brought a sardonic chuckle. Survive all the shit he'd been through only to get wasted by some asshole with buck fever.

The alert was sure enough out, and there was indeed a certain degree of pandemonium. Convict escapes custody, murders guard, steals state vehicle. Armed and you goddamned well better believe dangerous. Thanks to a monitor of the statewide police frequency, on-the-spot reporters were having a field day. They knew about the incident as soon as the cops did.

The hospital was a boiling mess of frenzied activity. Uniformed and plainclothes officials buzzed around like angry bees in a raided hive. Curious onlookers who got in the way were ordered off. Things like this flat and simple didn't happen in a small community like Corinth. This was better than the fistfight they'd had at the last annual church picnic. Generate excitement? Well, I guess. Insults were heartily exchanged between the town cops and the local rowdies, some push came to shove, resulting in a few arrests for disorderly conduct and interfering with an officer. Meanwhile the neighborhood ladies stood around speculating on the scandal of it all. And the air in the parking lot crackled with radio communication, a cacophony of mixed messages and transmitter static. Police cruisers, town, county, and state, squealed in, squealed back out again, leaving black trails of burned rubber, sirens screaming.

The superintendent of corrections was tall and heavy-framed. He was wearing a suit slightly too proper for the present gala, and his rugged, rock-jawed features gave him the look of a determined general. But right now he was looking a little peaked. He was leaning against his car door, an elbow on the roof, his hand massaging his forehead. His other hand limply held the microphone from his mobile unit. "Jesus, I should have known it!" he kept mumbling. "I should have known it."

The paunchy sheriff, standing alongside him, sucked in his gut and hoisted up his gun belt. The sheriff scratched his head. His bristly mustache twitched. "Ain't no sense in blaming yourself, Dick," he said, shifting uncomfortably. "Nobody can guess when a thing like this is going to happen."

"I should have guessed!" Dick Collins exploded. "The two-to-nine officer who assigned only one guard to that lunatic should have guessed!" He dropped the microphone, letting it dangle from its cord, and snatched a sheaf of papers up off the car seat. He shook the papers angrily under the startled sheriff's nose.

"Aggravated assault, Stevens. He hit a guy in the back of the head so hard, he almost broke the poor fucker's neck. He had weapons on him that you couldn't get in a terrorist training camp. Which means he's probably a goddamned shit-crazy shooter. Look at this shit! This guy's been in Vietnam since Ho Chi Minh was a baby. I couldn't have guessed? Long-range recon, says here. Special tactics, says here. What the hell is 'special tactics'? I take it to mean that there's a killer commando on the loose who's accumulated a mental history two miles long with a high-flying death wish at the top of the list. You know what they call him, Stevens? They call him 'Crazy Jim.' That alone ought to tell a man something.

"So because I didn't guess, because that idiot two-to-nine officer didn't guess, I've got a dead officer in there, and an armed lunatic—trained to kill, mind you—running around out there!"

Sheriff Stevens adjusted his Smokey the Bear hat and avoided eye contact with the flustered superintendent. "Well, Dick, the best we can hope for is to catch him fast. We've got roadblocks along every route to the Interstate, and that Warden Service chopper should be airborne in about ten minutes." He laid a hand on Collins's shoulder. "He can't get far, Dick. We'll have him before dark." Then the sheriff got in his car, switched on the blue bubble, and drove off.

Collins stood there a while longer, massaging his forehead, staring absently at the hectic activity moving in and out of the hospital. Ridley in there, in the basement morgue. Just one more day, he was thinking. Just one more day and that colonel—what the hell was his name?—Colonel Jarvis would have been in control of the nut. The inmate transfer request had come in only a few days ago. Official government request, no less. Walker was theirs. Unstable, they called him. They had the proper facility for his treatment, his protection, and everybody else's protection, they said. Everybody else's protection? Is this what they meant? Well, sure. Fine. Collins liked to run a tight ship. If they wanted a potential troublemaker, then take him away. Due to Walker's combat profile, the transfer had even been approved by the governor himself.

Collins sighed, squeezed the tension out of his eyes, and ran his hand through his thick, graying hair. And now the little bastard has poked a hole in the bottom of the boat that was going to take him away. Could it be possible that Walker somehow found out about the transfer? Inmates weren't generally given such information until the last minute, since removal to a new, unfamiliar facility tended to spook them. So why? He either knew something or he had intended to escape in the first place.

Collins got in his car and announced over the radio that he was cruising back toward the prison. There was nothing more he could do here. He had already questioned the traumatized lab technician, Arlene McPherson. She had confirmed Collins's worst suspicions—that Walker was not your typical loudmouthed braggart seen so often in the penal institutions. There were plenty who talked a big fight, or dreamed a bold exploit, but few who had the guts to carry anything out. And those who did have the guts were psychologically unprepared for the stress of a manhunt. They usually blew the game early. Most were rounded up like lost pups and trucked back to the pound within hours of the escape attempt.

Not Walker.

"It all happened so fast!" the trembling nurse had said,

even her voice shaky. "I've seen guys fight in school, you know. But, my God, I've never seen anything like that! He was like a blur. I don't see how anyone could have stopped him. I didn't even know what was happening until I saw that officer falling. Then . . . he grabbed me. I—I was sure he was going to kill me. It was like he was giving off . . . well . . . some kind of evil glow! I'll never forget that weird look. Never!" She had shuddered.

No, Walker was not a cowed fugitive running blind. He was cool—cool, hell; he was as cold as an iceberg—and he was deliberate. He had taken the gun, he had taken the van keys, and knowing Ridley, he probably also had money. The inmate had walked—not run, walked—out to the van and drove off like it was a leisurely Sunday afternoon. No doubt aware of a critical time factor, coupled with the seriousness of his actions, what he did took iron nerve. It also took a deadly kind of skill . . . and that's what bothered Collins the most. Walker had killed an armed guard, twice his size, with nothing but his bare hands. Collins didn't really believe the killing had been intentional. Just too much force. If Walker had been lost in a delirium of homicidal insanity, he probably would have murdered the nurse too. But that was a moot point. The result was still the same. Ridley had been taken out by swift, precise action.

No, Walker was not a big-talking punk. He was a professional of disaster. That much was obvious. Why hadn't anybody been able to see it before? How could anyone be so quietly elusive as to conceal such a deadly nature? And then Collins had a sick feeling that the disaster could get a whole lot worse.

Recognizing the superintendent's car, the cops waved him through the first roadblock about three miles up the road.

Myrna, Collins's wife, would have a shit fit over this one, he was thinking. She was always yammering about the ERA, prisoners' rights, faggots, you name it. Always wasting her time attending every female bitch session in the state instead of cooking meals and cleaning house like a woman ought to be doing. It was because she was getting plump and turning into a bored busybody, he was sure. Well, he couldn't wait to rub her nose in this one. She had it in her liberated mind that all those poor, misguided, disadvantaged boys up on Buckley Ridge were savagely brutalized without recourse to legal protection, and no presentation of solid fact could convince her otherwise. Well, she was wrong, goddammit! They were a bunch of dangerous, scheming ingrates, every fucking one of them! Of course, guards like Ridley didn't do much for giving the place a good name. The man had been reprimanded three times over the past year for misconduct toward an inmate. But you needed a few men like Ridley around to deal with some of those animals. Jesus Christ, just because he was an ass didn't give someone the right to beat him to death!

Four o'clock. Collins put a feeler out on the radio. Still nothing. Where could the miserable little son of a bitch have gone? It would be dark in a little while. It had been an unusually mild autumn, so if Walker had abandoned the van somewhere, he wasn't likely to freeze. Besides, he probably knew how to handle himself in the woods.

Collins's jaw worked. The great Maine forest, miles and endless miles of it, loomed into acute focus, every tree distinct, then blending with the mighty mass. The superintendent snatched the microphone up again and jammed the transmit button.

"Unit 16 to Unit 30, listen up! Get the fish and game commissioner on the line and patch me through. Get on it!"

CHAPTER
THREE

He had been hunkering in the bushes for the past fifteen minutes, as motionless as a gnarled stump, staring at the cabin the way a starving man watches a glutton eat. His eyes, eerily riveted, unblinking, undistracted, sought movement, any movement at all. Were it not for the pungent aroma of autumn leaves and the chilly northern breeze making his sweat turn cold, he might have been squatting in the jungle, awaiting ambush.

In this time he had not detected any sign of life from the cabin, with the exception of a slowly smoking stovepipe. He had noted four-wheel-drive tracks in the mud, coming in, then going back out again. How long ago, he could not tell. Recently, though. Probably hunters . . . and with the coming of dusk they could return at any time . . . but that was a chance Walker had to take. He was in no way equipped to deal with the wilderness. Low-cut city shoes, flimsy shirt, light jacket, no supplies. Only a green fool would try the rugged forest like that. He needed whatever gear he could plunder from that camp, and he didn't have any more time to waste. Not only might the owners return at any time, but he knew that that chopper circling a few miles to the east wasn't looking for poachers. Not that a chopper would do the pigs much good after dark, he mused, not unless it was carrying infrared heat-detecting equipment, or liquid crystals, or some goddamned thing . . . which wasn't likely. The sophisticated shit was reserved for war. For killing slant-eyed people. Still, he wasn't putting anything past the fuckers. It had been over ten years since the war, so no telling what kind of super death-technology they had developed since then. And maybe they had been waiting for an occasion such as this to experiment with it. Try it on an escaped con just like they tested the M16 rifle on the gooks.

He didn't see anything unusual about this paranoid line of reasoning. After all, *they* had created him . . . state-of-the-art. Years ago, so far back he could hardly remember, he used to be a normal boy. But they took his body and turned it into an iron-muscled death machine, capable of marching for days on end and fighting for hours without respite. And they took his innocent boy's mind and they used chemicals on it, and they used diabolical indoctrination, and they used key words, and they used codes, and they gave you a target, and they made you want to *kill*! And then, when the killing was done, they sent J. J was going to slow you down, baby. J was going to slow you down forever!

With the .38 pistol drawn and cocked, Walker approached the cabin, moving like a dark ghost floating on a low wind, utilizing the deepening shadows for cover. He could see the door now and relaxed. No one home. There was a padlock in the hasp, but it was not fastened, a trait among Maine sportsmen signifying that a wanderer or a lost person was welcome to come inside.

The cabin was not big, but it was cozy, woodsy. The kind of place where the owner could get away from his old lady, suck down a few brews, play poker with a few friends, shoot the shit, and party up. So it was well stocked.

Another thing about Maine sportsmen—they had all kinds of guns. There was a 12-gauge pump-action shotgun and a bolt-action 30-06 rifle with a sling on a gun rack on the wall beside the bunks. Walker took them both down and put them on a round oak table in the middle of the room. He hurriedly ransacked some drawers and found ammunition for both. He loaded the shotgun with .00 buckshot, which was commonly used for ripping the shit out of big game at close range. He was glad the tubular cylinder along the underside of the barrel wasn't plugged, so it could hold six rounds. He laid aside a big pile of buckshot shells and, chuckling, discarded the numerous bird shot. He wouldn't likely be shooting quail.

Walker laughed when he hefted the 30-06. The rifle was long and big and heavy, the kind of gun you'd use for tearing off the front end of a moose. Or an elephant. The box magazine seemed pathetically short when he thought of the banana clips he was so familiar with. It held five rounds, plus he could put one in the chamber. He found two boxes of bullets holding twenty rounds each. One box had softpoints, good for splattering meat. The other box had steel-jacketed, heavily loaded, torpedo-nosed shells. In a high-power rifle of this caliber, such ammunition made it as good as having an armor-piercing weapon. Walker loaded up with a predisposition toward piercing armor.

With over sixty rounds between the two guns, he was satisfied that he was formidably armed. At least for one swift, ass-kicking firefight. So let the bastards come now. Anybody. The commando had gained the terminal extensions to his hands, without which he was not a complete man.

Clothes were plentiful. Kicking out of his street shoes, he put on a thick pair of wool socks. He found a pair of army field pants and pulled them on over his jeans. He had to try on a couple of sets of lace boots before finding a pair that fit him reasonably well. He then pulled on a heavy wool sweater and covered that with a camouflage duck-hunter's windbreak. A mottled rabbit-fur cap, with the earflaps tied up, and a pair of leather gloves completed his outfit.

There was a battered canvas rucksack hanging on a nail beside the door. He took it down and went to the pantry

area. Under the sink was a case of beer and some bottles of
whiskey. Hey, hey. Good ol' boys. He took a big drink from
one of the whiskey bottles. The months in jail had left him
with a clean system. The whiskey burned bitterly, forcing
him to gasp, making his eyes water. Then the warm glow
flooded him. He drank again, this time washing the sting
down with a cup of water.

Enough fooling around. Light was fading fast in the
cabin. He threw a few cans of beans, canned meat, dried
beef, and a few other instant-food items into the rucksack.
Moving with speed, he ransacked drawers and cupboards
everywhere, taking items he wanted and flinging things all
over the place. He found an army-surplus bayonet, honed to
a fine edge, and strapped it on, chuckling. Assholes. What
did they know about this shit? Goddamn babes in the woods.
They wanted to play with the real stuff, did they? Hah! He'd
show them what these things were really designed for. He'd
show them what kind of a man employed the use of these
killing tools. He caught a glimpse of himself in the mirror on
the chest of drawers and laughed. He looked like some kind
of wild-eyed leftist guerrilla, straight out of the hills. Yay,
fuckin' Che! Viva the revolution and screw your tacos too!
Overt'row de worl', amigos!

Among the more important items he found were a Silva
compass and some sportsmen's maps detailing all the best
fishing and hunting sites in the North Maine woods. The
topographical maps covered broad regional sections, but
they were good enough for roughly accurate navigation.
After all, it wasn't as though he had a specific target area. In
fact, he had no plan at all other than tactical escape and
evasion, and for now that was purpose enough. Avoid J.
Either avoid him or obliterate the threat. . . .

He put the maps in the bulky pockets of the camou jacket,
along with all the ammunition, keeping the shotgun shells in
separate compartments from the bullets.

Now all he had to do was wait for transportation to show
up. The stove was still warm, with a big log smoldering to
coals. This told Walker that whoever lived here had been

gone most of the day and should be back this evening, since the place was set up for the weekend tomorrow. And he knew that anyone spending any time out here at all needed a solid four-wheel-drive in good working condition.

He took the whiskey bottle and sat down at the table, guns at hand, to wait. He drank. And as he drank, the old, familiar ache crept over him. Frustration. Anger. He wanted his woman. He wanted Claudine so bad, it hurt. But even when he was in her arms, he was lost. He was unequipped to deal with the tender emotions she would extract from him. And that would scare him. So he would turn cold. And run.

It was a bitter kind of loneliness. A feeling like he was trapped in a time and place where nobody had any use for him anymore. He had already been used. And now, as J could testify, and why J was coming, he was obsolete, no longer needed in a world of rapid change where the older models must be replaced by the new. What does a society striving for technological perfection need with an antiquated jungle fighter when there are no more jungles? When the jungles have already been conquered, stripped for everything they're worth? And leaving for someplace else, somewhere more happy, was just a futile dream. Heaven was nothing but a cheap joke, and the gods laughed at mankind's dumb struggle for utopia, luring them on with dirty tricks a human being wouldn't play on a scumbag. War was the only reality, and death its own reward. Death was the only thing that had any real power. Death could take you out of the whole sick game with the throw of some cosmically loaded dice. But it had a terrible price. It insisted that you not go down with dignity or grace. It demanded that you go down clawing, squirming, choking desperately for that last foul breath of a worthless life.

It had been dusk, just like now, when he had first been slapped in the face by what reality was all about. They had been out on patrol for over two weeks, gaining nothing but a bad case of the nerves. They were moving toward rendezvous. Fatigue was a general state of being, having lived on monkey meat and snakes, sleeping in perpetual wetness.

Everyone was in a dreamy haze, lost forever on some dark, hostile planet that stank like heavy mulch.

Suddenly it happened. From way up front came the sound of big popcorn popping. Or the abrupt clapping of morbid applause. Four or five guns were doing a wild dance in the thick, surrealistic steam, flinging red everywhere. Somebody was screaming, "Hit it! We're under attack!" and there was yelling and shooting everywhere.

Walker was utterly and horrifically fascinated. He felt detached from the whole thing, as if this were too incredibly preposterous to be happening to him. There was a lieutenant on his knees beside him, face buried in his hands, blood flowing freely from between clawed fingers. He was groaning sickly.

That's when the reality slapped Walker. His numbed brain finally recognized the fact that they were being ambushed. Un-fucking-believable! The mighty ass-kickin' Americans cut down by a bunch of fuckin' gooks who couldn't even speak English!

He didn't know it yet, but he had already hit the dirt. He was in the mud, deep in it, fucking it, pissing in it, and chopped leaves were falling around his head like green confetti. He made out a crouched shadow in the bushes up the slope, a flash-suppressor laying out burst after burst of automatic fire, cutting big dripping chunks out of the kneeling lieutenant. The lieutenant kept trying to fall forward, but the hammering slugs kept jerking him upright.

Then a red, wet stitch went up the front of the bushwhacker's black shirt, and Walker was aware that his M16 was bucking in his hands like a thing alive . . . and he was screaming. He didn't know what he was screaming, but it was hyper enough to rattle the bleeding kid who was laying alongside the dead lieutenant. The kid started screaming, too, while he watched the life ooze out of his ripped and ragged belly.

Then, as suddenly as it had happened, it was over. Guerrilla warfare. Swift, fleeting carnage. Hit and run. Whatever Cong weren't dead were simply gone, just gone. And

Walker sucked himself up out of the mud, got up, shuddering with some kind of weird laughter. He was thoroughly amazed at the human wreckage around him. God, he was all wet, and he smelled like shit.

And then his head hurt with the pain of remembering. Think back! There had been so many of those gunfights that sometimes they all seemed to run together. J! Where was J? Yes, he was there, as always. Drifting down the line after the music was over, moving like a slowed-down piece of film, almost ethereal, shadowlike, stepping gingerly over the blown-apart bodies. His alien eyes, roving like those of a clacking robot, would absorb and calculate the awful damage . . . and then he would smile his twisted smile. He would smile upon what was left of his terrified little-boy commandos with a godly benevolence. Good job, men. Now get up off your chicken asses and let's go find some more of these fuckers to kill! It's your job!

Now he was tired. Too much too fast, with not enough years gone by to assimilate the shock. He drank deeply from the whiskey bottle and wiped away the sweat that had beaded on his brow. He gazed around the camp, gloomy dark now, and a heartsick feeling consumed him. This was all he had ever wanted. A little place of his own, out in the wilderness, with Claudine, where he could hope for the elusive peace. Where nobody could bother him. Where Claudine could comfort him. Where he could share with her his nightmares, his frightening rage, and his emotional pain. Where he could learn to relax and enjoy the clean smell of the evergreens, fish for trout in lazy streams, listen to the birds, feel the warm sun.

He took an angry drink.

But the scumdog pigs wouldn't let him alone. They were after him, always after him, driving him, driving him, driving him . . . *mad*! The warm sun was nothing but a total eclipse, and life was a black moon on a kill-squad night, and the evil you weren't supposed to fear in the valley of the shadow of death wore tiger fatigues and carried automatic rifles, and hell was a sucking chest wound.

Then he heard the far-off growl of an engine. He leapt to his feet, slung the 30-06, and checked the leader round in the 12-gauge chamber. Peering through the window, he could see a pair of lights way in the distance, bobbing through the dark forest.

Harry "Fishhook" Wilson was the kind of guy who thought the bomb should have been dropped on Tehran, hostages or not, just to teach the Khomeini bastards a lesson in American diplomacy. Bullshit on détente and fuck the Russians. Support first strike. Give 'em all an MX right up the poop shoot. Alexander Haig should have been elected president. Now *there* was a real man who would have done the right thing and blown the hell out of someone, somewhere.

He finished off a beer in slurping glugs, burped heartily, and flung the empty can out the window. He slammed his pickup down a gear and gassed 'er through a wet hole, the all-terrain treads flinging mud thirty feet in the air. This last stretch of trail to the camp was rugged and narrow, just the way Fishhook liked it. He was having a ball negotiating it. That's what these fancy heaps were made for, by God! He hadn't put a scratch on 'er yet, thanks to his four-wheeling skill along these backwoods roads. Trees, white in the bright headlamps, whipped by like a hippie light show. The vehicle lurched and bounced, straining its tight suspension, shaking up the considerable booze in Fishhook's considerable paunch.

"Crack me 'nother one of them beers, Wally," he said, exhilarated by his ride. He hadn't gotten his deer yet, but by Jesus, it was sure fun as hell ramming around the woods trying to find one!

Wally leaned against the passenger door, orange cap askew, looking kind of stupid, drunker than the lords of London, oblivious to his head thumping against the window in rhythm with the rough motion of the truck.

"I said gimme a goddamn beer, you jeezlus drunk!" Fishhook roared. He reached over and shook his partner violently.

"All right! All right!" Wally roared back, pushing away the offending hand while trying to bring himself into focus. "Gee, Christ! Gotta git mah thang workin', ya know. Man can't work without his thang!"

Fishhook glared, red-eyed. "Then git your ass up out of your coma, git your goddamned thang workin', an' gimme a goddamned beer!" Both men burst into drunken laughter.

Fishhook tipped up the fresh can and glugged for a long time. He burped long and loud. "Wish to God the fucker'd cross my path," he growled, wiping his wet mouth with the back of his hairy hand.

"Whuzzat?" Wally slurred. He made a clumsy attempt at coming alert (Christ, but don't this deer hunting wear a man down), and in the process he spilled some beer in his lap. He made an even clumsier attempt at mopping it up, but the bouncing truck was foiling his efforts and making him spill more.

"That sum'bitch who escaped," Fishhook said, giving his friend a mean glare. "Jeez Christ! Why'n the fuck don't you wake up? What in Christless hell do you think we been listenin' to on the radio all day?" He took a tighter grip on the wheel, and his jaw gravitated forward. "Goddamn sum'bitch. I'd blow his fuckin' guts out. Yer goddamn right I would! That's the trouble with this country today. Too many of them shitbags crawlin' around. Blow his fuckin' guts out if I catch him. Legal too." The idea of legally shooting a human being excited Fishhook in a strange way.

Wally laughed, then sucked down a major portion of his own beer. "Bullshit! If that sum'bitch got anywhere near you, you'd have a shit hem'rage an' you know it. You wouldn't blow nobody's guts out."

"The hell I wouldn't!" Fishhook was angry now. He glugged beer and wiped his mouth again. "What you gotta do when you catch him is you drag him inside your house. Law says if you catch a shitbag like that inside your house, you got a right to shoot him. Drag him inside your house then blow his fuckin' guts out. You betcher goddamn ass that's what I'd do if I caught him!"

Wally didn't say anything this time. He didn't like the tone of his buddy's voice. Sometimes Fishhook got mean when he got drunk. Everybody knew about his beating his wife and kids once in a while. But most times he was just a good ol' boy—maybe a little quarrelsome once in a while. But Wally didn't like this talk about killing. Not a bit. It had a creepy sound to it.

He drank again from his beer, then yelled, "Watch out, goddammit! Yer gonna run the camp over, ya dam' drunk!"

Heehawing loudly, Fishhook brought the truck to a skidding halt just when it appeared he would crash into the porch. "I'll leave the lights on till we git the gas lamp goin'," he said. "Wouldn't want ya to stub your little toe in the dark. Git your gun, now. Git your gun. Man hadn't ought to have a gun if he don't know how to take care of it!"

He turned on the cab lights and reached around and got his own gun from the window rack. It was a lever-action 30-30 bush rifle, the same as Wally's. And although it was illegal to transport a loaded firearm within a vehicle, Fishhook kept it loaded just in case. After all, what's a fifty-dollar fine compared to an eight-point buck? he reasoned.

They piled drunkenly out of the truck, stumbled up the step onto the porch, and made for the door but froze when a flat, hard voice barked, "Stop! Stop where you are! I have a gun aimed at you! Don't make any move except what I tell you to do. If you make any move I don't tell you to make, then I will kill you. Now lay your weapons down. Slowly. Now!"

"What the fuck . . ." Fishhook craned his neck a little. The truck lights were blinding. He strained his eyes against the darkness, trying to locate the threatening voice. "Hey! Who the fuck's out there? What the fuck you think you're up to? C'mon outa there 'fore you git your guts blown out!" He was angry, quivering angry, but at the same time he felt ice in his belly. He also felt like he needed to take a wicked piss.

"Hey, Fishhook!" Wally whispered, his voice trembling to the point of pleading. He felt the keen edge of danger real enough to slice through the haze of his intoxication. This was no joke. It was mighty cold right now, a strangling, naked kind of cold. "Hey, Fishhook, that's him! That's the escaped killer they're lookin' for! Maybe we better do like he says!"

"Shut up!" Fishhook's voice was harsh, strained. "Ain't no fuckin' murderin' jailbird gonna jump me on my own property! These shitbags been jackin' folks around long enough. Not me, by God!"

Terrified now, Wally sucked air deep. "For God's sake, Fishhook—"

Quicker than anyone would have thought a fat drunk could move, Fishhook suddenly dropped into a low crouch, hipping the deer rifle and swinging it to bear in what he thought was the general direction of his assailant. There was the snapping, metallic click of the lever slamming home a shell, then a slap-blasting roar. The rifle bore erupted in a short spurt of flame, sending a whipping sound chewing through the brush.

Walker saw a shadowy gook hunkered in the bushes, laying out round after round of automatic fire, ripping great, dripping chunks out of the kneeling lieutenant. Lying neck deep in the slimy mud, smelling thick jungle stink, he was aware that his M16 assault rifle was bucking in his hands like a thing alive. They come to kill you, man. They come to kill you because that's what they do for a living. They come to blow your little-boy body away!

The shotgun was bucking in Walker's hands like a thing alive, belching fire, thundering monstrously, filling the crisp night air with an acrid stench. The bodies on the porch jerked, danced, sprung red leaks, slammed against the cabin, fell like broken mannequins in an obscene sportsmen's advertising display—the twisted artwork of a deranged window dresser. Walker's gun was hot and smoking, his eyes out of focus, lost in another world. "Tough shit!" was the title given to this macabre pièce de résistance.

And then, when reality gradually washed away the illusion of high combat, a sickness filled his belly. Something wrong. Something god-awful wrong—like the fierce, burning pain in his left forearm, and his sleeve heavy with a dark wetness that was dripping off the ends of his fingers. Incredible, he found himself thinking. The enemy's wild shot in the dark had accidentally scored a hit.

CHAPTER
FOUR

You couldn't really call it a camp or a house because it was more like a mansion, but the owner, a wealthy potato grower who had interests in the lumber industry, preferred to call it a lodge. It was made of tight-fitting white pine logs and consisted of a huge central building with two wings sloping down from each side. There was a long, wide, railed deck out front and a railed-plank catwalk leading down to the private docks where two light planes sat bobbing on pontoons.

The building rose from a gentle slope, allowing a spectacular view of the lake and surrounding mountains, now breathtaking in their autumn glory. Besides a small airstrip cut along the beach edge, the only other access to the place was an unkept jeep trail that was rough enough to deter most sensible people. Anyone foolish enough to abuse a vehicle long enough to reach the end of this road met with disappointment, anyway. Intruders, which meant anyone without a personal invitation, were quickly turned away.

Governor John Brandon finished his martini and then

fixed another one from the well-stocked mahogany bar. He strode over to the big bay windows and took in the magnificent red sunset over the lake. Friday night. He could forget about weighty problems until the first of the week. He had been looking forward to this much-needed, well-deserved vacation for a long time, and he was eagerly anticipating a brisk and refreshing day's hunt tomorrow. It could really be a wonderful weekend, except for one thing, he thought, slightly bitter, as he took a sip from his drink. He wished Nancy would quit whoring around.

She was over by the fireplace, which was crackling warmly with big logs, flickering patterns across the thick bearskin rug. Glass in hand, she was chatting merrily with Larson and Gorman, who in turn were laughing with her at some private joke. It hurt the governor to see her act that way, and he knew it embarrassed his colleagues. No one liked knowing his boss was the butt of nasty little remarks. A loose wife was definitely a problem in the public-office business.

It was the way she carried herself. It was as though she wanted everyone to know how much she enjoyed sex. When she laughed, she threw her pert blond head back, arched her back, and thrust her tight ass out provocatively. She had to use her ass suggestively because she didn't have a whole hell of a lot in the way of tits. She was pretty effective at compensating, though, the governor thought. Her high, tinkling laughter made him grimace. He knew she would somehow find a way into bed with one or both of those guys before the night was over. He knew there would be a few red and sheepish faces at the breakfast table in the morning.

He threw his drink down and headed back for another. What the hell, let her have her cheap fun while she could. He swore this was going to be his last year in politics, and when he stepped down from office, he had a little surprise in store for his dear wife. The charming tramp was going to get the shitcan. The fear of public scandal, the ax she had held over his head for so long, was going to be snatched right out of her hand.

He felt a hand on his shoulder. "How's it going, John?" It was Jack Archer, looking concernedly at the governor's glass.

The governor gave his friend a big why-everything-in-the-world-is-just-wonderful type of smile. Brandon's big, even teeth and his boyish face made him the envy of any hard-sell campaign manager. "Why, just fine, Jack. This is quite a spread you've got here. I want to thank you for inviting me out. You don't know how bad I've been needing this little trip. Only, I hope I'm not hurting your business."

"Oh, not at all, not at all," Archer said, making a Scotch and soda. He was the chunky-beef-stew advertisers' idea of clean, rugged, outdoorsy. He had the checkered shirt with the half-rolled-up sleeves, but there was no pine pitch on his hands and no soot on his fresh jeans. "As I told you before, I'm not entertaining any out-of-state sportsmen this year. They help with the upkeep of this place, to be sure, but sometimes they're so goddamned snobbish, it makes me wonder whether it's worth it or not."

The governor chuckled. "Come on, Jack. Since when did you ever need any help upkeeping anything? The way I hear it, you're not just in the potato industry, you *are* the potato industry. And a good thing too. Wise business management in a major crop like that means a lot to this state. You have a right to be proud of yourself."

It was Jack's turn to laugh. "It's not as rosy as you might think. But then, what is?"

Shrewdly but casually Archer watched the governor watching Nancy, and an anger welled up inside him. He and the governor went back a long way together, practically to boyhood, and it was Jack's considerable contributions that had been a major factor in securing his friend the governorship. John was too good a man for that high-class slut. Jack couldn't understand how someone as intelligent as Brandon could have gotten himself mixed up with her. Then again, he could, because hot lips and a tight ass bought more than any political promise ever did.

It was obvious what she wanted, the way she was sidling

up to Larson and Gorman, both young, handsome, energetic. Both were razor-keen, lightning-tongued lawyers for the Eastern Pulp and Paper Company, riding a fast corporate gravy train straight to the top. Both were here as a personal favor to Eastern's aging president, to conclude important paper company contracts concerning cutting rights to a section of state land.

Nancy kept brushing her knee against Gorman's thigh, making as though it were accidental. Jack knew the governor was seething inwardly, even though he admired the way the man was controlling himself.

"Well, Governor," he said heartily. "What do you say we go back in the den and take a look at those new rifles. I'll have Melinda make us some coffee."

"Quite a breed of new lawyers they're churning out these days, here," Brandon mumbled, then quickly said, "Sure, Jack, I'd love to. I ought to get the feel of my cannon before that big buck jumps me tomorrow."

Nancy caught her husband's eye as he and Jack passed. Bad electricity crackled between the two, but she smiled cordially and so did he.

"Having a good time, darling?" she asked, expertly hiding the smug tone, laying light fingers on his cheek.

"Wonderful," he replied, his teeth clenched as he kissed her lightly. He exchanged a few strained amenities with Larson and Gorman, then hurried after Jack.

Brandon was thankful for the change of atmosphere in the den. A fire was burning in the cut-stone fireplace, making it warm and cozy. The room was tastefully finished in dark wood, lending it a relaxing air. There was a big moose head hanging on the wall, staring glass-eyed. Big stuffed chairs faced the fireplace.

White-haired Dr. Simms sat on a low, leather-covered couch, sipping brandy with his elderly wife while Jack's wife, Melinda, was leaning over the hearth, poking new life into the fire.

Melinda rose and turned when the men came in. "Well,

there you are," she said sweetly. "Would you like some brandy, darling? Governor?"

Jack was a lucky man, thought Brandon. Melinda was anything but ravishing, but she was kind and gentle, with a charmingly warm personality that made a man feel like his home was his home. And she was loyal.

"Maybe later, dear," Jack said, striding to the gun cabinet. "We could use a little of your excellent coffee, though. The governor and I thought we'd examine these new rifles."

"Good-quality equipment, if I say so myself," said the old doctor, rising perhaps a bit slowly, his knees bent slightly under his big weight. "I should think the governor would get a bang out of that .32 special. Good little deer rifle. Has a good scope too."

There was a radio communications room off to the rear of the den. The room held expensive electronic equipment that was the backbone of this isolated chalet's contact with the outside world. Suddenly the small door burst open and a young man wearing earphones stepped out. "Call for you, Mr. Governor," he said in an excited voice. "It's really urgent!"

Brandon grimaced. "Damn! I told that secretary not to get in touch with me unless it was a dire emergency. This had better be damned important or she's had it! Excuse me for a moment, please."

But he was more than a moment. In fact, he was in there for quite a while, and when he finally came out, he was clearly shaken. Noticing all eyes upon him, he sighed heavily and then said, "Great news. An inmate from that new Buckley Ridge facility has escaped custody. He killed the guard who had taken him to the hospital for X rays this afternoon and even stole the prison van, for God's sake. He's considered armed and extremely dangerous." Brandon rubbed a hand across his tight, thoughtful lips. "Just the kind of press that place needs after all the flak we went through to get the funding to build it."

Dr. Simms took a big drink of his brandy, his purple jowls quivering with indignation. "My God, what's this country coming to? We do everything we can to help those young people these days, and all they want to do is terrorize and destroy. Absolutely no ambition. Not very damned many of them even want to better themselves. I used to be against the death penalty, but by God, I'm beginning to think that's just exactly what they need!"

"Now, dear," fussed his petite little wife, "don't go getting yourself upset. Your heart, you know." She wore a most vacantly puzzled expression. "I heard that Buckley Ridge was a very reasonable place. Well, you know, considering what those criminals do. I think they get more than they deserve."

"How long ago did this happen, John?" asked Archer.

"Around two. Anyway, believe it or not, that's not the worst of it. Seems this guy is some kind of ex-commando, Vietnam vet, and is as loony as a jaybird. Come to think of it, I seem to recall signing an inmate transfer order on him a few days ago. It sticks in my mind because the request came from the Department of Defense. They pointed out that this individual suffers from an unusual form of combat trauma, and they wanted to move him to a military hospital facility in hopes of getting a better understanding of that sort of problem.

"Well, Dick Collins told me that when they catch up to him, they expect anything but a peaceful surrender. In fact, Collins wanted to tell me in a roundabout way that he expected the holy shit to hit the holy fan. Pardon my French, ladies. I think I'll have that brandy now, if you don't mind, Jack."

Jack poured two glasses and handed one to the governor. He drank from his own, then said, "Hmm. Dick Collins. Isn't he the guy you appointed superintendent of corrections? Seems there was a lack of security on his end of things. If they suspected the man was dangerous, why wasn't he better guarded?"

"That was my point exactly when I talked to Dick. He assured me that he would get to the bottom of it. He also assured me that they had a line on the fugitive and would have him soon. And I assured him that they'd better, or someone's head was definitely going to roll!"

The doctor's wife was tsk-tsking to Melinda. "I just don't understand it," she was saying, her tiny old face wrinkled with perplexity. "Those young people have so many opportunities these days. Whatever possesses them to go out and act like that?"

The governor lifted his glass to his lips, and as he did, he caught a glimpse of two silhouettes outside the window, heading hand in hand down the wooden dock ramp. One was Nancy and the other was the unmistakably trim figure of that lawyer, Gene Gorman.

Dick Collins wasn't very hungry, but he picked at his macaroni, anyway. He was pissed because the governor had jumped on him so hard. What the hell, you had crazy people in the world. Collins couldn't be held personally responsible for every psycho the system snatched up. But he could see the governor's point. Buckley Ridge was supposed to be the latest in modern rehabilitation, offering vocational training, work-for-pay projects, special counseling, and a number of other personal initiative programs. There had been a lot of controversy over the money for the facility, in view of its projected impact on lowering the rate of criminals returning to jail time after time, and now the first notable product that it had turned out was an escapee who killed. God damn that Walker!

Ralph Mendel had been the two-to-nine officer on duty at the time. Collins knew him well. Mendel was a good man, the kind of man who gave the inmates every break he could. He had a big family and needed his job. Collins hadn't had the heart to rat him out during that conversation with the governor. He knew he was just buying time for the man, though, but, Jesus Christ, somebody had to take the rap. And whose job was more important? That's just the way the system worked. Chain of command and all that. The soldiers were supposed to bite the dust before the officers.

Collins's stomach was tied up in knots.

Myrna, sitting across from him at the kitchen table, was shoveling down the ol' grub like a sow at the trough. She was deliberately ignoring Richard, as well as deliberately annoying him. She certainly was not extending him any sympathy, since she loathed his chosen profession in the first place. If he wanted to play the great redeemer of lost youth, the benevolent warden parading proudly among his caged charges, then let him play it. And let him suffer the damned consequences too! Maybe this would finally encourage him to turn toward a more respectable career.

To say Dick was annoyed would be putting it mildly. He finally slammed his fork down. "All right, Myrna, say it!" he shouted. "Go ahead. Say it. Get it off your mind."

Myrna looked up and stopped in mid-chew. She swallowed. "No, Richard, I'm not going to say it. You never listen to anything I have to say, anyway."

He banged a hand on the table. "No, no! I want to hear what you have to say."

She laid her fork down, too, then leaned toward her husband, her chubby face resolute with her convictions. "All right, Richard, you want to hear it, I'll say it. First of all, that boy was forced to fight in an illegal and an immoral war. He was used like a pawn in a deadly game of political chess. And don't tell me that anyone had any consideration for his life because he was most certainly expendable and he knew it. So in exchange for his service he finds that he was lied to, and he finds himself treated like a criminal. So he finally goes out and acts like a criminal, just the way he was taught. Then everybody goes nuts and says, 'My goodness, he can't act like that in our sanctimoniously clean society. So lock him up. Lock him up in that perfect little hotel up on that hill.' Wait until he's finally had enough, and he strikes back. Oh, it's a tragedy, all right. I'm not denying that it's a tragedy. But just what the hell did you expect, Richard?"

Collins was blustering red. He was bursting with a multitude of mighty retorts but was mercifully saved by the front door bell ringing. He pushed his chair back angrily, stood up, and stamped out through the living room to answer it, hoping against hope that it would be welcome news concerning Walker's capture.

However, he was unprepared for what stood on the porch beyond the door: three army men wearing crisp military fatigues bloused above shiny black boots. They bore an aura more sinister than anything Collins could ever remember feeling.

The man in front, holding the briefcase, stood ramrod erect. His tight-jawed face looked as though it could have been chiseled out of lava rock, seemingly devoid of any emotion whatsoever. And he had eyes reminiscent of steel ball bearings. Those twin chips of blue ice drilled Collins unmercifully, taking his measure, making him feel uncomfortably self-conscious.

"Superintendent Collins?" The man stepped across the threshold, and Collins gave a startled gasp and took an involuntary step backward. The voice! The voice had an eerily robotic quality. "My name is Colonel Jarvis." A hand was extended.

Still staring, Collins found himself shaking a hand that felt like cold rock, behind which must lay unreal strength. "Yes. Uh, yes, of course," he stammered. "Won't you come in, Colonel?"

With deathlike slowness the colonel turned and nodded to the two men still standing on the porch, and they retreated to the car that was parked at the end of the driveway. Closing the door, Jarvis brought his ruthless gaze back to Collins. His every movement seemed to enhance his alien texture, which had so unnerved Collins.

"I have just come from the prison," Jarvis said, removing his black beret, which bore a strange, lightning-riddled insignia. "As you probably know, I'm here to pick up an inmate. One James Walker. It appeared to me that the personnel at the prison were somewhat secretive. They told me that I had best talk to you. Well, I can assure you, Mr.

Collins, that I have all the necessary paperwork in order, right here." He extended the briefcase.

Collins sighed heavily. "Ah, yes. Well, I think you'd better come in and sit down."

Jarvis, standing like an unblinking statue, didn't move.

Sighing again, Collins finally came out with it. "The prisoner escaped. Earlier this afternoon. He killed the guard who was assigned to take him to the hospital."

With the faintest nod Jarvis finally moved. He strode across the thick, shag-carpeted living room floor and made himself comfortable in a recliner. "Maybe we should talk," he said, those damned eyes piercing like laser beams.

Then the phone by the stairs rang. Collins answered it, and as he listened, his face began to go pale. "Jesus Christ!" he exclaimed a couple of times, then one pathetic, "My God!"

Myrna had been standing just inside the kitchen door, and ever since that strange army man had entered her house, her heart had gone cold. Now she was scared. Her hands were clasped to her breast. "Richard?" She was unable to hide the worry in her voice. She knew with women's intuition that this whole thing was turning bad serious.

Collins hung up the phone with a certain tiredness. He looked first to the weird-eyed military man, then to his wife. He drew a deep breath. "They think he's killed two more men out in the Moosehorn region. They think he killed them, then blew their camp up and stole their vehicle. They think that because they found the stolen van abandoned a few miles away."

Jarvis rose, and the rising seemed to take a long time. "Get your coat, Mr. Collins," he said.

Myrna gasped, then shuddered. "Oh, my God, Richard! Please be careful!"

Collins took time to hold her and kiss her, forgetting about their earlier differences. He was no longer interested in getting back to her. It had lost its significance.

"Myrna, dear, I'll be late, so don't wait up. In fact, I

would prefer it if you would go spend the night at your sister's."

She tried to cling to him, tried to hold him back as he went out the door into the chilly night with that most creepy man, who must surely be somehow linked to the killer's destiny.

CHAPTER
FIVE

Shit! Just shit! What rotten luck. He hadn't meant for that to happen. It wasn't supposed to happen that way. How was he supposed to know that that drunken civilian fool meant to go for a firefight? *Shoot to kill.* . . . The buckshot had made a red mess of them both. The fat man's head had been dangling from his shoulders by some drenched strands of sinew or something. Walker didn't like to think about the other one. It reminded him too much of the time he kept trying to pick up Pete Turowski's guts, after Pete had tripped a Bouncing Betty. And the guts kept slipping out of the commando's hands, long, greasy, thick fart smells oozing from the perforated membrane. Turowski's got the other half of my tent, he kept thinking, his arms elbow-deep in his friend's entrails. Here's the other half of my shelter half, he kept thinking. Goddammit, Turowski, you ain't gonna sleep in my tent looking like that!

What a rotten fucking mess.

And now there was the mess on the outside of his left forearm. Son of a bitch was hurting like hell. He used his knife to cut the sleeve and examined the wound under the truck lights. It was a nasty flesh wound, not deep enough to shatter bone, but the bullet had done an excellent job of tearing a substantial chunk of meat out of him. He knew he would never be able to function properly if he became weak from loss of blood, and he would never be able to afford falling victim to fever if the wound became infected. He would have to perform tactical field surgery immediately.

He went inside the cabin and lit a gas lamp. He hastily scrounged for items he would need and put them on the table. He drank deeply from a bottle of whiskey, then poured some of the liquid directly over the wound. The alcohol burned like white fire, and he had to force himself not to scream, though sweat was now dripping down his face. As soon as the initial sting subsided, though, he immediately threaded a needle and punctured his injured arm, coldly proceeding to draw the ragged edge of flesh up tight.

That done, he paused and drank again, letting this fresh assault of pain pass. Then he went to the propane gas stove, beside the sink, and turned a burner on high. He unsheathed the heavy bayonet and held the blade into the blue flame until the steel began to glow. Without hesitation he laid the hot metal against his wound. This time he was unable to stifle the scream that tore from his throat, and he swooned sickeningly at the rising smell of his own searing flesh. Then he staggered back to the table, sat heavily, and tightly wrapped the wound with gauze. Sweating profusely, he drank again, giving himself a moment to recover.

When he'd felt he'd been sufficiently desensitized by alcohol, he went out to the porch and dragged the butchered hunters inside the cabin. He then stoked up the wood stove and left the loading door wide open. He went back to the gas stove, shut out all flame including the pilot light, opened the oven door, and turned on all the knobs. There was a spare propane cylinder around back of the building. He had taken the cylinder and put it in back of the truck. He had taken both 30-30s, thrown them on the floor of the cab, and hauled ass, hitting it hard down the narrow camp road, skidding, sliding, putting fresh dents in Fishhook's new pickup.

He was back out on the primary logging road now, driving fast and heading deeper into the woods. With the window rolled down he inhaled the crisp, cool air through his nostrils to clear his mind. He marveled at the incredibly still blackness of the night forest. Then he felt the dull thud of the explosion when the gas finally caught up with the flame in the stove. Through the rearview mirror he saw a long ball of light streak skyward, trailing bits of board, shingles, and flaming tar paper. Then it settled down, the fire lighting the black sky dimly in low, flickering patterns.

Shit! That was dumb. Now the pig-dog motherfuckers had a flare to zero in on. Well, to hell with it. At least now they would know that a commando doesn't fuck around! But, boy, would they ever be on his ass now. So what? Déjà vu. It happened before. On night patrol. Like now.

There had been four of them, slithering in deadly silence through the midnight jungle, somewhere up the Ho Chi Minh trail. Way up. Kill squad came looking for enemy movement, and they found it. They jumped a gook patrol, regulars, NVA, had it out with them. Fried the fuckers, made a lot of noise. Comes to find out these gooks are only an advance scout for a massive assault force shortly behind, all well-armed regulars. Hundreds, maybe thousands, who could tell in the dark? The Starlight scope was nothing but a shimmering mass of movement. And four pathetic little Yankees going, "Oh shit!"

They hastily called artillery and an air strike, then beat feet into the black jungle. Only the jungle wasn't black anymore. It was bright with flares, tracers, rocket grenades, tearing the forest into chopped salad. Walker had no clear recollection of how they ever made it back. Except they all didn't make it back. Just Walker and Pete Turowski, dragging each other into some Marine outpost, beat, torn, delirious with shock and fatigue.

Two weeks later, on a similar mission, Turowski tripped a

Bouncing Betty, and Walker picked up his guts, and they kept slipping out of his hands.

Walker was having a hard time figuring out what was the matter with him lately. Every time he thought he had a grip on things, it slipped away like Pete's guts. It was like his mind was drowning in some murky swamp somewhere. Lost in a weird, hazy, dark space. Every once in a while he would come to the surface gasping for fresh air, fresh insights, a clean look at a good world. Then he would be sucking mud again, drowning in gore. Life was just a tangled mass of slippery guts. Where the hell was he going, anyway? What the fuck was going on? Escape. Run. Haul ass like a jackrabbit with the hounds on your tail.

Oh, Lord, if only he could be with Claudine. Lord, I'm tired. I'm tired of war. Let me rest. Let me find a nice warm den, safe from the howling wolves. Oh, yeah. Find a lost cabin way back in the high country. Lay back and let peace numb me like a morphine injection. Fuck civilization. Live off the land. They'd forget him after a while. And then God would come for him someday, laid in his woman's arms, waiting, waiting way out in the wilderness.

He hadn't really wanted to waste those hunters, but neither was he particularly bent out of shape about it. You pick up a gun, you step into a war, you pay whatever it costs. And sometimes it costs plenty, baby. You fire on another soldier, you do it knowing you stand the same chance of eating lead yourself. If you don't know it—tough shit. Tough shit either way. War is just plain tough shit. Walker knew. He knew what a Chinese boot knife in the back felt like. He knew what RPG shrapnel tearing his belly apart felt like. He knew what an AK-47 round through the leg felt like. And he knew what a rifle butt smashing his face in felt like. He knew what tough shit was.

Ridley was a different story. Walker heard about it while monitoring the CB. It caused him to stop the truck, yank the unit out by its bolts, and heave it into the bushes. Good! He was glad the rotten, contemptible son of a whore was dead.

He hoped the dirty bastard had choked on his own puke. So why was he standing by the side of the road, trembling with a mighty rage?

He jumped back in the truck, cracked another of Fishhook's beers, and tore up dirt. He didn't need that goddamn CB, anyway. He already knew what the pigs were doing. They ware converging on the scene of that blown shack. Bunch of pigs waddling importantly around the blown barn door, grunting, squealing, trying to figure out which way the horse went. Walker could see a chopper spotlight dancing like a tiny firefly way, way off in the darkness.

The moon was rising full, and it was a sharp, crisp harvest evening. Night in the woods was always absolute, complete. But in spite of the dark shadows down among the trees, Walker could see well enough to drive without headlights. He just stayed in the middle of the long, winding black ribbon, hoping to hell some major sort of wildlife didn't leap out in front of him. He barreled right along, hitting ruts hard, the truck throwing rocks and leaving a trail of dust behind it. It was an eerie yet thrilling sensation, like flying a fast ship through hyperspace in the middle of a meteorite bombardment. Walker swilled down beer after beer, space juice, smiling, feeling good, loving this bumpy, freewheeling rocket ride through the dark, fathomless universe. Shee-it, this truck wouldn't be fit to use for a garbage can by the time he was finished with it.

Then an icy hand grabbed his heart and put the squeeze on. Adrenaline shot through his system like liquid lightning, and his conditioned commando brain snapped alive. There were headlights bobbing ahead, way ahead, tiny pinpoints in the night. A blue bubble was flashing, streaking the dark with its swinging patterns. Border patrol or game wardens, no doubt, were speeding toward the explosion, on a collision course with the perpetrator. This was the Maine woods no more. This was no longer a space ride in a rocket ship. This was the jungle, and this was fuckin' war!

Walker hit the brakes hard, sliding to a halt, throwing gravel everywhere, glad he had already pulled the fuses for

the brake and backup lights. Without a moment's hesitation
he opened the glove compartment, grabbed a box of kitchen
matches, a roll of electrical tape, a flashlight and a file that
he had put there earlier, and put them all in the pouchy
pockets of the duck jacket. He got out, dragged the propane
cylinder off the truck, rolled it up front a ways, and positioned it about halfway in the road, crosswise. He taped the
box of matches to the side of the tank, then hastily dragged a
bunch of dead branches over it. A hurry-up job, but it would
conceal the tank's immediate identity, at least until the gook
motherfuckers found out they done stepped in shit.

Gooks! Christ, don't it make my mind scream, my head
burst from within!

The vehicle was coming at an alarming rate of speed. But
it was weaving and bobbing with the road, going up and
down gullies, so there was not much chance that whoever
was in it could have gotten a clear view of any activity ahead
yet. Maybe.

Walker jumped back in the truck and backed it up sixty
yards or so, pulling it off the road as far as he could without
getting it stuck in the drainage ditch. Hands flying deftly,
surely, he grabbed the 30-06 rifle, taped the flashlight to the
side of the barrel, and ran the file across the rear of the front
sight bead. So now, when he switched the flashlight on, he
would not only be able to see his target but he would be
zeroing in with a tiny silver disc as the light illuminated the
bead.

He could hear the revving of the hot engine now, and light
was crisscrossing the road. Eyes glaring, drunk with the
specter of war, teeth clenched, snarling, he leapt to the far-
side ditch, ran down it a ways, and took the prone position,
heavy rifle laid out before him. He slammed the bolt forward
and locked in a torpedo-nosed, steel-jacketed shell, sufficient to blow the ass off an Indian elephant. What the hell
did that redneck bastard want with ammunition like this,
anyway, Walker absently wondered as the Warden Service
vehicle, a jeep wagon, loomed into view. Power tripping,

that's all. Like that bayonet, which was now strapped securely to a commando's leg where it belonged.

At first Walker thought the jeep wasn't going to stop. He thought it was going to speed on by, see Fishhook's stolen truck, and radio for help. Damn! There would have to be a gunfight. He needed one of those vehicles.

But the 4X4 wagon did slow down. Blue lights rotating, it approached the object dominating the road cautiously. When it pulled alongside the camouflaged cylinder, the driver eased his head out the window for a closer look, feeling sure there was something wrong but not sure what. It was the last thing he and his partner ever wondered.

Walker's powerful flashlight cut across the headlight beams and illuminated the matchbox taped to the cylinder. The heavy, big-game rifle kicked like an angry mule, its booming shot like a clap of thunder, echoing loudly through the woods. The tank went off like napalm. It blew apart in a tremendous, roaring flash fire that lifted the jeep over sideways, into the ditch. Walker felt the heat of the explosion roar over him, and for a second he thought the oxygen was going to be sucked out of his lungs and the hair singed off his face. Then the jeep caught fire and another gas explosion shattered the night air, throwing metal and glass, like shrapnel, everywhere.

Snarling like a slavering, rabid wolf, he jumped out of the ditch and ran for his own truck. "Make that one shot count," J used to say. Well, you sorry pricks, I guess I made that motherfucker count, didn't I? Yeah? Well, I'd give anything on God's good earth to cook you down with a burning blast like that. J! His mind wouldn't stop screaming. J! My whole squad all gone. All killed. The team. The high-tech team. Shot down and killed. And J stepping over the dead bodies, slowly, deliberately, his hands clasped tightly behind him, eyes of ice always there to coldly calculate the damage.

Walker started the truck up and raced the engine. He watched the fire in the road, the burning jeep, like a man hypnotized. Like a Boy Scout in awe of his first camp fire. Thinking. With the mess he'd left behind, with the pigs

snorting down his tail, there was only one way to go, and
that was forward. He might get through those flames without
blowing his own vehicle up; then again, he might not. The
alternatives were almighty slender, and time now was surely
a critical factor. The pigs had another flare to zero in on.
Shit! Why didn't he just send them a map with specific directions!

His decision made, he popped the clutch and the pickup
lurched forward. It gained speed, hit the far side of the
ditch, banged against a couple of trees, slid almost out of
control, then spun back on the road again, and Walker was
in the clear. The fire was just a devil's dance in the rearview
mirror, falling behind fast.

He drove fast, oblivious to caution, not sure whether he
could hear sirens or if his ears were just ringing. All he
knew for sure was that he had to get somewhere soon . . . tall
order when you're out in the middle of the goddamn
woods! And then he saw the battered, bullet-riddled sign
that read, PRIVATE ROAD. DO NOT ENTER. VIOLATORS WILL
BE PROSECUTED TO THE FULL EXTENT OF THE LAW, in great
big bold letters.

Walker chuckled. Now PRIVATE ROAD meant to him that
that road led to somewhere where somebody didn't want you
to be. And at this stage of his evasion tactics, somewhere
was infinitely better than nowhere. Because he damned sure
couldn't stay on the main logging road any longer. After that
number with the wardens, they'd be down on him like stink
on shit.

The private road was overgrown with weeds and bushes,
and it was deeply rutted. Walker rammed through, bouncing
from one side to the other in a teeth-jarring ride, glad Fishhook had kept his truck in such good shape. Well, at least it
had once been in good shape.

The place was crawling with police activity, engines running, lights flashing, men prowling around the burning ruins
of the camp, firemen trying to contain the blaze so as to
avert a forest fire—without getting in the way of the cops.

A helicopter was circling overhead, rotors beating loudly, its powerful searchlight probing the surrounding area, hoping to turn up something. Flashlights dotted the woods all around as men thrashed through the brush like a bunch of African beaters trying to flush out a beast.

Collins, standing hump-shouldered by a city squad car, hunched in his coat against the night chill, was having words with the chief detective from the Corinth Police Department. The detective had a plastic bag that contained six spent shotgun shells. He was saying, "Oh, they're dead, all right. We'll come up with a few charred bones once we get those flames under control. Maybe. I figure it was a damned hot gas fire. Might have disintegrated the poor bastards. We'll get something, anyway.

"Now these shells came from that wooded area right over there. I figure your man had it out with those boys. Why? Well, if he's anything like you say, I don't figure cold-blooded murder, though it might as well have been when you stack the odds. He probably just wanted that truck. Evidence indicates that those guys had been drinking. They must have gotten trigger-happy, and of course your man let 'em have it. And from the looks of things they let Walker have it too. There's blood over there where we found these shells. Got no way of knowing how bad he's hit, though. Let's just hope it's bad enough. Don't need him thrashing around out there like a wounded bear." The detective scratched his balding head, then absently commented, "Don't know why he blew up the camp, though, unless he freaked. He must have known we'd come running to this fire. Maybe it was just one of those war things he felt like he needed to do. Say, Dick, you don't look too good. You feeling all right?"

No, Dick didn't feel too good. He felt sick. My God, just one little error in judgment. But hell, the prison always sent one guard for one inmate. Sometimes one guard for even two or three inmates. There had never been a reason to do things any different. One man. One lousy little mistake. Collins was seriously considering retiring from his position as superintendent before he had another chat with the governor. It would be a hell of a lot less embarrassing, although he guessed that he was now probably too late for anything to save Ralph Mendel's job at the prison. In fact, if anything else happened, the entire corrections staff was apt to be put through the wringer. The governor himself was just so much more fat floating in a bubbling pot. His had been the final signature on the bill approving the new facility. God. Walker had to be stopped. Dead. In his tracks. Yeah, but how? The commando was as slippery as a greased weasel darting through the barnyard, voracious, blood-starved, taking a single huge bit out of every chicken on the farm, and streaking too fast for anybody to draw a bead on him. One chicken after another. Taking a big bite.

There was one small consolation, though—the little bastard had been hit. Hopefully bad enough to at least slow him down.

Ray Smith, the game commissioner, was standing with Collins, looking tousled, exasperated—and mad that someone was defiling his woods like this. "I been to 'Nam too," he was saying. "I got a good idea what we're up against."

Collins laughed sarcastically, bitterly. "You got a good idea what we're up against, do you, Smith? I'd say it was pretty goddamn obvious what we're up against!"

Commissioner Smith's face reddened, but he let the rudeness ride. He knew Collins was under a lot of pressure, and he might shortly be feeling the same heat himself if that convict wasn't stopped soon.

"You know what I mean, Dick. The man is no common run-of-the-line grunt. Back in the jungle those boys were a spooky lot. One of the things you didn't do if you were ever around them was you didn't ask them any questions. Weren't very many of them, either. They wore tiger fatigues like a real tiger wears his skin. No unit patches, no dog tags, no ID, and carrying the absolute latest in light automatics. They'd take off in the middle of the night in black, unmarked choppers. Heh, figure that out, why don't you? Anyway, you might see them again in a few weeks, maybe months, maybe never. You knew that wherever they were, they weren't rightfully supposed to be there. If they stepped in shit, nobody was going in after them. They knew it. And they stepped in shit all the time. Rumors from the forward camps had it that wherever those boys touched down, they made a nightmare out of what used to be just a bad dream. Charlie was terrified of them."

The commissioner looked at Collins, then at the detective. Both had been paying fascinated attention.

"Tough, those boys," Smith continued. "If Walker is anything like I think he is, we're going to get a bellyful when we catch up to him. I figure he's a walking arsenal by now, and you can bet your last ace in a showdown that he knows how to use every item he has on him. And I figure he knows a few tricks of the war trade that no ordinary man could ever anticipate."

Others had been listening to Smith's speculations concerning the escapee. Among them were Jarvis and his two soldiers, who had returned from prowling the dark. Collins noticed that the two thin-lipped, silent henchmen never stepped in front of the colonel or even directly alongside him. He found himself thinking that all three could have been poured into the same mold. They seemed to communicate without speech, as though each could read the other's thoughts. Who knows, maybe they could.

Jarvis stepped forward, his face glistening waxenlike in the artificial light of headlamps and flames. "You seem to know quite a bit about that sort of thing, Commissioner," he said, his oddly robotic voice holding the faintest trace of contempt.

Smith turned to face the man, not liking the exaggerated rigidness of his military posture. In fact, he didn't like Jarvis at all. Something about the man gave a body the creeps. Smith didn't much care for his alien presence among them.

"I know enough," the commissioner replied quietly. "I know that Walker must be something special . . . or you wouldn't be here to claim custody of him. Military Intelligence, isn't it?"

This news put the men in a nervous silence as Jarvis smiled, a thin, twisted smile. "Yes, Commissioner, Military Intelligence. Walker is a deeply disturbed combat veteran. The Army must assume at least a measure of responsibility for the unfortunate condition. That is our interest in him."

Smith nodded, then chewed his lip in thought. "Well, considering the section we're in, I'd say we ought to make our operational headquarters at the Ranger Station out on Moosehead Point. From there we can organize our strike teams, and come morning we'll have aircraft cover every sector from—"

He didn't have time to finish. Sheriff Stevens came running up, puffing and wheezing heavily. "Just lost radio contact with Ellis and Parks! They were driving a Warden Service jeep, southbound, coming to us." He was gasping for air. "Chopper just verified a large flash, ten-twelve miles due north. Possibly an explosion!"

Smith's mouth fell open. "Jesus Christ! Those are my men!"

"Well, let's get on it!" roared Collins as he ran for his car. "Get that chopper over there!"

"Rotten motherfucker!" Smith hissed through tight teeth.

"Son of a bitch!" said the detective in awe.

Meanwhile Colonel Jarvis, observing the flurry of activity with critically squinted eyes, wore an expression that might even have passed for pity. He alone knew that that commando intended to tear these country boys a new asshole.

Sighing, he gave the faintest signal to his men, and they headed for their own car.

CHAPTER

SIX

There was no question about it—that chopper had to come down. It was already hovering over the last fire zone, and it was making increasingly longer exploratory sweeps around the area, that damned probe light illuminating everything under it. There was no way a man in a truck could outrun it even on a good road, much less a beat-up trail through the pucker brush. It was only a matter of time before it was going to spot the road Walker had taken moments earlier. That searchlight would expose the fresh wheel tracks through the overgrowth as clearly as the luminous dial on a diver's watch. And then it would shortly be finished. The pigs, no doubt pissed off by now, would swarm all over him. Probably even cut him down before he could position himself for a stand.

Walker swore angrily and fought off an overwhelming sense of defeat. They just had too much shit to throw at him. Goddamn! Goddamn! It couldn't end now. He couldn't let that fucking mosquito, that glaring eyeball in the sky, ruin him now. Suddenly it seemed so hopeless, so utterly useless.

He was a fool to think he could ever be free. He was a fool
to think he could extricate himself from the slimy, far-reach-
ing tentacles of the monster. They were going to catch him.
He might as well sing his death song, because he wasn't
going back. They were not going to take him back! Lord! his
soul cried. Release me from this puny, clumsy, worthless
shell I am trapped in. It's no good. It shits and farts and
smells bad when it ain't washed. It falls apart when hard
things hit it. It's sick all the time. It's a piss-poor design, and
life inside it ain't worth a fuck. Release me from the damned
thing and let it rot. It's cold. There ain't no camp and there
ain't no sunshine. Just cold, God, cold.

Then he got mad. Hard-eyed, snarling mad. Raging mad.
There was a camp out there somewhere. The sun beat down
warmly on it. All day. And a crackling fire kept it warm at
night. And when the heat from this trouble died down, he
could go for Claudine, because only she knew how to comfort him. And nobody—fuckin' nobody . . . was going to
stop him from reaching his dream. The surge of rage swept
hotly through him, and suddenly he felt an absolute and total
lack of fear. The sick fear had eaten away at his insides for
so many years that there was nothing left for it to feed on.
There was no more feast in there. The trembling, frightened
kid had been gobbled up. The nervous, paranoid man had
been consumed. There was nothing left in there but an iron
shell. An empty, hollow bombshell. And that shell was
slowly filling up with chemically unstable rage. Mind-bend-
ing rage.

He wheeled the truck in among the thick stands of trees as
best he could without lights. He snatched up the 30-06 and
got out, his jaw clenched with the rage of his deadly purpose, and he made sure the clip was filled to capacity before
angrily jamming it into the belly of his beastly piece of artillery. He stared glaze-eyed at the searchlight swaying in the
sky, hovering, circling, getting closer with each sweep. With
rotors beating and engine growling, it was like some futuris-
tic beast of prey hungrily seeking out a plump, gushy mor-
sel.

"Fuck you!" Walker suddenly screamed. "You fuckin' eye in the sky! I'll give you something, you cocksucker! I'll give you a fuckin' cataract!"

As though shot from a cannon, he took off, running back toward the main logging road. Rifle thrust before him at port arms, he ran low and fast, leaping rocks and mud holes, dodging brush, feet pounding, legs pumping with great exertion as though the gooks were cutting a rapid-fire trail behind him. He found a spot, a small clearing by the side of the road, and went for it immediately. He crawled under the thick, dead grass, swearing, panting, bringing the butt of the big gun to his shoulder.

The chopper was hovering a short distance across the road. It dipped down for a closer look at something in a deadwood bog, then rose again, *whap-whap* chugging. Searching. The pilot was probably beating his gums over the mike, relaying idiotic information to a bunch of frantic pigs. Amazing how similar this sensation must have been to the Cong hiding in the jungle, Walker found himself thinking.

Walker got a side view of the thing. Similar to a Loach but no class. No rocket launchers. No quad-60s hanging out the doors. *Where am I?* Piece of shit. They didn't have no shit like that in the war. Junk. Airborne junk. He wondered if it had a self-sealing fuselage. Piece of shit—even if it did, it wouldn't help against a burning close-range thirty-odd slug. It was coming down any goddamn way! Walker was going to blacken that fuckin' eye . . . just as soon as it got a little closer. Come on, you fat, nosy bird! Get your ass over here! Let me show you a nice little trick only a scumdog pig would fall for! Pigs! Gook motherfuckers!

He touched the button on the flashlight that was still taped to the rifle barrel, then immediately switched it back off again. Whaddaya know, it worked. The pilot spotted the short flash and swung the chopper over to investigate. The rotors beat heavy wind down on Walker's precarious hiding place as the big light washed over the area, certain to put a shine on where Fishhook's truck had plowed over brush while leaving the logging road.

Hissing like a cornered cobra, Walker flung himself to his knees, swung the rifle skyward, and put a slug right in the middle of that damnable light. It went out with a loud crack and a tinkling of falling glass.

The chopper backed off, shaky, wavering, uncertain. Walker was on his feet now, slamming shell after loudly cracking shell into the dark bulk as fast as he could work the rifle bolt. The chopper shook, veered off, then started to spin crazily, its rotors twisting erratically. Then it trailed smoke on a headlong flight toward earth and crashed hard down the road. Mighty thunder rocked the forest, and a giant ball of smoke and fire erupted skyward, brilliant, deafening.

Walker was jumping up and down, shaking the rifle above his head like a man gone insane. "Tough shit, mother-fuckers!" he was screeching. "Life is a great big bitch, ain't it, you dirty cocksuckers! Life is a black moon, baby!"

He ran back to the truck, jumped in, and tore off down the trail—private road, my ass—oblivious to any and all obstacles, banging the shit out of what used to be Fishhook's fine wheels.

Collins, face twisted tightly, hardly daring to breathe, was speeding down the rough, rutted logging road as fast as he was able. With Ray Smith riding with him, handling the radio, they were caught up behind the dust from a paramedics' wagon when they lost contact with the chopper. The pilot, who had been communicating seconds earlier, had suddenly been cut off in mid-sentence, just as he was saying something about a flash of light.

Smith was gripping the radio microphone so tight that it was hurting his hand. "Come on, Jimmy," he kept saying. "Come on! What the fuck's going on up there? Come on!"

Then the fireball hit the sky, a distant flash of flame in the night forest, and everyone in the line of vehicles heading toward it felt the tremors from the explosion. Both Smith and Collins gasped, staring forward in horrified disbelief.

"Oh, my Jesus!" Collins croaked the words, forcing them through a strained throat. Almost fourteen years in the corrections business and he thought he'd seen them all. He couldn't imagine anyone causing this much damage, much less an inmate of his! "Jesus! God Almighty! He's killed him too! How far, Ray? Oh, God, how much farther up there is it?" Tears were welling in his eyes, and his nose started running. He sniffed, wiped the back of his hand across it. He was shaking, feeling sick, following the taillights of the paramedic wagon like a man in a trance.

Ray Smith was still staring at the orange, flickering speck way out in the black wilderness. His jaw kept clenching and unclenching, and his Adam's apple kept bobbing up and down. He was having a hard time absorbing all this. I mean, Jesus, this was a state forest, a friendly and familiar place, not a goddamn war zone! He'd never seen anything like this except in Vietnam. And from a a safe distance, at that—from the security of the company mail room. Never riding straight into it like this. Jesus, he was a fish and game commissioner, not a fucking Marine! And now he was starting to get scared. He had lost three men to violent death in less than half an hour, a record that had never been duplicated in the history of his department. And now he was starting to feel the fear "those boys" had felt when they walked deliberately into that night jungle, stalking some shadowy black death and marveling at the senselessness of it all. And he felt the rage that went with it. The helpless rage that attended loss without meaning.

He was still hanging on to the mike as though it were the thread of life itself. "Eight miles." He had to choke down his sobs, and his words were coming out hard. "Maybe six, eight miles before we even get to the jeep that dirty bastard zapped." He squeezed his eyes shut tightly, then took a deep breath. "Jimmy was a good boy. Ellis. Parks. Good boys." He let the breath out long, wheezing, then gulped air again. He looked at Collins, clinging to the wheel. The superintendent's weathered face had taken on a worn, broken look, craggy with deep wrinkles. Smith could only imagine the turmoil eating away at the man's insides.

"That's a monster you boys got loose out there, Dick. A

monster. And I swear to God I'm gonna kill it. I'm gonna
stamp it out just like a disease!"

Collins got hold of himself. He met the commissioner's
wet, red-eyed glare. "No, you're not, Ray," the corrections
man replied tightly. "He's mine. He's my fucking meat.
And I'm gonna blow his head clean off his goddamned
shoulders!"

The radio had been silent, everyone awestruck by the explosion of the chopper and the inevitable death of its pilot. It
crackled back to life now, and the first person on the line
was Sheriff Stevens, driving directly behind Collins. And
the first thing Stevens had to say was, "I'm gonna kill that
crazy motherfucker . . . and there ain't a son of a whore alive
that's gonna stop me!"

"Get this fucking thing in gear!" Smith snarled. "Get
around those medics and burn dirt!"

The car roared forward in a surge of speed. Designed for
the civilized highway, it hit the ruts hard, threatening to destroy the suspension and rattle the whole machine apart.
Meanwhile the commissioner got on the mobile unit and
jacked around from station to station in an attempt to raise
some more aircraft, even though he had a queasy feeling
about it.

Sitting in the passenger seat of the military vehicle following the string of local law-enforcement officers, Colonel
Jarvis's steel-cold eyes glared straight ahead, and his sharply
outlined jaw bulged, slightly thrust forward. "Looks like
we're going to have to bring in Chip-One and the Double-
D," he quietly commented to the driver, who was wearing
captain bars.

The faintest sardonic smile twisted the captain's lips.
Hands tight on the wheel, not liking the roughness of this
hillbilly road, he replied, "You got that shit straight, sir."
And then the captain asked, somewhat uncomfortably, "Do
you think he's still pissed off about what happened in Nam
Dinh, sir?"

Jarvis continued to stare straight ahead, but he was remembering. He was remembering his own total surprise when Walker had walked into the rendezvous, calm as you please, having survived a hellish infiltration that no one had a right to live through, especially since, once the deed had been done, word had been surreptitiously slipped to the enemy camp's commanding officer that there was a saboteur in their midst. Could Walker have possibly understood? Yes, his eyes spoke of deep understanding, but he'd said nothing. Maybe it was because his eyes also spoke of deep retribution. It was time now to consider the possibility that Walker was luring his beloved colonel into the trap of traps. And damn the bloodshed. Perhaps Jarvis had trained those men too well.

"He was a soldier," the colonel finally replied tightly. "Nobody ever promised a soldier that he has to be happy about anything. Victory is all that matters. Victory is all that a soldier should live for. Or die for."

Somehow those words sounded ominous, even to himself.

The clear night sky was alive with a million twinkling stars and a big silver werewolf moon. And it was crispy with a heavy frost, whitening the summer-gone grass along the beach. Gene Gorman and Nancy Brandon weren't feeling any chill, though. That's because they were in heat. They had some blankets spread out on the boat-house floor. They were grappling with each other's half-naked bodies, touching, groping, breathing heavily, whispering urgent passions. Nancy's blouse was around her slim, bare waist, and her pointed little nipples were exposed, hard, waiting. Gorman's pants were bunched around his knees, and Nancy had a hot hand around his stiff member, stroking it. He gasped, then went down on one of those luscious tits, slurping and sucking. But that wasn't what Nancy wanted sucked. She was twisting, writhing upward while pushing Gorman's head down toward her steaming thighs. Good boy, she was thinking. Get that pretty face down where I want it . . . ohhh! So when the chopper crashed some five, six miles distant, neither one of them paid much attention to the faint echo of the

explosion. They didn't even notice the flash fire hit the sky.
Nancy had her eyes closed in ecstasy, and it was kind of
dark and musky where Gorman was looking.

Actually Nancy and Gorman were the only ones who
could have informed the house of any unusual occurrence
... such as a chopper blowing sky-high. Roger Billings, assistant to the governor's secretary as a part-time job while he
was finishing law school, was in the radio room where he
was supposed to be. Much earlier he had been listening to
the cops bickering back and forth for a while, concerning a
jailbreak, before finally growing tired of it. Being young,
being half in the Heineken bottle, and buzzing out with exotic herbs and greens, he had long ago tuned himself into an
FM station where they were playing a Rolling Stones special. Billings painfully remembered how angry the governor
had been at that last interruption. Well, we couldn't have
Hizzoner pissed off while he was on a hunting trip, now
could we? So, earphones on, feet propped up, cold beer in
hand with a full cooler beside him and enough smoke floating around to blast the brains out of a mule, Billings laid
back in his swivel chair and grooved to the tunes. He didn't
know anything about the blown jeep or the crashed chopper.
He didn't even know anything about the shotgunned hunters.
He hadn't the slightest idea what a berserk commando was,
much less what one looked like. All he knew was that some
dumb con was on the lam and the cops were hot on his ass.
Big deal. Happens all the time. "Midnight Rambler," yeah,
yeah, what a tune!

The governor and his company were entertaining themselves in the den with an antique phonograph, the kind with
the side-cranking handle and the French horn—looking
speaker. They'd crank the old sucker up and listen to such
two-pound ancient classic records as "Too Old to Cut the
Mustard Anymore" and laugh and reflect on days gone by.
Nancy's and Gorman's absence was uncomfortably conspicuous, but nobody was saying anything about it. Particularly
not Larson.

Larson was by the big, cut-stone fireplace, drink in hand,

fidgeting uneasily, laughing nervously at the jokes. In the spirit of audacity among the wealthy and the powerful, he was supposed to have his turn with Nancy later on, but being on the ambitious side, he found himself wondering if a quick screw with what everybody knew was the governor's immoral wife was worth jeopardizing his scale up the treacherous political ladder. Guiltily he wondered if these older and very influential folks knew about his tormented intentions. There was a noticeable lack of conversation coming his way, or so he thought, so they probably did at least suspect.

Of course the governor knew. He didn't enjoy his present position by just falling off the cabbage truck. But what the hell . . . Nancy was asking for it. Hard as it was to swallow, he could hardly blame Larson, a blue-blooded young lawyer with a lawyer's scruples. After all, he had once been a young lawyer himself, so he knew what kind of scruples it took to get to the top. Besides, he was having too good a time with his friends, Jack Archer and the blustery old Doc Simms, to let it bother him right now. She'd get what was coming to her when the time came.

He poured from the gin bottle. For the present he didn't much care about anything.

CHAPTER
SEVEN

With hard-slitted eyes and lips pulled back across clenched teeth, the commando saw the moonlight glittering on the lake from some distance away. A short distance farther, he saw the lights of the lodge. He was truly surprised. He had just whanged and banged that truck down a trail on which he wouldn't take a goddamn mountain mule. And now there were lights! Immediately he drove into the woods as far as he could get it, hoping nobody down there had heard the growl of the truck's engine yet.

Coming upon an occupied situation like this so suddenly (especially after such a bitch-ass ride) made him do some instant calculating. Like end of the line, baby. Snarling in desperation, he took the rifle, the shotgun, and the rucksack and went around and put the tailgate down. He laid everything on the truck bed, then took another look at the light through the trees. Target area, if there ever was one. There was nothing else to be done. Alternatives were about as slim as a string across a booby trap. The road ended here. There was no reasonable solution other than going into that place.

He knew he could not simply take off through the woods and hope to lose his pursuers. Not without careful preparation, which he didn't have time for, and especially not in the dark at such a specific location. Those goddamned imperialist running dogs, which they no doubt had an ample supply of, would tree him like a wounded bear in no time.

While entranced by those lights, everything he'd ever learned about hostage-taking situations went clicking through his mind like a computer readout, the heavy-metal clacking once again pervaded his brain, and the pain came to his head like a raw wound. Even still, some sensibility, some human thing yet gnawing at his guts, hoped it wouldn't turn out like the hunters. But if it did, it did. Life is a bitch. Who knows, maybe someone would get lucky and beat him to the draw, something a soldier lives with every day. Maybe someone would get lucky and mercifully put him out of his own misery. Until then . . . a commando does what he has to do.

Face tighter than a Mardi Gras grinner, eyes a pair of hard slits, he reached into the rucksack and brought out a couple of chunks of charcoal wrapped in a plastic bag. Air hissing quietly out through clamped, tightened teeth, he began to blacken his face and hands. It was a silent, ominous ritual. It conjured the spirit of death.

He made sure his pockets had only the things he required in them, and then he fastened them securely. He took a careful inventory of himself. No rattle. No shine. He could see his breath (high condensation in the chilly night air) so he tied a scarf around his neck. He could tuck his face into it whenever he needed to, to absorb the steam. He made sure the earflaps of the rabbit-skin cap were securely tied up, because he needed to hear even the slightest whisper of sound. Recon. Night patrol. Your life depended on it.

Finally he checked his weapons. The six-shooting .38 revolver rested snuggly under his belt, hard against his belly. And as a man who lived on the borderline, he wasn't the slightest bit concerned about the safety of the hammer laying on an empty chamber. Walker had that sucker loaded to the gills.

The bayonet, in its hard sheath, was tied securely to his leg, so there would be no drag in case he had to whip it out and ram it through some sorry fucker's throat. He made sure both clip and chamber were fully loaded in the 30-06, and then he slung the big rifle crosswise across his back. He tightened the sling and tested the sliding catch-buckle to make sure he could slip it, duck out of the sling, and have the weapon in his hands in a split second. He decided that with what he had for arsenal, Fishhook's and Wally's deer rifles would be about as worthless as tits on a wart hog.

The pump shotgun was his baby right now, and double-zero buck was the language it spoke, sufficient articulation to rip the face off a bear. With the methodic coldness of a jungle fighter, he made sure the pump cylinder, running down the underbelly of the barrel, was full and that there was a shit-kicking round slid securely in the firing chamber, and that the safety was disengaged, ready to back up anything the man behind it had to say.

War! Nostrils flared, he took a deep, sucking breath before pushing himself away from the side of the truck, spinning, coming down in a low squat. *And the commando was ready.*

And while he squatted there, under the brilliant moon, shotgun thrust before him, he gave himself the briefest moment to reflect on Claudine. Claudine knew what words to use. Who knew how she knew what words to use? She just knew. Maybe she could stop it; maybe she couldn't. And then the horror. J. What if J ever touched her innocent, peaceful life? J would eat her like a shark at the feeding frenzy. Rage! My God, can't you put anything inside my belly besides rage!

The commando moved out, dancing darkly from tree to tree, making no sound, assuming that the occupants of his target may have been warned and were armed and waiting. You take no chances, pal. Many is the soldier burning in hell because of chances. Hey, but this was an old feeling, this feeling of war, of imminent contact with the enemy. His every sense, all humpteen dozen of them, was working on hyperalert, bringing the whole picture into acute focus. For a split second the entire universe and the riddle of existence became remarkably obvious. Then it was instantly forgotten, the marvelous message lost inside a pounding heart, the mind of the man distracted by the intensity of life at hand.

The lights in that house by the lakeshore had a warm, inviting glow. Hanging low by the line of trees, everything white with the deep autumn frost, shotgun looking to cut somebody down, Walker experienced a sense of awful sadness. It made him remember what it was like when he was a kid, out in the winter dark, standing forlornly in the cold, wet snow. On that white-covered hillside the lights of his own house didn't look as nice as those of the neighbors', the homes of the kids he played with. The neighbors' lights seemed warm in their family fold, loving, caring, the shining windows a powerful talisman against midnight terror.

The lights in Walker's house were different. They conjured unpleasant scenes within. His mother and father fighting. Drunken screaming. Hitting. Tension like a stranglewire drawn taut. Tension as unstable as quasi-nitro about to explode. Walker had been brought up on the edge of singing nerves, and it eventually gave him the gift of ultrakeen perception. He could smell out danger as clearly as a dog smells shit. In the jungle, walking straight into it as point man, point man always being the first to buy the bullet, he never overlooked a booby trap. Keeping in mind that you only overlook a booby trap one time, baby. And he never failed to detect an enemy presence—any kind of ambush site. Not after he'd first got slapped in the face by what reality was all about. When danger came to his team, it thrummed through his soul as though somebody had thumped a banjo string, vibrating, making his nerves scream. He was so good at point that his buddies all thought he was some kind of psychic. But he was no psychic, nor anything like it. It was merely a lifetime of conditioning. How to anticipate and avoid the blows of a drunken father.

How to keep from being the target of violent frustration by a semi-hysterical mother. All favorable traits that "they" could use.

And where he was now, skulking under a bomber's moon, armed to the goddamned teeth, contemplating an assault on a lodge by the lake, was not unnatural at all. His peculiar orientation into a restless world had prepared him for every deadly second of it. Every desperate movement, every act of violence seemed fitting in the broad scheme of things. The bite was just *in* him. And now the odor of danger was falling around him like a suffocating fog. He knew. He knew just like a mutt knows when it's on death row at the local pound. He knew "they" were coming to terminate him.

Knowing that, he no more reasoned with what he was doing than Rover gave thought to fetching the stick. He just does it. Surely something J could appreciate. High performance. And the pressure on him now was plenty enough incentive to assure high performance. That's what they made him for, drilled him for, trained him for, and that's what he lived for. High performance. And when it came down to a final performance, it was going to be a memorable grandstand play, worthy of a standing ovation. That's because you never came out with your hands up, no matter what. The gooks would only kill you, anyway, and it would end up much worse than if you'd died gunning it out with them, especially if you weren't an officer and didn't have any hostage value. Like those Marines who had finally surrendered after a fierce firefight, when they were pinned down and their support never came. The last of the patrol was found hanging upside down from tree limbs, naked, with long, thin strips peeled from their hides and their nuts hacked off and crammed in their mouths.

No, better to die with honor, with enemy shells ripping the shit out of you. At least while you were choking on your own blood you were taking a few of the dink bastards with you on the way down. Fuckin' slopes. At least you had the satisfaction of knowing you weren't going to hell alone. Damn! If you could hold your feet long enough to hammer off just a few more rounds, your dying eyes could see gook brains glop all over the jungle floor, and gook guts spilling out and making the elephant grass red. They might be killing you, but by merciful God, it was coming at a high price.

But that was war . . . and the gooks knew and respected what it cost to kill a man like Walker. How about now? Did they know? Well, if they didn't know before, they were finding out what tough shit was awful quick!

Walker breathed a tense sigh, signaling to himself that he was ready to move out from the hillside he was perched on. He was ready to advance. And he was ready to die if it happened that way. So he moved on, crouched low, gliding like a ghost from one shadow to the next.

There was a humming sound in the distance. Walker identified it as a motor noise coming from a building separate from the house, set off by itself in a grove of trimmed pine. He rightly reckoned it to be a gasoline-operated generator, which meant the house had its own independent power supply, and from the looks of the antennas rising from the rear of the main building, they also had their own communications system. Fancy. Those definitely weren't poor folks down there. All the better. Cops might kill you all if you had nothing but penniless hostages, whereas the rich ones might bring you results. Any terrorist could tell you that. Walker smiled at thinking of himself as a terrorist.

Then he was not smiling anymore. He became angry. He was not a terrorist, and political ideals meant nothing to him. If anything, he was an anarchist in the truest form. He recognized the authority of no government on the face of the earth. Shit, government? Government was the real source of mankind's afflictions. To hell with that. He was a simple commando on the most important mission of his life. The nature of his self-imposed assignment was to gain freedom —or to die trying. How could there possibly be anything odd or criminal about that? Wars throughout history had been fought for the sake of freedom. Or so they told him. But this was only another war, except this time the objective was clearly defined. A great American hero once said,

"Give me liberty or give me death!" Walker was saying it now.

Stealthily, doing the low crawl across the wet, frost-filled grass, his war-conditioned brain transcending the fierce pain in his wounded arm, he approached the rear of the house. There was a shaggy hedge around the whole building, so he took advantage of it and filtered through shadows between the foliage and the wall. Crouching under each window, eyeball peering up over each sill, checking them out one by one, he soon had a mind's-eye view of the inner layout.

He stopped short by the window of the back den. There were sounds of laughter coming from within, tinkling glasses, old-fashioned music. Squatting low, directly beneath the sill, with shotgun brought up tight against his chest, he reckoned it was the cocktail generation doing whatever it is that they do. It was still early in the evening, so it was reasonable to expect them to remain so occupied for a while yet. All good signs so far. He had not yet encountered any indication of an armed reception committee, which he had his cold-slitted eyes glaring for. Could be possible that they were unaware.

Still, he was taking no chances. He was hurting to sneak a peek inside the window but decided against it on the odd chance that someone might inadvertently glance out and see him, thereby calling the alarm. He'd helped put men in rubber body bags on odd chances. Besides, he could just about guess from the voices that there were about five or six people in there, mixed company. And they didn't sound like they were anticipating anything other than a good time.

There were a few smaller cabins, unlit, farther down the beach, in the direction of the generator house. Finishing his recon on the main lodge, Walker checked them all out with extreme caution, in the event that guests or maintenance personnel might be living in them. Then he checked the hugely impressive generator itself. His first impulse was to sabotage the machinery, blow the fucking thing sky-high, but he could think of no logical reason for doing it, so he left it alone. This unreasonable impulse to blow things up was something he had to curb, before it got him in serious trouble. He knew damned well that he didn't need to put his prospective hostages on alert. He needed absolute and total surprise.

Satisfied that the guest houses were empty, he cradled the shotgun in his elbows and low-crawled along the bush line of the beach. Then he was in the shadows of the catwalk, slithering in the direction of the boat house, sand and gravel sneaking up his sleeves and down his boots. A minor irritation when you put the assault into perspective. A goddamn sight better than jungle mud, anyway.

Then he saw the planes bobbing lazily on either side of the wharf. He stopped. His heart stopped. His breathing stopped. Planes! Were his eyes deceiving him! No, there they were. The winged craft put a whole different picture to his plight. Now, by God, his chances were real! It was no longer a showdown to the death, surrounded by the wolves, hacking away at him bit by bit, mercilessly assuring him that he was doomed to a snowball's odds in hell. Planes! And some goddamn sorry fucker inside that house knew how to fly them!

He heard voices in the boat house and froze tighter than a fish on ice. Ears strained to the max, he listened intently for a while. He couldn't suppress a smile. A man and a woman screwing on the sly, complimenting each other on how good it felt. He would have liked to give them a break, but wartime is no time for benevolence. Even the most harmless-appearing situation could turn out to be a death trap. Forget it, pal, and you'll be spilling your woes to those in hell who lost it on the fast draw.

Walker snaked under the catwalk and emerged by the building's sliding door. One quick glance and he jumped inside, landed in the low crouch, shotgun cocked and leveled. "Don't move!" he whispered harshly. "Don't even twitch or I will kill you!"

Both Nancy and Gorman had been on their feet when the commando surprised them. Nancy was in the act of pulling up her panties, and Gorman, shirt open, had just finished fastening his trousers. They stared at the armed intruder in utter shock, eyes wide with fear, disbelief holding their mouths partially open.

Walker could tell instantly that a hysterical scream was preparing to rise up out of the woman. His movements nothing more than a black blur, he vaulted forward and slapped her hard enough to drop her to her knees.

Well now, that maneuver constituted more bullshit than the surprised Gorman cared to stand. He became outraged. Tall, well built, he played a tough game of tennis, was highly competitive, and had been on the college wrestling team. He intended to beat the shit out of this crazy little punk, maybe even cave his skull in with one of those guns he was carrying.

"Now see here!" he began indignantly. Tightly corded neck muscles bulging, handsome face thrust forward, fists clenched at his sides, he went for Walker, but no courtly game he ever played left him prepared for the swift, precise violence of a gun butt ramming him with murderous force in the middle of the belly. Although he might not have appreciated it on his long journey downward, a different man administering such a blow in so critical an area quite likely would have killed him.

The air went out of him in a loud, burping whoosh, his legs turned to jelly, and ten million tiny stars exploded in his brain. He fell to the floor heavily, then struggled sickly to his knees, clutching his stomach tightly, gasping raggedly for every tortured breath. Nancy was shuddering and sobbing, suddenly aware of the cold. She clung desperately to the stricken Gorman, now choking on his knees, her small breasts buried against him.

Walker low-squatted so he could be at eye level with Gorman. He laid the cold, yawning shotgun muzzle up against the lawyer's throat. "This is a 12-gauge pump," he quietly explained, as though he were talking to a ten-year-old. "It is loaded with double-ought buckshot. If I pull this trigger, it will tear your head right off your shoulders. It would not be good for you to forget that!"

"W-what do you want?" Nancy was whimpering, the side of her face red and stinging. She dared not look directly at the deadly intruder's horribly blackened face, and particularly not at his fierce, burning eyes.

"Shut up!" Walker snapped. "Just shut up and listen. I am an extremely desperate man, and I think that you know by now that I'm not in the mood for any fun and games. If you like living, then you will do exactly what I tell you and not make any more stupid moves. I don't make jokes. I'm not a stand-up comedian. If you think I won't kill either or both of you, you're living in a suicidal fantasy." He grabbed Gorman by the hair and jerked his head upright. "Do I make myself clear?"

Gorman, the fight knocked completely out of him, nodded as best he could. He felt like kicking himself in the ass for his preconceived notion of the "little punk." A little commonsense strategy might have altered the situation (although he somehow doubted it). This dude was wired to the gills.

"We're going up to the house," Walker said. "Pull any kind of funny shit—anything at all—and I'm going to blow you away."

He picked a blanket up off the floor and threw it disdainfully at the woman, signifying that he didn't have the patience to wait for her to get dressed. Fearfully and in shame, she huddled into it. She helped Gorman struggle to his feet, clinging to him, both of them a little unsteady. The defeated lawyer gave her a look that said, "I'm sorry I let you down, darling."

And she returned him a scornful, twisted look that said, "You weak-kneed, lily-livered bastard!" And that hurt him more than the gun butt to the guts had.

"Move out!" Walker ordered. And he herded his subdued prisoners up the catwalk, forcing them to stagger along as best they were able.

For a reason he could not name, the governor did not find himself surprised when Nancy and Gorman came stumbling into the room, half naked, looking like they'd taken a beating. It was as though some unspoken, hidden thing deep inside his belly had always meant to tell him that he would finally be hit in the face by this. So he did indeed have some difficulty being surprised when a most savagely visaged, armed man slid smoothly from behind the two, stalking cat-like to a position where he could cover the entire room and watch the door at the same time. Curious, maybe. But not surprised.

Melinda Archer had been in the process of changing records on the old phonograph when the commando, like an ominously silent storm cloud, darkened the room with his presence, a surrealistic image of danger suddenly risen from some faraway swamp in some faraway jungle. That clenched face held no smile; those frozen, staring eyes held no mercy. She stopped what she was doing, her mouth half open, her heart in the grip of a hand like ice, and she stared in horror, thoroughly speechless. She wasn't the only one gawking in wide-eyed disbelief. So was her husband, Jack, his cocktail glass half raised, as was Doc Simms and his wife, and Tim Larson, Esquire.

If they were gawking wide-eyed, then so was Walker. That face! He knew that face! Awestruck, he suddenly realized that he had the governor of the state under the gun. It took a few seconds for the magnitude of it to sink in. Was this an act of God? One simple quirk of fate and he had enough hostage power to assure successful negotiations. *Hai*, war was wondrous and full of miracles in its ruthless give-and-take.

But just now the governor wasn't looking at the commando. Brandon's lips were pressed together in a tight slit. His eyes, cold, slightly glazed by alcohol, were on the girl and the lawyer. It was a disgusted expression. Hurt and disgusted. And Gorman, still clutching his midriff in pain, looked as though he'd rather shrivel up and drift away than remain under that chilly glare.

Walker, with shotgun barrel covering all the odds, looked from one to the other, and then to everyone in the room. Suddenly he understood. He found himself under the influ-

ence of an unreasonable sense of embarrassment, a stranger
having stepped into an unpleasant family dispute. But circumstances being what they were, these people had best
right away understand why he was here.

His tone carrying an inflection of respect, Walker said,
"I'm sorry, Governor, but all of you are my prisoners."

Lips still tight, Brandon nodded, acknowledging what the
ferocious-looking young man had just announced. He took
note of Walker's calm bearing, deliberate desperation, the
steady, unwavering shotgun barrel, the slung rifle, the big
knife strapped to the leg, the thin-bearded face painted for
black-night work. He also took note of the ripped jacket
sleeve, pinned together so it wouldn't flap, and heavy with
dried blood. Brandon recognized his professionalism, and
that gave him some measure of relief. This was no scared
kid liable to shoot at the slightest sound. This man, lurking
before him like a mountain cat hungry for a meal, was the
real thing . . . whatever the real thing was. And obedience to
his orders would surely mean the difference between life and
death. Brandon couldn't resist a certain feeling of respect.

He nodded again. "I understand your position, Mr.
Walker." He raised his hands slightly. "Easy. I know who
you are and what you've done. You'll get no provocation
from anyone here."

The commando nodded too. "Good," he said. "That's all I
wanted to hear." He let the barrel of his weapon slowly rake
the room, just so everyone understood.

Suddenly Nancy broke away from Gorman and threw herself in Brandon's arms. The blanket slid to the floor from her
bare back, forcing her to push her little titties against him.
"Oh, John!" she whined. "Darling, it was horrible. He hit
me. He's crazy! Oh, John, he's going to kill us all!"

The governor firmly pushed her out at arm's length. A
revulsion built up inside him as he glowered at his wife,
shivering before him in nothing but panties soaked at the
crotch. Goddamn sow in heat. He took her by the arm and
none too gently marched her toward the couch where Doc
Simms and his wife were sitting. The old folks' hands were

on their knees, clearly showing that they harbored no deadly intentions.

"Get over there and sit down!" Brandon roughly ordered. He picked up the blanket and threw it at her. "Cover yourself up, goddammit!" Then he shifted his blazing eyes back to Gorman. "Get over there with her, Studly. You not only deserve each other, but I hope to Christ this gunner delivers you both into eternity!" And Gorman, like a whipped dog, silently obeyed.

With whatever dignity he could muster, Brandon turned back to face the grim-lipped commando.

Jack Archer was a reasonable and intelligent man. He was still standing motionless on the other side of the couch, elbow on the fireplace mantel, drink in hand, attempting to appear calm and collected when in truth he was scared shit-less. He knew enough about the human condition to know that this black-faced boy wasn't just wired . . . he was a god-damned A-bomb about to happen! The vibes were thick enough to float a battleship.

Archer tried to think of something, anything, but he knew with dead certainty that any action at this moment would result in nothing short of disaster. Doing his best to maintain his composure, he peeked across the fireplace at Larson— and that's when his heart went damned near up his throat. It was clear that the young lawyer was fidgeting with some kind of indecision. His whitened face even showed his fear. It also showed a desperate resolution. God, no! Archer thought with alarm. Surely that fool wasn't going to try something stupid!

Larson, standing cowed-down like everybody else, was within arm's reach of the expensive ebony gun cabinet. He kept casting furtive glances at the drawer beneath the rifle rack, where he knew there was a loaded pistol. He knew it was loaded because he'd been playing with it earlier, liking the important feel of it, thumbing shells into it, thinking to plunk a few cans down by the beach later on.

He was drunk. Shit-faced drunk. And his drunken figuring had it that a heroic display in this time of stress would mend the tension between the governor and his wife and certainly remove the heat of suspicion from himself, maybe even move him on up that coveted ladder. Lawyer to the end. To the end, all right.

He licked his lips, waited for his moment, then moved.

Before Archer could yell to stop him, Larson jumped for the drawer, yanked it open, snatched out the pistol, and turned . . . but way too slow. Teeth bared like a slavering, rabid wolf, Walker gunned him down. The shotgun belched smoke and fire in a deafening roar, drowning out the screams of the women, the recoil rocking Walker's body backward. Larson's whole chest blew apart in a spray of red. He was sent flailing back against the gun cabinet, smashing the glass doors. Then, mouth open, eyes rolling in his head, frozen in a picture of his own death, he finally slid to the floor, and the shaken cabinet crashed heavily on top of him, mercifully covering the crimson mess of his upper torso.

Just then, the door to the radio room at the rear of the den swung open and out stepped Roger Billings, higher than the space shuttle, earphones perched atop his head.

"Dear God!" gasped Archer, as the crazy-eyed, snarling commando spun on his heel. The smoking shotgun barrel zeroed in on Billings's chest as flawlessly as a compass needle seeking north. Breathing in that room stopped, and the specter of instant murder loomed like a thick, choking fog.

Billings's face went whiter than a Klan sheet, but fortunately his arms had the sense to automatically shoot themselves skyward. And then the moment passed, and the gasps of relief were clearly audible, and Billings realized how close he had just come to exploring the hereafter.

Witnessing the commando's unusual quickness, the women were cowed to terrified silence, and the men were drenched in nervous sweat. This was a nightmare. This was supposed to happen somewhere else, to somebody else. This was supposed to be something you watched on the late news with a shaking head, in the safety and security of your living room. It wasn't supposed to invade the sanctity of your private life. The war monster had no business crouched in your midst, hard-eyed, showing his teeth, ruthlessly efficient, killing off your numbers. The sudden reality of Larson's death gave those standing the odd sensation of rubbery legs.

"I—I have an important transmission for the governor," Billings said awkwardly, feeling somewhat disconnected. He also felt nakedly conspicuous staring down the black bore of that shotgun, with that crazy guy crouched like an unmoving statue behind it. Queasily he avoided looking at Tim Larson's legs sticking out from beneath the overturned gun cabinet.

"Everyone sit down right there by the couch!" Walker barked, motioning with the gun while sidestepping toward the radio room. Even though he still wore the visage of a six-foot-three, great big black-ass drill sergeant, he understood what the kid had just been through. It didn't ease the tone of his voice as he growled, "Okay, boy, relay your message."

Billings, still standing in the radio room door with his hands raised, still keeping them raised, all of a sudden had a good idea of what it was like to be on the proverbial spot. He fidgeted, shuffled, and had a hard time holding his bladder. He looked to the governor for some indication as to what he should do, and Brandon nodded solemnly.

"Well, uh, er, sir. A report just came in that the, uh, convict who escaped today has killed two men near the twenty-one-mile marker on the access road, and then he blew up their camp. The, uh, convict commandeered a vehicle and proceeded north on the access road where he encountered a Warden Service jeep. The jeep was blown up and the two officers in it were killed. He then shot down a surveillance helicopter, killing the pilot. We have been warned that he is definitely headed in this direction and that we should evacuate immediately." He gulped, then added, "I think he's already here, sir."

Brandon, Archer, the women, the old doctor, stared slack-jawed. They stared at Walker in horrific fascination.

"Get over there on that couch," Walker ordered the shaken Billings. "And stay put. Every fucking one of you. And you get your ass over here, Governor. We're going to have a chat with those officials of yours." He cast a warning mean-eye at those huddled on and around the couch. Blackened lip pulled back over his teeth, he said, "Let your friend over there remind you of what will happen if anyone tries any more shit. I have enough ammo in this fucker to wipe you out entirely. Do you understand that? Entirely!" He let that sink in, then added, somewhat contemptuously, "If you had been commandos, you could have killed me in the instant that man distracted me. You had a chance, but you didn't know how to take it. That's the difference. Not my fault. You are not commandos, which simply means that you had better not forget what grade you're in, kiddies. When a soldier is in a forced confrontation with hostile enemies, he is not differentiating between the learned and the unlearned."

"We're not murderers...like you!" Melinda Archer hissed. Her tiny fists were clenched, and she was trembling.

"Hush, Melinda!" snapped Jack in alarm. He grabbed her in his arms, tightly, protectively.

Eyes so slitted that they practically showed nothing but white, Walker slapped a look on her that spoke of true amazement. "Murder?" Then he roared the word: "Murder!" He gestured wildly with his weapon at the fallen lawyer. "Is that what you call murder? Well, let me tell you something, lady! He was a man in a war situation, just like I was when I was a nineteen-year-old kid. That son of a whore meant to blow my shit away. So he died with a gun in his hand, killed by the enemy. Me. If I had made a stupid mistake in the war, I would be dead too. What's the big difference between him and me? What's the difference between him and a Vietnamese soldier? What are you going to tell me next? Are you going to tell me that none of you asked me to come here? That none of you asked for the war you're in right now? Well, you listen to me, every shit-fuckin' one of you. None of us asked for your goddamn motherfuckin' war, either!" His voice had risen to harsh fury, and the captives became overwhelmed with the prickly sensation one gets when suddenly aware that he is in the company of an unhinged mad-man.

The commando calmed down, then said in a more deadly, hushed tone, "Now you know what tough shit is. Governor, it's time we got on that radio. No doubt your troops are worried."

CHAPTER
EIGHT

She was pushing herself nervously back and forth in the rocking chair in front of the radio, her hands clasped tightly in her long-skirted lap. Tears wet her high, Southern-girl cheeks. A kerosene lamp on the flowered table, turned down low, was the only light that graced her quaint log cabin. And that light washed warmly over her terribly hurt face. She did not want to believe the monstrous things that the radio announcer was saying.

How well she remembered her first encounter with him. Her husband had abandoned her years ago, leaving her with this isolated homestead farm. She stayed because she had grown in love with the farm and the rolling hills beyond. She loved her flowers, and her vegetable garden, and her chickens, and her goats. And she loved the peace and serenity of country living.

She first saw him while she'd been working her garden. He came strolling across the meadow with a lazy grace. He was carrying a backpack and a rifle, appearing as though he'd just spent much time in the woods. Except the rifle was not like anything she had ever seen before, and somehow that made her uncomfortable. It was short and compact. It had air vents and a pistol-grip handle. It had a long, curved magazine, which would hold more ammunition than any hunter would ever need. And he carried it high before him, supported by a sling across his shoulder, as though at any moment he expected . . . well . . . war.

She'd smiled at the ease of his movements over the rough backcountry ground. She'd smiled at him when he approached. "Been out hunting?" she had asked.

And, oddly, he had looked at the ground like a bashful child. "Don't hunt anymore," he'd mumbled. Then he'd asked, "That the road to Fir Grove over there?"

He had long, flowing hair that whipped in the breeze, and he had an aura of self-assurance that Claudine had instantly fallen in love with. "Yes," she'd replied. "Exactly six miles to town. Been out camping long?"

"Couple of weeks."

"Oh? Where?"

"Back there."

If there was one thing that stuck in Claudine's mind, it was the amazement she had felt when the strange, quiet man had gestured toward the west. Vast, trackless wilderness, and he'd not been anywhere near any hiking trails. Just wandering out of the dark forest like that had felt almost spooky.

She had set her hoe aside and straightened her hair. "Well, you look like you could use a cup of coffee."

Dimples had creased his cheeks with a light smile. "Yes, ma'am, I sure could."

And once inside her tight, lonely, cedar-log cabin, she'd refused to let him go. That he'd been hurt more deeply than anything she could imagine was obvious. But she had always known in her heart that she could teach him the ways of peace. And he was learning, except for times when his strange emotions would overwhelm him. She never understood it, except deep inside where her soul was. She knew he was different. But she also knew he was good, that he treated her with profound kindness and more respect than she had ever known.

Then came that terrible day of the phone call. "Sometimes freedom comes at a price," was all he'd say in explanation, while arming himself with those horrible guns of his. And then prison. And now this.

She shut the radio off. And the tears came in dripping streams, and sobs racked her slender body.

There was nothing even remotely salvageable from either the jeep or the helicopter, both destroyed within a scant couple of miles of each other. Nothing but burned, twisted wreckage. The firemen had put out what flames remained, and the paramedics had zipped three scorched leftovers into their rubber body bags.

"Looks like a fuckin' war zone," commented one medic while gawking with great trepidation this way and that. He helped load the last body bag aboard the hospital transport.

"Tell you one thing, they sure as hell don't pay me for this kind of shit," whispered another, also nervously glancing around. "C'mon, let's get these stiffs to the morgue."

So, using one excuse or another, the medics and the volunteer firemen, who emphatically embraced the status of noncombatants, slowly drifted away. What lay ahead was not in their contract. At least not until it was over. That's what you paid SWAT teams and soldiers for.

The area surrounding the entrance to the private road Walker had taken was a blending mass of headlights and a psychedelic display of spinning blue and red bubbles atop numerous vehicles. The state troopers were there. The Sheriff's Department and his deputies were there. The Warden Service and whatever men they had on call were there. And Collins, the man who could possibly be held the most accountable, was there with every officer he could spare from the correctional facility. All the men were armed with everything from pistols to riot guns to automatic rifles. Some amused themselves with anecdotes about other manhunts they'd been involved in. Others brandished their weapons with self-importance, anxious to shoot somebody. Most milled around their vehicles in small groups, holding secretive, uneasy conversation, each segment of law enforcement, without saying it outright, hoping the other would be the first ordered to go down that trail.

Collins was at his car radio. Ray Smith, Sheriff Stevens, and a few other officials were hovering closely around him. So was Colonel Jarvis, for once wearing an expression of deep concern. It showed by an ever so slight loosening of his rock-hard visage. But what was it that concerned him?

"The operator has gone to get the governor!" There was excitement in Collins's voice. "At least we know the little bastard hasn't got there yet. Unless he's outside casing the place. God forbid! Jesus, the governor! Those people have got to get out of there. What the hell's taking so long? What are those men over there doing? Where's that state trooper captain? Christ Almighty, don't let anyone start down that trail until I've talked to the governor!" And on he babbled. And as he babbled, he locked glances with the steel-eyed colonel, and an inexplicable chill swept over him.

Finally the receiver crackled, and everyone jumped as though a shot had gone off. A slow, deep voice came over the radio.

"Good evening, Mr. Collins. It's a little warm for this time of year, wouldn't you say? Some might even think of it as hot. It's a fuckin' hot day in November, Collins, you treacherous pig!"

Collins stared at the radio in unrestrained horror, his worst nightmare come to life, feeling somewhat like he was in the middle of *The Twilight Zone*. Visions of the floating eye and Rod Serling's deep narrative went sailing through his stunned mind. It occurred to him that it was an odd thing to be thinking at a time like this.

"Oh, shit!" groaned Smith and Stevens, almost in unison. All units had been on that frequency. All had heard.

Collins never would have thought silence could be so deafening. The microphone in his hand felt like some kind of creepy, crawly thing. He pressed the transmit button and cleared the colony of frogs hopping in his throat. "Walker!" he choked. He coughed and cleared his throat again. His chest felt tight, as though someone had put a rope tourniquet around his rib cage and was applying steady pressure. Christ, he wasn't having a heart attack, was he?

"Walker," he said again, his voice more clear this time but quavering. "Is—is the governor with you?"

There was a short laugh, then a snort. "Yes, the governor is with me. You know, Collins, I put in a request over two months ago to see you. I wanted to talk to you about the possibility of work release. You didn't acknowledge my request. You ignored it, you son of a bitch. Instead you set me up to be shuffled off to some military installation about which you know nothing. You shrugged me off as just another sniveling convict whining for his freedom, undeserving of your precious attention. Obviously, as Mr. Big, you had higher and loftier matters to concern yourself with than the stupid, illiterate, bitching bums under your charge. I mean, there were the press conferences, there was the hobnobbing with the big-shit politicos. What goes on inside those fuckin' zoos you oversee from the outside is of little interest to you. So long as nothing causes a public furor, then everything is running smoothly, right? Up yours, you prick. It's not running very smoothly now, is it? All you've ever been concerned with is your public image, your sense of position, your status. How does it feel to squirm, motherfucker? Tell me, Mr. Collins, are you putting in a request to speak with the governor?"

Collins's ears burned. His face was flustered with rage and embarrassment. The whole state force was listening to this shit. Oh, Walker was a smartass, all right. Bastard probably knew that the press was picking that crap up too. Even still, the superintendent couldn't shake the feeling of guilt. Walker was right, he had ignored that request slip. He had in fact wadded it up and thrown it in the wastebasket, just like he had done with hundreds of others. I mean, you couldn't grant an audience to every petty complaint that came across your desk. None of these guys here knew that. So why did

he get the impression that everyone was looking at him like
he was some sort of a reptile?

But the governor's life was at stake, which was all that
was important right now. So, swallowing a bitter portion of
his pride, he said, "Yes. Yes, Mr. Walker, I am putting in a
request to speak with the governor." I'll kill him, he
thought. I swear to God I'll kill the murdering little cocksucker!

Walker's voice came back on, but he was not exactly
gloating, as Collins thought he would be.

"All right. You may find my tactics repulsive. But in the
final analysis you will agree that they are not quite so despi-
sable, nor so treacherous, as your own. You may talk to the
governor."

"John!" Collins gasped. "John, are you all right?"

The governor's voice, somewhat strained, came on.
"Calm down, Dick, and remain calm. Do you read me?"

Collins wiped the sweat from his brow. Even with the
growling of engines and numerous lights streaking the dark,
a hushed silence pervaded the air. "I read you, John."

"Good. Now listen carefully, because I'm going to relay
my wishes and those of Mr. Walker. He refuses to speak to
you again, since he considers it beneath his dignity." There
was a short pause, during which a few officers shuffled uncomfortably. "There are eight of us being held hostage. Take
it down: me and Nancy. Jack Archer and his wife. Dr. Ro-
land Simms and his wife. Gene Gorman, an Eastern Pulp
and Paper representative. And Roger Billings, the assistant
to my secretary and our radio operator. We are all fine and
well, with the exception of Mr. Tim Larson, who has been
killed in action—as Mr. Walker puts it. Mr. Larson tried to
be a hero."

So the maniac has already killed somebody in there, Collins groaned inwardly. Christ, what a nightmare! Then he
suddenly blurted, "How is he armed? What are his plans?"

"Shut up, you blundering idiot!" came the harsh reply,
and Collins shriveled. "Do not interrupt me again. If you do
that again, communication will be terminated."

The radio went silent again. Everyone figured the governor must be getting his instructions, which was true.

"All right, listen up. You are to send no one into this area. If there are people in this area, call them out immediately. If Mr. Walker detects any movement outside, one of us will be killed. If any aircraft approaches this area, another of us will be killed. Any attempt to surround this place, or execute any movement of force, will result in all of us being killed without hesitation.

"Dick, you'd better be listening very carefully. I don't want any more heroes. You are quite aware by now that Mr. Walker is highly proficient at whatever it is he's doing. But believe it or not, he is also something of a man of honor. I believe that if we do as he says, no one else will be hurt. I don't want anyone else hurt, Dick. His orders are my orders precisely.

"We can see the lights of a patrol boat out on the lake. Mr. Walker intends to show his good faith by releasing some of the hostages. They will get into one of our boats, and that patrol boat will pick them up, then it will immediately leave the area.

"Instructions stand as stated. Any attempt at a double cross and we all die. If that happens, Dick, Mr. Walker feels confident that he can slip through any dragnet you could possibly lay. He fully expects to leave a body count that will stagger you. He fully expects to personally slit your throat.

"Stand by. And I mean do absolutely nothing but stand by. Over and out."

Collins leaned against his car, slumped, staring like the broken man he was. He wasn't immediately aware of it, but his hand had been absently caressing his throat. He drew the hand away as though a jolt of electricity had zapped it. Jesus! It was like having some kind of a monster in your backyard! He looked to his trusted friends Ray and Sheriff Stevens for a word of support, but both were intently interested in the ground, toeing the dirt. No one wanted to be the first to make a decision on this unholy mess. There seemed to be little doubt that Walker would indeed carry out his threat if his instructions were not followed. And there was also the possibility, judging from his incredible performance so far, that he could indeed exfiltrate a dragnet and . . . well . . . carry out the rest of his threat.

Then Collins moved his tired eyes to Jarvis, who appeared to be lost in an unpleasant reverie of his own. "Care to comment on the situation, Colonel? After all, you probably know more about the man than we do. Why do I keep getting the feeling that there's more to that guy than we know about? Good Christ, he's a one-man walking disaster!"

Jarvis had one hand on his hip while the other massaged his forehead, as though he were afflicted with a bad headache. "He was exceptionally well trained, that's all," Jarvis replied, almost with regret. "As a result, he's seen a lot of combat. That's the problem. He thinks this is war. He thinks this is just another combat situation. He sees us as a hostile enemy force. Worse, he sees us as the aggressor. That's why we were coming for him: He's ill. He probably doesn't even know he's in the real world. He probably thinks we all have slanted eyes. Which means that he'll likely carry out his threat if we move in, something I'd advise against trying for the moment. You'd be surprised at how well he can pick up movement in the dark. Or even sound. Jungle fighters get that way."

Collins sighed and ran his hand through his gray hair, now tousled. "Damn! Shit! Well, can't you talk to him or something? Wouldn't he listen to you?"

At this Jarvis looked away. "I don't think that would be a very good idea at this time. I would venture to guess that he's less fond of me than he is of you. If he hears my voice and knows that I'm in on this, no telling how he'll react." The colonel paused in thought. "We might have an ace in the hole, though. He's created an attachment to a girl. Out of character with a man of his nature, but he's done it nevertheless. According to my map, this road leads to a cutoff that goes directly into Greentown Junction, the area where she lives. I'm sure I can convince her to have words with Walker. She might even be able to talk him out—if he hasn't shut down communication altogether. The trouble is, I might not get there before he goes for a tactical evasion. I'd say it was worth a try, though."

For the first time that evening Collins's face lit up with hope. And there was a measure of excitement in his voice. "You may have something there, Colonel. I know the girl you're talking about. Claudine Ford, I think her name is. She never missed a weekend visiting day at the prison. And I don't know of anyone else who ever came to see him. Yes, you just might have something. And the cutoff is about three miles up the road. Then it's about another fifteen, twenty miles to the junction, no doubt where Ellis and Parks were coming from, since there's a Ranger station there. If you hit it hard, you might make it in a half hour, forty-five minutes. You've got a radio, but I'd like to send a couple of men with you. I'd best stay here myself."

"Thank you, Mr. Collins, but I think it would be better if I handled this alone. Too many officials might put her on guard. Don't worry, I'll get her on the air." Then Jarvis nodded to his men and they headed for their car.

As Collins watched the military vehicle peel out, an inexplicable set of chills creeped up his spine. He could not shake the feeling that things were not quite on the up-and-up. Not just the colonel but also Walker. Walker. No man alive had the right to function with such terrifying accuracy.

A group of officers down the road were having a time holding a noisy assortment of newsmen at bay. One stubby, short-legged reporter broke through and came running toward Collins. Two officers quickly jumped in front of him and began hustling him back, roughly informing him that he was in a restricted area.

"Mr. Collins!" the reporter yelled as he was being manhandled, trying to wrestle himself free. "It appears the fugitive is holding all the cards. What do you intend to do? It's our understanding that you are responsible for him. A court of law sentenced him to your custody, did it not? Is society safe from men imprisoned for their crimes? Or do you run a

Boy Scout camp for killers who can come and go as they please?"

Collins shook his head while looking at the dirt. Well, it was time to put on the knee boots because the shit was getting deep. By morning he would be under a hard and unforgiving public eye. His job was doomed even if he rescued the governor and killed Walker. He himself—and he just plain knew it in his guts—was doomed if he didn't.

Finally he said, "Sir, I intend to do exactly as the governor of this state has ordered me. No further comment. Officers, get those men away from here! We will have a statement for the press once we have evaluated our tactical advantages. Until then, all unauthorized persons are to stay clear of this area. We consider it a danger zone, and we are not discounting the possibility of booby traps."

He turned back to his own men. He lit a cigarette, dragged deeply, let the smoke roll out in a long breath. He sighed heavily, hoping to hell Myrna wasn't tuned in to this catastrophe.

"Well," he mumbled, "at least we know where he is, whatever comfort that is. And he's pretty well surrounded, even if we can't close it up. He can't leave there without us knowing about it. And he's at least releasing some of the hostages." He sighed again, looking over the conglomeration of milling troops. "All these cops and not a real professional among us. Isn't this rural Maine for you? We need to send a reconnaissance team down there, but I don't dare send any of these guys. Like the colonel said, he'd spot 'em for sure." He turned abruptly to the sheriff. "Stevens, get on the horn, will you? I guess the FBI will want a piece of this action. See if you can raise us a hostage negotiating expert." He hesitated, chewed the filter of his cigarette, then said, "And see if SWAT can send us every long-range sniper they've got to spare."

Using a pair of high-powered binoculars, Walker watched carefully as the motorboat carrying his released hostages made contact with the Warden Service patrol boat. Dr.

Simms and his wife, Jack Archer's wife, Gene Gorman, and Roger Billings were helped aboard. Then the boat swung around and headed up the lake, as instructed. Walker, with some amount of grim satisfaction, watched the bobbing lights recede into the darkness.

He had his remaining prisoners at the front of the house, seated on a divan in front of the bay windows. A comfortable distance away he had the shotgun resting on a plant table, trained on them, his finger on the trigger as he alternated quick scrutiny from the prisoners to the boat. He needn't have worried excessively, though. After witnessing the ghastly spectacle of Larson getting his chest blown out, no one was eager to provoke a repeat performance.

Jack Archer's opinion of Walker as a mad-dog killer was undergoing doubt and confusion. Jack lived in a world where things were cut-and-dried. A man was one thing or he was the other. He didn't like contradictions. And a wild-looking man with his face blackened out, who shot people down and at the same time showed mercy and spoke intelligently, constituted a contradiction. But was Walker really a contradiction? He was a real something, to be sure. It's just that Jack didn't know—or didn't want to name it.

"Mr. Walker," he said. "I want to thank you for letting Melinda go. Also, you did the right thing with Dr. Simms and his wife."

Nancy, cowering uncomfortably between Archer and Brandon, started whimpering again. "Sure, you let Jack's wife go. You let the doctor's wife go. But what about me? I'm a woman too." She rose and slowly began to advance across the floor, swaying her shapely hips seductively. "Would you like to know how much of a woman I am?" But she stopped dead in her tracks, midway across the floor, when the shotgun rose, its yawning black maw staring her straight between the eyes. Her heart froze in terror at the commando's utter lack of expression. She was confused. She was extremely pretty. Men adored her, pampered her, gave her whatever she wanted. And *he* was nothing but a man, wasn't he? With a horrified shudder she suddenly realized that he intended to shoot her—my God, of all places—directly in the face!

Archer was embarrassed. Not for Nancy but for his friend, the governor. Brandon gave her a sour look, then shook his head. "Oh, for God's sake, Nancy, straighten up. Get back over here and sit down. If you can't stop being a whore, at least stop acting like one!"

She complied, her knees wobbly. But her husband's severe rebuke was not what drove her back to her seat; it was the commando's squinted, terribly ruthless glare. He'd said not a word, yet he'd struck her down as surely as he'd done in the boat house. As she resumed her seat her enviable beauty was distorted with anger, hatred, and profound humiliation.

Walker eyed the woman coldly, and a sick kind of disgust filled his belly. Cong bitch. Using the wiles of her sex to lure men to their deaths. Maybe she had a tube inserted up her cunt, filled with razor blades. Maybe some gook would burst out of nowhere and put a knife through your ribs while you were in the throes of passion.

The clacking started at the back of his head again, and he clenched his teeth against it. But it was mild this time, and mercifully it went away.

It was amazing how differently people conducted themselves in a crisis. There had been a scene with Melinda not wanting to leave her husband, and Jack insisting that she go. The old and feeble doctor had been absolutely determined to have a last look at Larson, on the odd chance that he might still be alive, before he would leave. Gorman and Billings had offered cheap sympathies to the remaining hostages but were in truth so glad to be getting out of the situation that it couldn't help but show on their relieved faces.

Finally the commando said, "I had a girl one time, quite some time ago. Right after the war. Long before this one. And she claimed she loved me." And he was unable to conceal the hurt in his voice. "Well, she used to bitch me out all the time. Just all the time. She'd accuse me of being an alcoholic, so I'd go to AA meetings. She'd tell me my mind was sick from the war, so I'd go to counseling sessions. But that didn't help. She still bitched. No matter what I did, she could always find a flaw in my character. You know, it took me a long time before I finally understood why she was making life so difficult for me. She had to bitch. She had to bitch long and loud because my shortcomings covered her own tracks. She used me for a scapegoat so she could retain whatever she had left of her self-respect. Because, you see, she was unfaithful to me. It's a sad thing, but an unfaithful woman is no man's wife . . . but every man's whore. There is something tragic about a married whore."

What he didn't tell them was that except for a very few street prostitutes, he had not felt the warm embrace of a woman for ten years since then. Until Claudine.

Nancy cringed in guilt, her face flushed red with shame. But Archer and Brandon regarded the commando in surprise and awe, mingled with some admiration. The contradiction. They were contradictions of each other; the one sitting passively in their crisp, new outdoorsy clothes, the gun holder looking like he'd just crawled out of the swamp. But those were not the words one thought of as coming out of the mouth of a crazed killer. Yet he was calmly speaking plain, unarguable truth, painful though it must be for him.

Walker moved away from the window. He eased behind the bar and laid the shotgun on the counter. "Governor," he said, "we are going to wait for a little while. Why don't you make some drinks for your people? You might as well relax. Besides, I think you all could use some refreshment."

With as much dignity as he could muster, Brandon did as he was told, although he was not doing a very good job of ignoring the yawning black muzzle of the gun. He mixed drinks for himself, Nancy and Archer, all the time surprising himself that his hands remained so steady. Then he returned to the divan.

Walker drank straight from a bottle of good bourbon, his face twisting as it burned down. "Governor," he said, "would you like to know why I made the selections like I did?"

Brandon took the invitation to talk as possibly an opportunity to lead the conversation toward constructive negotiation. And there was also the remote possibility that the commando might get drunk enough to be overwhelmed. Jack Archer was a strong and alert man—definitely no lightweight. And Brandon, an avid jogger who worked out regularly at the gym, was in pretty fair physical condition himself. This kid might fall victim to his own schemes yet.

"Yes, Mr. Walker," he said. "I would indeed be very curious to know the reasoning behind your selections."

Walker smiled, showing deep dimples on the thin, tight, bearded visage. He took another drink, and his blackened face twisted at the stinging bite of the straight whiskey, but the smile returned. "The doctor and his wife were old—too old for this kind of shit. It is shameful, it is a disgrace to make war on old people and children." There was a bitterness in his voice and a haunted, faraway look in his eyes.

You been out in the boonies, man. You been stepping in shit. Your cage is rattled. You never knew you could know so much fear. They'll kill you. They do it for a living. Any one of them. You come walking through these villages, great American saviors. But they're sitting there, squatting in front of their hootches. Old men, women, kids. And they'd be looking at you out of eyes filled with more hatred than a man can imagine. They want you dead. They want you gone. They're clearly not in the mood for being saved. And you're scared, man. Your whole body feels like a naked target. You just hope you don't get shot in the nuts or in the face. Because you know that anything can happen. Anything. You can *feel* it. And sure enough, it does. You're on the far perimeter of the village, moving out, just a patrol coming through. Some armored personnel carriers, APCs, from another unit coming up behind. Then, with no warning whatsoever, some stupid son of a whore comes bursting out of a hootch and lobs a grenade at one of the APCs. It's not like your nerves aren't already singing and riding the borderline, man. It's not like you'd shit yourself at the snap of a twig. No sooner does the grenade go off on the other side of the village than you hear a crashing sound in the bushes. So you spin around with your rattled cage and your high-strung nerves, and you drop a clip into it. Rock and roll. Full automatic. But what do you do when you find out that what you greased was nothing but a kid taking a shit? A fuckin' kid. And how do you live with what happened to the rest of that village when everybody else plain and simply freaked?

He drank again, his voice softened, and he looked at Jack. "Mrs. Archer looked to me like a good woman. You're a lucky man, mister. You don't get too many of them anymore. Her desire to see you again assures me that you will not be foolish. As for that lawyer, he was a coward. Cowards are dangerous. The same goes for that radio operator. Now, why have I kept you three? Well, in the case of the governor, his value is obvious." Then he looked at Nancy, and the look was not pleasant. "There are certain kinds of women who should know what it's like to stand beside their men. You know, for better or worse and all that."

There was dark hatred in Nancy's eyes. Walker ignored her. "As for Mr. Archer, he is a man. If he reaches inside himself, he has what it takes to function under these what you might call adverse conditions. And function he will—as long as I have the drop on him. But should I make a mistake, he ought to be able to disarm me, maybe even kill me. That's the best edge I can give you. Not to mention, of course, Mr. Archer's invaluable ability as a pilot. There you have it."

When Brandon realized the implications behind what the fugitive had said, he was stunned. By keeping Archer, the strongest and ablest of the lot, the man was offering them a chance to free themselves should the opportunity arise. Most kidnappers would have preferred to prey upon the old and the weak, minimizing danger to themselves. Walker was indeed a brave man; given the unusual circumstances, he was fair. Brandon felt envy and respect. Perhaps a twinge of guilt. When he was sitting in the governor's chair at the

State House, holding the gun, as it were, many of his decisions had not been so brave nor so fair—nor so absolutely decisive.

Brandon also noted another favorable aspect, adding weight to his refined personal image of the kidnapper. Walker had never once asked a favor. He had not begged or demanded a pardon, release, or otherwise. It was as though he had the intelligence and the decency not to compromise the governor's office. He was man enough to take full responsibility for his actions. What Brandon didn't know yet, though, was that Walker despised politicians as corrupt little wimps, playing with power and money, and he wouldn't lower himself to ask the slimeballs for the time of day.

"I admire your courage, Mr. Walker," Brandon finally said, after sipping from his drink. He was slowly gaining a thread of hope by the way the commando was hitting that bottle. He would surely become unsteady soon. "Not many men would, ah, do things the way you do. But tell me, do you really expect to get away with all this? I mean, look at it realistically. In the long run. Your future. You know you'll never be safe. Because you've killed they'll never stop looking for you, no matter where you go. No man can live under that kind of pressure for long. No offense, Mr. Walker, but whether you realize it or not, you are ill . . . and who can blame you after what you've been through? I understand that now, even if I didn't before. Jail is no place for you. I think perhaps I can arrange the right kind of treatment for you if you give it up now. If this goes much further, you're sure to be killed. You must come to terms with reality. You must come back to this world. Now. Here. Where we live, work, play. We are not in Vietnam, Mr. Walker. We are home. You have to understand that these acts of hostility are unacceptable."

Walker laughed. He drank from his bottle, then laughed again. "I hate to say it, Governor, but you must think I just fell off the cabbage truck. What you're offering me is plain bullshit, scraped right from the bottom of the bucket, and you know it. You're trying to convince me that spending my life in an institution for the criminally insane is preferable to a lifetime of hunted freedom. Well, sir, I will take the hunted freedom any day. And I'll gladly take death before I ever take any kind of incarceration again. Nice try but no cigar. And socially acceptable or not, you're still in the middle of a motherfuckin' war!"

The commando moved from behind the bar and hit the light switch by the door, throwing the room into darkness. The hostages fidgeted. It was getting time for something to happen. A dark and ugly something . . . pertaining to war. There was no denying their predicament.

"The reason we waited," Walker explained, "was so they could have time to remove anyone who might have been close. But that's only temporary. I'm sure they're arranging for SWAT teams, negotiators, and snipers. We'll be gone before they can organize anything workable. Now let's go to the plane. You will hold hands and walk down that ramp. And you better hope to God nothing happens between here and there. Because any bullshit—and I mean *any* bullshit at all—and I am simply going to open fire. Now move out!"

They saw the commando, a ghostly shadow in the darkness, bring the shotgun to his shoulder. But as they started down the catwalk Walker thought he heard a plaintive, pleading cry from the rear of the building, where the radio room was. The sorrowful cry of a woman. A woman he loved. Combat stress, he was sure. How many times had he heard strange, haunting, ethereal voices under combat stress. How many times . . .

CHAPTER

NINE

It was late. She had turned the radio off hours ago. She didn't want to hear about hopes destroyed beyond recovery. She didn't want to hear about lost lives and wasted lives, or inevitable conclusions to the insane games men play on each other. Still, she sat and slowly rocked, and she stared and she wept. The lamp had gone down low, casting gloomy shadows over her cabin, over her peace. So lost was she in the pervasive gloom that she didn't hear the car pull up in her yard. She didn't hear the light tapping at the door. She didn't hear the door open. She didn't need to hear all that, anyway. Somehow she knew.

She slowly lifted her large, liquid eyes and let them rest upon the ironlike, unbending man who stood before her, his lightning-struck beret in his hands, oh, so perfectly symbolic of the thunderbolt that had shattered her dreams for a happy future with the man she loved. Two other soldiers stood lurking in the dim, dancing shadows behind him, as though they might be flickering, unearthly sentinels standing watch over the Demon of Doom. Yes, somehow she knew. And the knowing, as only a woman can know, filled her heart with a sickness more heavy than anything she could ever remember.

A subtle change—so subtle as to go without notice—crept across Jarvis's hard, tight face. And for an instant there might have been a warmth glowing in his ice-cold eyes as he gazed down at this broken girl, rocking, her high cheeks streaked with wet. For the briefest moment his jaw was no longer rigid, his lips no longer drawn thin. "We need your help, ma'am," he said, his voice no longer robotic but whispering like the wind through the valley.

And then her tears came again. But her low, husky voice was also quiet. "Why? What do you need me for? Do you need me to help you kill him? Because you have come to kill him, haven't you?"

Jarvis lowered his head and looked at the floor. Shit. What the hell did she know about it; smug and accusatory in her blissful ignorance. What the hell could she know that gave her the right to hit him with a question as cold as a blade through the belly? What was he supposed to say to her? Was he supposed to tell her that he'd had a daughter once, oh, so goddamned many years ago? Was he supposed to tell her that his daughter had been raped and murdered, her stabbed body thrown like garbage into a stinking ditch? Was he supposed to tell her that he'd chosen war for a living? War against the filthy slime called humanity?

The hardness, cold as the steel of his being, gradually reclaimed the colonel.

"We need your help," Jarvis repeated. "Walker has taken hostages at a lakeside camp. The governor is among those hostages. He won't talk to any of us, but maybe he'll listen to you. I've got a radio in the car. I'd be obliged if you'd come give it a try."

Claudine did her best to hide the shock, giving the appearance that she'd known something like this would happen all along. Then she remembered the secretive phone call, the day her lover left with his guns, the day her world crumbled apart. With absolute trust in the instinctive revelation that swept over her, she knew that this evilly mechanical soldier was somehow responsible. It was difficult for her to control the anger rising within her, but she knew she must.

She rose from her rocking chair. Her long skirt fluttered as she planted herself directly before the unmoving Jarvis. Her big, wet eyes cut him no mercy. "Suppose I do talk to him," she said calmly. "What does Jim get out of it? Suppose he gives himself up? What consideration can he expect from you people, a swift bullet between the eyes?"

This woman is too damned perceptive, Jarvis found himself thinking. Then, attempting not to sound too officious, he replied, "You know we can't simply turn him loose. That would be an unrealistic expectation in view of the fact that he's killed a few men. But if you can talk to him, maybe we can avoid more needless killings. Including Walker himself. You must realize that what he's doing is extremely serious. He's sure to die if he keeps it up. On the other hand, I might be able to help him if he surrenders."

A ray of hope swept over Claudine's sorrowfully bitter countenance. "How? How can you help him?"

Now Jarvis was sure of obtaining the woman's help. "Well, I'm familiar with Walker's history. He's suffering from a combat-related illness known as post-traumatic stress disorder. In other words, he's still living in the war." Jarvis hesitated, then lied, "I believe I can convince the authorities to release him to a military hospital. He'd be there for quite a while, I imagine. But it's better than prison, and at least he'd still be alive, with a chance for release someday."

Claudine let this information sink in, allowing herself to believe that there might be some validity to it. She felt she had no choice but to trust the colonel, even though her insides cried out against it. But as the man said, it was Jim's only hope for survival. "Okay," she softly said, lowering her eyes. "I'll try to talk to him." But she could not bring herself to feel good about her decision.

* * *

Even though it was chilly in the cockpit, Jack Archer was sweating. Nervous sweat was trickling down his forehead, and his palms were cold-wet on the yoke as he guided the light airplane through darkness, lights out, revved up, barely skimming the treetops, flying low enough to shake any man's nerves.

The governor and his wife were in the backseat, a blanket wrapped around them, huddled together for the convenience of warmth, not love. The commando was in the copilot seat, his rifle and shotgun between his knees, and in his hand was Ridley's .38-caliber pistol, its black barrel aimed casually at Archer's head. The growling of the engine pervaded the oppressive atmosphere inside the small cab. The commando occasionally examined the map in his lap, which he could read well enough under the illuminated dials of the control panel.

"Good God, man, this is suicidal!" Archer exclaimed tensely, his eyes straining hard into the moonlit night, his clean-shaven, handsome, sporty face showing a picture of his worry. "We're way too low! If we drop into an air pocket, I'll never be able to bring her up before we crash into the trees. I've got to get some altitude so I can at least see where the hell we're going. I can't fly in the blind like this. I told you before, I'm no bush pilot."

Since they had become airborne, Walker steadily had been drifting in and out of a kind of eerie mental phase that was causing the act of swallowing to become difficult for the hostages. It was as though the danger of flying this low was rejuvenating warped cells. It might have been a subtle lover's embrace with death that thrilled Walker like a mysterious woman. The hostages preferred to attribute it to an excess of alcohol.

The commando laughed and raised his gun a little. "Bullshit. That line might work on the scenic flight with a load of tourists, but I don't buy it, pal. You don't have international airport conditions when you're flying millionaire moose hunters in and out of these woods, now do you? Just keep one thing in mind... I know enough about flying that I can handle this rig without you if I have to. Shitbox ain't nothing but a goddamn Tinkertoy, anyway. Some kid could fly it around on a kite string." Walker's voice held contempt as he talked. The gun waved menacingly. "Don't worry. If we hit an air pocket, my reflexes are quick enough to nose her up, even if yours aren't."

Archer was a good pilot, and he was proud of the fact. But now the commando also knew he was a good pilot, which put a major crimp in his plans. Archer had hoped he might be able to intimidate the madman once he got him in the air. Should have known. The son of a bitch had probably spend more time bailing out of planes than most people spent on the ground. The commando was deliberately keeping the aircraft low enough to avoid detection by radar. Archer had underestimated the man again. But still he had to try. Walker's insults angered him, though.

"I tell you, we need more altitude!" the pilot snapped. "I need more visibility at the very least. And what if we go into a stall?"

"And I said bullshit!" Walker angrily repeated. "Listen up, shitbird, because I'm not going to tell you again. You use that line of trees as your flight line, you keep her nose north-northwest, and you keep her flat out. There's a nice big moon out, the sky is clear, and visibility couldn't be better, so long as you keep your running lights out. Nice try, pal, but you're not going to hype me. You take this thing up into radar tracking altitude... even by accident... and I'll definitely blow your fuckin' brains out!" He paused, then added with a mischievous smile, "So let her stall. Shit, at this speed and height I could jump out right now and hit the ground running."

"Well, don't let us stop you," Nancy suddenly remarked. The words just slipped out of her without forethought. She hated the commando. She hated his blatant self-confidence, as though the entire state police force was little more irritating than a pack of pups yapping at his heels. She hated him for not being weak, subject to her manipulations. She hated

the cocky ease with which he handled his polished professionalism. She didn't like the exotic internationalism about
him because, sickeningly, it made her thighs tingle. She certainly hadn't forgotten the way he had shamed her, humiliated her, caught her with that wimp Gorman. Worse,
though, was the cold way he looked at her. She was a beautiful woman and spent much time, money, and effort culti-
vating her image. She was accustomed to having important
men fawn over her, their eyes begging for her favors. But
this criminal whose skullish face was painted like some savage, this dirty convict, this bearded animal looked at her like
she was scum. As though he, of all people, was too good to
be in her company. And she hated her husband and she hated
Jack for being so powerless against him.

She was seated behind Walker, with Brandon behind
Archer. Walker had insisted on this arrangement so he could
keep both men to one side of the plane . . . and so he could
quickly kill either or both of them at the first sign of treachery.

Walker peered over his shoulder and gave Nancy his ug-
liest of glares. "If I jump, bitch, I'll be sure to take you with
me."

She instinctively cringed against her husband, suddenly
remembering how really dangerous this man was. The whole
side of her face still hurt from the brutal slap he had given
her in the boat house. That he had even touched her made
her skin quiver in revulsion. An excited sort of secret revulsion.

Brandon, although he loathed his wife's unfaithful activities, felt it was his duty as her husband to defend her. "You
have us at your mercy, Mr. Walker," he said, protectively
tightening his arm around Nancy. "That should be sufficient
for your purpose. I don't think it's necessary to fling vulgar
insults around." Ever the politician, he was careful not to
enrage the commando. In a lower, yet audible, voice he said
to Nancy, "Dear, I do wish you would keep your big mouth
shut!"

Walker let out a disgusted sigh. Soft moonglow filled the
cabin, making Mr. and Mrs. Brandon's grim faces shine.

Walker shook his head. Two hogs in a gunnysack. They deserved each other. But maybe that was normal living among the rich and the powerful, he guessed. What did he know? They shared wives all the time, had hot-tub parties together. Martinis and slinky wenches and power and corruption—it all went hand in hand. And then, when the party was over, the monsters would go back to their machines. And they would move their pins around the big corporate board. And then would come the orders for the common units to move out.

It was a rock and roll war with practically nothing but teenagers who should have been playing pinball instead of with rocket grenades. Your political orientation is so refined that you thought a radical was something you put on your car in the wintertime for better traction. And without warning you're slapped in the face by reality. Shooting and killing everywhere with a bunch of squirrelly little people who waste each other for a living. You have it out. You grease a few. You lose a few. You come back staring vacantly. You instantly proceed to blow your own mind away. Then, when the pins move, word comes in for your next mission. They drag you out from under your dream in some opium den. They carry you puking out of some sleazy, shit-smelling dive. And suddenly there you are again—a bunch of drunken, blasted-out kids lying on the chopper pads, armed to the teeth with some of the most sophisticated weaponry ever seen in the history of creation.

Then comes the injections.

The needles were there. Then the pathetic sight of one kid commando helping the other jack the injection up his arm. And it didn't matter what kind of coma you happened to be lying in. It didn't matter if you were shuddering on the ground with the d.t.'s. You were coming up out of it. You were coming up out of it ugly, hard-eyed, and mean. And the back of your head would be clacking, and murder would be making your mind scream from within. And you would unmercifully harass and harry the Cong all up and down the

Annam Range. And then you were back, suffering combat fatigue, staring, pushing people out of your way. Whatever was left of the team, that is. Whatever wasn't left was in rubber body bags over there somewhere. And then it would start all over again. The terribly vicious drinking. The mind-numbing opiates. The orders for a new mission. All over again, like a needle stuck on a broken record. Over and over.

"You know, Governor," the commando said, sighing again. "This is getting to be awful goddamn tiresome. You know that? I mean it. This is getting fuckin' tedious. I mean, if I was to do the right thing, I would throw the lot of you out of this fuckin' rig right now. What good are you? You're used up, in case you don't understand. I have successfully evaded capture, I can land this plane myself if I have to, and I don't need a single one of you for a goddamn thing. You know, it's true, we used to do that in 'Nam a lot. Let me tell you how it worked. We'd take two prisoners up a few hundred feet. Don't say a word, just boot the first one's ass out the chopper door, then ask your questions to the second one. And when he gets done babbling ninety miles a minute, boot his ass out too."

That brought on a nervous silence. Even Archer was not willing to mention altitude again, for the time being. Christ, was this guy high-strung or what!

Brandon was frowning with worry. And he was becoming increasingly more worried as the plane flew deeper into the night forest. He was finding it an effort to fight back an inner terror. For one thing, there was no telling what the commando had in mind. Brandon could only hope the man would let them live. But even if he did let them live, the plane was already below a fuel point that would allow them a safe return to civilization. To Brandon, city born and bred, the prospect of being stranded in the remote wilderness was no less fearsome than being held hostage by an armed terror-ist. Even though his most imminent danger was directly be-fore him, he couldn't keep from thinking about scary tales he'd heard. Tales he'd heard in the gaiety of cocktail parties and comfortable lodges. Tales he'd scoffed and ridiculed with good strong hunter companions. Tales about ill-tempered bears; tales about ravening packs of Maine coyotes, half wolf, half wild dog; tales about ferocious forty-pound bobcats and the odd cougar who tracked down and lay in wait for unwary men. . . .

Brandon cleared his throat uncomfortably. "Mr. Walker," he said. "I have to know what your intentions are. My God, you can't be serious! To say we're out in the middle of nowhere is a gross understatement. You know we don't have enough fuel to make it back. Surely you're not going to abandon us out here!" His voice had risen and there was fear in it. "And where will you go? There's nothing out here for you. Listen, fly us to the nearest town on your charts. I'm sure we can make arrangements for you that are agreeable to all parties. Think of the innocent people aboard this plane. I have a certain responsibility toward them, you know. You can't simply leave us out here to die!"

Walker had his head back and was laughing, which only added to the governor's discomfiture. It was a madman's laugh. Stripped of his considerable ability to negotiate, Brandon felt helplessly naked. How in the hell is a man supposed to bargain with a goddamned crazy person? The governor cursed himself roundly. It was his own ego, his own sense of power, his own sense of well-being that had gotten them into this mess. He had flatly insisted that his security men take the weekend off, comfortable in the knowledge that no one in his right mind would have dared approach Jack Archer's exclusive lodge. Besides, Gorman and Larson had been there to finish drawing up important paper company cutting-rights contracts. And those two were considered pretty tough customers around the sporting circles. That they might possibly be harassed by some audacious young man wouldn't have raised anyone's hackles, but being brutally terrorized by a lunatic leftover from a dead and forgotten war was something you just didn't spend a lot of time thinking about. It was like trying to predict that a bridge might collapse because you just so happened to drive over it at the precise moment of maximum stress. This was, quite simply, an accident of fate.

Walker controlled his laughter, aware that it was unnerving his guests. "You'll have to forgive me, Governor," he said. "I thought you were a sportsman, you know, great white hunter. I didn't know you were scared of the woods in the dark."

Brandon bit his lip in fury. The time would come, he thought. The time would come when that bastard would get his. And, oh, wouldn't that be a lovely day in court? Brandon knew of one young fellow who was going to hang from the highest yardarm. Examples had to be made. Precedents had to be set.

"Relax," the commando continued. "Just relax. I told you that if you do as I say, no one will be hurt. I mean that. You'll be rid of me just as soon as we land."

"Which is when?" asked Archer irritably.

"Which is when I tell you, motherfucker!"

The Ranger station at Moosehead Point had become headquarters for the statewide search effort. After helplessly watching the plane lift off the lake and make a sweeping arc into the darkness, there had been nothing left to do except notify the Air Force radar tracking station at Loring Air Force Base. But the directional information Collins had given to the officer on duty wasn't precise enough. The plane must have drastically altered course and must be flying at absolute treetop level unless, of course, it hadn't already crashed. The computers were not picking it up. And Walker was not maintaining radio contact.

The small, log-cabin-type office building on the edge of the great and windy Moosehead Lake was packed with a colorful and impressive collection of official importance. Wardens rubbed elbows with state troopers at the big wall maps, all jabbering noisily and frantically shifting red and green map pins. The communications network crackled electrically, jamming the airwaves with mostly useless and obsolete information.

In the midst of all this commotion two hard-eyed, rock-jawed men in dark fatigues and fatigue caps with the brims pulled low sat quietly at the coffee table, sipping hot brew and chain-smoking. They each had a long-range 7-mm rifle with a modified banana clip, and which was equipped with a sophisticated laser-dot precision scope. Their grim faces tight with the purpose of their deadly mission, they were both about as warm as the middle of January. Sitting at the table with them was a portly, balding fellow who was enthusiastically giving them a lecture on dog technology, particularly the great, drooling, sleepy-eyed, tail-thumping bloodhound sprawled at his feet. Every so often the big hound would thrust his flop-eared, wrinkled head up for an affectionate pat, monstrous jowls just a-quivering and slobber a-flying. The two snipers would occasionally give the handler an understanding nod, give a brief, dubiously nose-curled glance at the snorting, panting mutt, then looked guardedly at each other. Although the snipers spoke little, the exuberant handler was undaunted. Round face lit with pride and joy, he emphatically continued expounding on the virtues of his unhandsome beast.

Outside, dozens of engines growled idly as four-wheel-drives and all-terrain vehicles stood by. Anxious men checked and rechecked a wide assortment of firearms, while others tested their walkie-talkies. Some goddamned con had kidnapped the governor, and by Christ, he was going to pay for it! But the men stopped what they were doing when a big black Cadillac came barreling upon them at a high rate of speed. The low-slung car skidded in among them, throwing gravel all over the place, and the doors swung open even before the vehicle had ground to a halt. Three very seriously clean-cut men piled out, dressed in plain dark suits that weren't sufficiently tailored to conceal the bulges under their armpits. Without so much as a glance around, they rapidly paced straight to the station house, their air of hurried importance raising a few somber comments from the on-lookers.

Collins was at a big wall map with Game Commissioner Smith, busily working out grid speculations on Walker's probable flight plan. The harried superintendent turned abruptly when the door banged open, and the three men swept brusquely inside, bringing more than the night chill in with them. The noisy chatter ceased as men were suddenly intimidated by an aura of power. Even the Dogman stopped upgrading his favorite subject. The two hard-eyed snipers gave the newcomers mildly curious scrutiny. Sheriff Stevens, who had been giving instructions to the radio operator in touch with the Air Force, twitched his mustache and shuffled uncomfortably. Everyone had an excellent idea who these men in the suits were, and nobody was anxious to attract their immediate attention. Stevens mumbled something about seeing after his men, then awkwardly stepped outside, shutting the door behind him.

The blood drained out of Collins's tired face. Instantly recognizing the clipped, iron-haired senior man in front as Mort Roderick, Chief of Security, the State House, Collins maintained his poise with difficulty. Even now the security man, with beady black eyes slitted in righteous rage, was swaggering directly toward the superintendent of corrections. Petty officials scuttled out of his way.

"I guess you know you're in a whole world of shit," Roderick said in his iron-hard, cigarette-raspy voice.

Collins swallowed hard, and the blood came back to his face in a hot rush. It had been a long, pressure-packed day, and the steam release on his mental valve was approaching critical. He'd be damned if he was going to stand here and be browbeaten by a glorified office boy looking for a scapegoat to pin the rap on. Roderick had earned his position by stabbing backs and sucking ass—the same as everyone else in this slime-infested system. Roderick's job was security. He was supposed to make sure that the governor and the governor's people were safe from mad dogs and assassins. It was obvious that Roderick had neglected his duty. It was also clear that Roderick didn't intend to ride this sinking ship to the bottom alone.

"Well," Collins replied coolly, looking straight into that slitty glare. "I guess you would know what a whole world of shit is, wouldn't you, Mort? Looks like Brandon kind of slipped out of your fingers, didn't he?"

Red anger compressed Roderick's wide face into a figure reminiscent of a bulldog waiting for the mailman. Then he let it slide with a sarcastic kind of snorting laugh. "Yeah, I guess he did. Just like Walker sort of slipped out of yours." Chewing his lip, he looked around the crowded room. His hard-squinted, roving eyes came to rest and locked on those of Colonel Jarvis, who was giving instructions to one of his aides at the radio-teletype machine. The colonel's other man was with Claudine. They were at the coffee counter, next to the snipers and the Dogman. After Walker had failed to respond to radio communication, Jarvis, for reasons revealed only to himself, had decided to bring the girl along.

The security man, big and ruddy, visibly paled.

"Good Christ, oh God Almighty!" Roderick's voice was little more than an incredulous, raspy whisper. He ignored Collins. He stepped slowly across the room. He stood before the ice image of the colonel, staring. "J! What are you doing here? He's yours, isn't he? He's one of those *things* of yours, isn't he?"

Jarvis stood as rigid as the stone he might have been carved out of. He had papers in his hand, which he passed to the captain at the teletype, then he slowly turned back to Roderick. "Yes, Mort," he said calmly. "He's mine."

Collins had stepped up behind Roderick, not liking the bad electricity passing between the security man and the army officer. "What do you mean?" Collins asked. "What are you talking about? I have a right to know what you're talking about!"

Roderick finally tore his eyes away from Jarvis's glacial gaze. "Got some place we can talk, Dick?"

Collins nodded. He handed his pointer stick to the distressed game commissioner. "Carry on with that probable flight path, Ray. Come on, Mr. Roderick, there's an office over here."

Jarvis, Roderick, and his two security men followed Collins to a small room at the rear of the building. The room was not much bigger than a janitor's closet, and one wall was nothing but filing cabinets. A big metal desk was fitted in one corner, on which there were three telephones. There was a uniformed warden on one of the phones, but he left when Collins gave a jerk of the head toward the door.

"I've only got two things to say," Collins said straightaway. "First, I want to know what you were talking about out there. Second, if you're here to chew my ass out, then you can just kiss off. I've got enough trouble as it is. And we're doing the best we can."

Roderick sniffed like a haughty woman. Then he showed clenched teeth in some facsimile of a smile. "Don't get all hot and bothered, Dicky boy. We'll see about kissing off when the time comes. As for the best you're doing, it isn't good enough. But lucky for you that might not be entirely your fault. I expect that there's a good reason why the colonel has come to grace us with his presence." He gestured with a jerk of the thumb at the ice-eyed military man, who had perched himself on the edge of the desk, his beret cocked at a jaunty angle.

Collins took note of the two security men, standing sentinel directly beyond the door, arms folded, appearing to be looking at nothing. They must have graduated from the same clone class at the same clone school. Maybe Myrna was right. Maybe Collins deserved every minute of this shit.

"Colonel Jarvis, you might say, is from Military Intelligence," Roderick announced, and Collins snapped alert. The superintendent knew something was wrong. He'd known something was wrong from the beginning. Roderick smiled his bulldog smile. "Yes, the colonel and I have had the pleasure a time or two. I worked Intelligence in the Army. The colonel and his boys came to be quite a legend on the battlefront. All I can say is thank God I wasn't attached to that outfit." Roderick licked his thick lips and noted by the cold-

ness on the colonel's face that it was time to observe proto-
col. "No offense, Colonel. I was aware that the governor
had signed an inmate transfer release. I wasn't aware that he
was one of yours."

"I'd like to know what in the hell you're talking about,
Roderick," Collins interrupted coldly.

The security man turned, not meeting Collins's question-
ing glare. He harrumphed. "Well, Dick, I'm sure the colonel
has information concerning Mr. Walker that will be invaluable to you in . . . er . . . apprehending the fugitive. In fact, I
should think the colonel ought to serve as your most immediate adviser. But we'll talk about that later. Right now let's
get down to a blunt and cold status evaluation." Roderick
took a rather thick notebook from his pocket, opened it, and
began to read.

"At approximately 1400 hours today your office received
a Code 76—inmate escape. The inmate, one James Walker,
in the custody of Officer William Ridley, was being escorted
by state vehicle from the Buckley Ridge Correctional Institute to the Corinth Community Hospital for X-ray testing."
Roderick paused and peered at Collins, who had sat down
and was nervously drumming his fingers on the desk. "If I
am incorrect anywhere, please set me straight, Dick," the
security man said, somewhat caustically. Collins said nothing, so Roderick went back to his notes.

"Mr. Walker was serving five years for high and aggravated assault, with intent to commit robbery. It appears he
struck a man behind the head with such precision as to drop
him cold, and he was loaded down with a number of unusual
weapons, which in itself should have marked him as someone who ought to have been kept under close scrutiny. Officer Ridley must have been one hell of a man, since no one
thought it was necessary to send anyone else along on that
trip to the hospital. As it turns out, though, he wasn't nearly
man enough. As soon as the handcuff restraint was removed, Officer Ridley was instantly set upon and killed by
nothing more than brute force, the type of which can only be
attributed to an education in hand-to-hand combat." Here

Roderick paused to look at Jarvis. The military man, with
cheeks corded, still perched on the desk, was staring into
space. Roderick went on.

"Mr. Walker then armed himself with the downed officer's
weapon, waltzed out of the hospital as casual as you please,
and made good his escape in the van belonging to the correctional facility. By approximately 1600 hours every law-
enforcement agency in the state had been notified,
roadblocks were in place, and an air search by Warden Service helicopter was under way. All of which Mr. Walker
successfully eludes simply by driving down a logging road
used by the Eastern Pulp and Paper Company. He abandons
the vehicle in a thickly wooded area and proceeds on foot,
when he shortly comes upon a camp owned by Harry 'Fishhook' Wilson. This camp, being stocked for the hunting
season, provides Mr. Walker with an undetermined arsenal
and such provisions as he needs for his survival. It is believed that Walker waited in ambush for the return of Mr.
Wilson, who was in the company of Wallace Anderson, for
the purpose of commandeering their vehicle. It is believed
that there was a dispute over the commandeering of this vehicle, and in the ensuing gunfight both Wilson and Anderson
were killed. We can determine that Mr. Walker is now in
possession of a 12-gauge pump-action shotgun." Shaking his
head grimly, Roderick paused to turn a page.

"By 1830 hours, or around 6:30, you were at the scene of
a fire which destroyed Mr. Wilson's camp. Shortly after
1900 hours, Mr. Walker encountered two officers of the
Warden Service at the thirty-two-mile marker on what's
known as the access road. Wardens Ellis and Parks were
killed in an explosion believed to have been created by a
rifle bullet fired into a propane cylinder. The Warden Service
helicopter, equipped with a powerful searchlight, was dis-
patched from the area of the burning camp for the purpose of
investigating that explosion. Before 2000 hours, that chopper was shot down and its pilot killed. After that incident
Walker knew he had to get off the access road, so he exited
down what he must have thought was an unused jeep trail. It

is unlikely that he knew this trail led to a private lodge owned by Jack Archer where, as luck would have it, the governor and his wife just so happened to be spending the weekend." Here Roderick grimaced and hissed, "Jesus!"

"By 2100 hours this evening you were aware that Walker had taken complete control of that lodge. Tim Larson, a popular and respected lawyer, was shot and killed when he tried to get his hands on a gun. Mr. Walker, after having made his position clear over statewide police frequency, released a number of his hostages. From those released, we learned that Walker not only has a shotgun and the .38 pistol he took from Ridley, but he also has a 30-06 elephant rifle, which explains what he used to down the chopper and penetrate the propane cylinder. Our man is literally armed to the teeth and has, as the expression goes, gotten his shit together. He's commandeered a single-engine aircraft and has the governor, the governor's wife, and Mr. Jack Archer in his power. With the aircraft he successfully evaded any approach you made or intended to make on the lodge. It is now approaching 2300 hours, and neither you nor anyone else has the slightest idea where the fuck he might be."

Roderick snapped the book shut and put it back in his pocket. In a gesture of professional understanding he laid a hand on Collins's shoulder. "Don't feel too bad, Dick. I expect that there's a lot about the man you couldn't possibly have known. I expect that there's a lot about him that none of us could know." Roderick shifted his beady eyes to Jarvis. "Isn't that right, Colonel? I mean, Military Intelligence wouldn't send their top torpedo for a simple line grunt, now would they? Walker was a member of that—that team of yours, wasn't he? Heh, Dick, I'll bet the colonel can tell us stories about Walker that'll curl your hair."

"I think Mr. Collins's hair has been curled quite enough already," Jarvis said lightly, in his oddly robotic voice. With his abrupt military movements and rigid bearing he crossed the room and closed the door, ignoring the puzzled glances from the security men beyond.

Jarvis turned his attention back to Collins and Roderick.

Long moments of silence passed before he finally spoke. And his weird eyes shone like a cat's in the dark.

"Mr. Roderick is right . . . Walker is not normal," he stated simply. "The information I am about to disclose to you is, to this day, highly classified. Keep in mind that the government of the United States has a more than passing interest in the outcome of this—what we will call an accident. If it comes to our attention that either of you has been discussing anything I have to say outside these doors, to anyone, anywhere, at any time, then you will most assuredly be, ah, held accountable."

Collins was suddenly aware of freezing little pinpricks snaking up his spine. He found himself acutely uncomfortable in the presence of this creepy colonel, if indeed that's what he was. He found himself wishing the man had never stepped into this mess. For some reason it had all the makings of something namelessly ugly, as if things weren't ugly enough already. And once you got your foot stuck in it, the vacuum might suck you straight to hell. And his guts told him that there was no reversing the ride on this colonel's skull train. Collins was getting scared. And he couldn't help it.

Jarvis casually leaned against a file cabinet. He rubbed a hand across his sharp chin. "There were only a dozen of them. They were specially trained to undertake missions of a nature I am not at liberty to discuss. The unusual training procedures were of highly complicated and sophisticated mind-altering exercises, which, still being in experimental stages, are also code classified. Suffice it to say that these experiments were successful at programming some of the most devastatingly lethal sons of bitches ever to walk this planet. Naturally no new development is without kinks that need to be ironed out. It appears that debriefing these human torpedoes is still a subject requiring some technical attention. Actually it has yet to be done with the older models, which, of course, makes them obsolete.

"I know what you're thinking, gentlemen. Relax. A lot of new weapons were designed and experimented with in Vietnam. That's common for any war. And in close combat, what better weapon than the soldier himself? A super trooper, if you will. Anyway, these men had an incredibly high success ratio. You just turned the fuckers loose and hell couldn't stop them. Walker has clearly demonstrated their unusual abilities by the ease with which he eluded you. Particularly interesting is the way he took that lodge even though there were six grown men in there with unlimited firepower at their disposal."

Collins listened to the droning voice with a growing sense of unease. When numbing realization finally swept over him, the unease quickly changed to a dark sense of crawling horror. His voice was little more than an incredulous whisper. "What you're saying is that you've created a dozen practically flawless killers which you turned on, and now you don't know how to turn them off!"

Jarvis chuckled, and the sound carried a bone-chilling note. "Oh, we turned them off, all right. Of those dozen, nine are now dead. A few of them had to be tactically terminated during the final days of the war. It wasn't safe to bring them back stateside. Most of them bit the bullet on the battlefront. Two are hopelessly insane, safely locked away in one of our institutions, where I intended to take Walker. Walker is the only one still at large. After the war he moved around so much that we lost track of him. We never considered him completely docile, but then again, he wasn't making waves. Until now."

"Yes," said Collins tiredly. "Until now. And now, Colonel, how do you propose we stop this berserk invention of yours? As Mr. Roderick has so clearly pointed out, this man is not normal. Good Christ, in little more than nine hours this joker has killed seven men and kidnapped the governor! Colonel, I want to know how we intend to stop that thing!" This can't be real, Collins kept thinking. How in the hell does anyone, even the government, go about hiding something like Walker? These things only happen in the movies. But Walker had indeed shown an unnatural talent for destruction. Could it be?

Jarvis had a disconnected look about him—the kind of glazed expression a wolf gets when he's lapping up fresh, bloodied meat. "I'd say it was pretty obvious. That plane has to come down sometime, somewhere. You'd best be there when it does. Once you get his position nailed down, your best and only bet is to set up a wall of concentrated gunfire from which there can be no escape. He'll force you into it, anyway. Nailing him down might be the big problem, though. But we'll find a way to work it out. Gentlemen, we have to."

A security man with a pot of coffee and some cups knocked on the door. Roderick rose and let him in. The security man wordlessly poured cups for everyone, served himself, then resumed his position outside the door. Collins was staring at the wall, not having much taste for coffee. Earlier, his feelings toward Walker had been nothing but murderous hatred. Now he felt a kind of sick pity for the misused sucker.

Jarvis's disconcerting chuckle sounded again, sending another wave of creeps up Collins's back. "Relax," the colonel said. "It's going to be a long night. First of all, consider the maximum fuel range on that plane. And you keep in mind that according to the hostages it wasn't full to start with. You can bet that he'll go down tonight, and it'll be somewhere in those north woods where he'll figure he has plenty of room to move. We'll spot that plane first thing in the morning. Then we'll be so hot on Walker's tail that he'll think his ass is being fried by a flamethrower!" Jarvis adjusted his beret, then headed for the door. "And now, gentlemen, if you will excuse me, I have business to attend to."

CHAPTER
TEN

"Look at this shit!" Walker cursed as the plane glided low over acre after acre of clear-cut forest ground, the result of loggers singling out a specific area and sawing down everything standing upright. Even the undergrowth and the earth was all torn up by the large skidder-tractors used to drag the logs. Walker's face was twisted with hate and anger. "Jesus Christ, in another ten years this'll be a desert." His beautiful forest, his sanctuary, his inner peace was laid waste beneath him, mile after mile. It was like watching an old moose, quietly powerful, big, dignified, majestic, being slowly worn down, then finally ripped apart by a bunch of yapping, slavering coyotes.

Walker drank from one of the pints he had brought with him. He hissed viciously, then shot the governor an ugly glare. "It's a fuckin' wasteland, ain't it? You and your fuckin' money-grubbing corporate leeches ought to be wiped off the face of the earth while the rest of us still got an earth to care about."

Brandon fidgeted in discomfort. The commando was

drinking again, and that was not good. It seemed to make him unpredictably angry. It never occurred to Brandon that perhaps the wasted forestland made the man legitimately angry, and not the alcohol. In any event, the hijacker had to be pacified before he reached excessive rage.

The governor cleared his throat. "I'll have you know, sir, that we have an excellent reforestation program in this state." He spoke as though addressing a large audience of voters. "Before you make hasty and uninformed judgments, I would like to tell you a few things about the forest industry in Maine—"

"Ahh, shut up!" snapped the commando. "I said it's a fuckin' wasteland, and that's what it looks like and that's what it is. And you and your shit-eating corporate pals— you know, the ones who bought your office for you—ain't gonna quit slashing the woods to hell until every last penny has been sucked out of every last tree. You've been playing on public sentiment with that reforestation crap for years. What reforestation? I don't see anything growing down there. Christ, you couldn't even grow peckerwood in that mess. The only time you care about public sentiment is when it's running your way. You sit up there in your little high chair and hire, at no small cost to the taxpayer, profes- sional public relations experts who can brainwash the people into the kind of public sentiment you want. Shit, the average Joe doesn't stand a chance against those goddamn high-tech vultures. But you're not running that line of jive on me, buddy. I know a fuckin' wasteland when I see one. Tell me I'm blind and I'll rip your goddamn throat out!"

Brandon clammed up. And this was a conversation neither Archer nor Nancy wanted a part in. They had all been with the commando long enough to know what riled him. And anything having to do with the Maine lumbering operations definitely riled him. But even though the governor had clammed up, his blood was boiling. He hated it passionately whenever anyone—particularly of the lesser educated classes—cut him off while he was expressing his learned views. Another dark strike against the commando. In light of the circumstances, though, it was best not to antagonize the man with the gun. Brandon had observed and duly noted that Walker had lately been continuously swinging through a variety of mood changes. Typical, the governor was sure, of the mentally deranged. Even now the lunatic was chuckling.

Walker drank again, hissed again, then chuckled again. "You know, Governor," he said, "I wouldn't worry too much about getting lost out here. No matter where you go, you're never very far away from one of those land-rape outfits of yours." Brandon ground his teeth but said nothing.

The plane, a floating shadow in the night, passed over the extensive clear-cut area, then skimmed treetops again, still nosed in a north-northwest heading. They were approaching an unidentified mountainous region, and Walker directed the pilot to fly between or skirt the higher ridges.

"There's water directly forward off your port wing," the commando finally said. "Land on it."

Archer's face turned white as he gawked incredulously where Walker had indicated. "Good God, man!" he gasped. "That's nothing more than a frog pond! There's no way I can land on that! It looks too shallow, for one thing. Limbs or rocks lying under that water would tear the pontoons to shreds. Worse, it's not long enough. We'd crash into the trees before I could ever slow this thing down. And if nothing else, we'd never have enough room to lift off again. No way. You're crazy! I won't risk our lives on that mud hole."

The mood instantly turned ugly. With the speed of a striking rattler Walker reached around and grabbed a fistful of Nancy's shirt and roughly yanked her forward. He jammed the .38 brutally against her temple. "Oh, Jesus! Oh, Jesus!" she whimpered. She was a quivering wreck, quite sure the lights would go out with a deafening boom any second.

Walker's upper lip had curled back over his teeth, and a weird glaze had transformed his blackened face into something namelessly deadly, making his narrowed eyes glint with the killer craze. The overall spectacle was most unnerving.

"You miss that lake, you dumb jerk asshole," he snarled,

"and I'm gonna splatter this bitch's brains. Then we'll make another pass. Miss it again and that faggot back there you voted for gets it. All in all, we got enough people in here for three passes. The fourth pass I make myself. Get the message? Now you'd best start letting off your airspeed, pal, and get your flaps down. Hit it!"

"For God's sake, do as he says, Jack!" Brandon screamed frantically. His heart was in his throat, and he felt like he was going to throw up. His civilized nervous system just wasn't geared for the stress of mortal danger. He had his arms stretched forward, as though to ward off disaster, but he dared not touch his wife.

"All right! All right!" Archer desperately shrieked. "I'll do it! Let her go! My God, I'll do it!"

"That's more like it," Walker growled. "And don't try any more of your dumb fuckin' tricks with me. You're way out of your class, chump. Shit, that lake's big enough to land a B-52 on." He let go of Nancy and she fell back into Brandon's arms, almost fainting, trembling violently, her face buried in her hands.

Brandon held her close, bracing himself for what he was sure would be a crash landing. He was scared. Never in the course of his existence had he ever encountered anything close to that strange man with the guns.

Archer gritted his teeth and took a firm hold of the yoke. "Hang on, we're going down!" he said tightly. A mighty rage had hold of him, but it wasn't enough to overwhelm his fear of Walker.

The commando was in fact right again. A man could land on a body of water that small, but it would be shittin' and gittin'. It would take every bit of Archer's skill, accumulated from many years flying experience, to pull it off. But without question they would be stranded. There wasn't half enough water down there for the plane to gain enough speed to clear the trees. Archer knew that that was what the commando wanted, anyway. He swore a silent oath to kill the crazy bastard the first chance he got. But he knew he had

better get over thinking of the killer as a stupid young fool
. . . before it cost him his own life.

When the pontoons first touched water, about a third of
the way across the small lake, Archer instantly knew that
he'd blown it, that he should have touched down sooner.
Everybody else knew it too. Nancy had her face buried in
Brandon's shirt, huddled tightly against him, and he was
hunched protectively over her, prepared for the worst. The
commando was grinning wildly, his foot braced on the control panel and his shoulder pressed against the door. Archer
wore an expression of desperate determination as he tried to
bring the craft's speed down, utterly frustrated that there was
nowhere to turn. One bank was just as close as any other.

Halfway across the pond they were still doing just under
sixty, and running out of water fast. Then suddenly the plane
was skidding up over a mud bank, bringing the dark forest
down upon them. Archer threw an arm across his face.
Nancy screamed. Then there was the rending crunch of ripping metal and the shattering of glass. Both wings were torn
to shreds before the thrashing bulk finally fetched up, caught
solid between two big spruce trees.

Archer's arm was lacerated by glass, and there was a
bloody gash on his forehead. Even still, he was the first of
the hostages to recover his wits. Without even giving himself a chance to consider his disadvantages, he made a desperate lunge for the commando, hoping to knock the gun
aside and strangle the bastard.

But the crash had not even fazed Walker. If anything, it
seemed to have increased his alertness. Easily brushing aside
Archer's groping arms, he whipped the pistol barrel into the
pilot's face with such force that a great spurt of blood came
gushing from the man's smashed nose. Archer fell back in
his seat, and the back of his head cracked the door hard,
knocking him cold.

Instantly Walker had the gun trained on Brandon, who had
shoved Nancy aside and was in the act of rising to the aid of
his friend. The uncanny speed of Walker's maneuvers under
the circumstances left the governor frozen in a look of dis-

belief. A normal man would have been thoroughly rattled by the crash alone. This man seemed alive with crackling electricity, and his face seemed weirdly illuminated, as though danger, as though a closeness with death, fed fire through misaligned circuits. There was a malignancy in Walker's glowering visage that Brandon could not even attempt to put a name to.

The governor let out a defeated sigh and slowly settled back in his seat. He regarded Walker with horror, knowing that the only chance they ever had of subduing the man was now gone. "That's not possible!" he whispered through a constricted throat.

Nancy was also staring at the commando, her eyes wide and round with fear. Her whole shaking body could feel the suffocating waves of pure death emanating from him. Perhaps it was the way the moonlight was making his darkened skin shine, but he looked like he was glowing oddly. She was speechless. She was utterly terrified.

Walker said nothing. Holding the gun in his left hand, he reached under the control panel and yanked out the radio wires, jerking them back and forth until they were completely torn free. Then he threw the wires into the governor's lap. Brandon looked at them as though they were living, squirming snakes. He gulped, realizing that he was now effectively cut off from communication with the world.

The commando heaved against the battered door until it finally banged open. He slid out, dragging his things with him. He tucked the .38 under his belt, shouldered the rucksack, and slung the rifle. He checked the shotgun to make sure of a chambered shell.

"Wait a minute! Where do you think you're going? You can't leave us out here like this!" From inside the crashed plane the governor's muffled voice sounded almost hysterical.

"Fuck you," muttered Walker. Then he disappeared soundlessly into the night forest.

* * *

It was a while before Brandon could completely comprehend the magnitude of their situation. The commando, incredibly enough, was gone, and in his place was the blackest, most nerve-racking silence the governor had ever known. Then Archer stirred and groaned, and Brandon snapped out of his personal trauma.

"Jack! My God! Come on, Nancy, we've got to get him out of this thing!"

Bitterly cursing, Nancy awkwardly crawled out of the backseat and helped wrestle the big man out of the cabin. They positioned him with his back against a tree, then Brandon hurried back to the plane and found a first-aid kit under the seat. Archer's face was a bloody mess, which Nancy refused to touch. Blood did not agree with her finer sensitivities. Brandon, ignoring her, went to work immediately, wiping away the superficial red so he could see where the real damage was. Mostly it was just minor cuts and abrasions, except for the smashed nose.

"He's gone, Jack," Brandon said nervously, while patching his friend. "He stripped the wires out of the radio. He left us out here with nothing. He stranded us God only knows where!"

"I think my leg's broke," Jack muttered, his voice oddly nasal.

"Didn't you hear what I said?" Brandon shouted, almost frantically. "We're stranded!"

"Relax, goddammit!" the pilot yelled sharply. Then he grimaced against the pain in his leg. He took Brandon firmly by the arm. "Listen, John, take it easy. If the man's gone, then we've got nothing to worry about. There'll be a massive air search—you can count on that. All we have to do is wait, probably just until morning. They'll see the wreck, don't worry. Meanwhile we're alive and free. There're blankets in the back of the plane. There's a flare gun back there too. Now build us up a good fire and put a splint on my leg. And for God's sake, stay calm."

Nancy hugged herself against the night cold. Under the moonlight she surveyed the scattered wreckage of the crashed plane, aware that they all could have been critically injured or killed. Yet the commando hadn't given a second thought to those odds. There was a slight sneer on her face as she watched her husband laboring over Jack. They looked the perfect part of a disaster. Sniveling cowards. Safely bullying people up and down the lobbies of the State House was where they belonged. Out here where a man needed real guts, they had none. Thoroughly intimidated by a glare-eyed convict. Yet... the convict could get exactly what he wanted out of those brave heroes of hers, then vanish into this vast, dark wilderness without even a trace of hesitation or fear. Oh, how she loathed him. She hated him for making her men look like pussy-whipped wimps. She hated him for ... that night. Shuddering, she wondered what it was going to take to bring him to his knees. She knew it would take a lot, but she was not capable of thinking in terms of awesome.

Brandon was up, stumbling in the dark pucker-brush, scrounging for firewood. "Nancy!" he called. "Would you please help?"

"Help what?" she retorted angrily, her arms tightly folded.

"Help gather wood for a fire, for God's sake!"

She threw her head back and sniffed. "Don't be ridiculous, John." She sulkily stamped over to the tree Jack was leaned against and sat down beside him.

Brandon, arms filled with dead brush, seethed in silent fury. He blamed the commando for this. And the commando would pay his pound of flesh. Oh, he most surely would pay. And then—then, by God—that snooty tramp he was married to was going to get hers!

CHAPTER
ELEVEN

The young male cougar prowled the dark woods restlessly. He was in pain. And he was pissed off. A few days earlier, with his belly knotted with hunger, he had jumped prey. Unfortunately his prey had been a slow-moving porcupine. The porky had defended the pouncing attack on itself by a quick swish of its spiked tail. And now the cougar, driven both by hunters with guns and his own kind, was strayed far beyond his northwest Canadian range. So he stalked with a limp, snarling with the hurt of the many quills that festered inside his mouth. Foamy saliva dripped from his powerful jaws. His tongue, infected with needle wounds, lolled crazily over bared, razor-sharp fangs. His feverishly yellow cat eyes glared weirdly. And the hunger. Lord, the angry hunger.

He hunted the night forest as mad as hell, favoring his stricken right paw. He padded with his limp along isolated game trails. He searched to appease the pain that consumed him. The pain made the low, dark animal growl and gnash at woodland shadows. The fury of the pain drove the cougar toward whatever it was that would give him relief.

He knew he wouldn't have to go far before finding evidence of the statewide tree-butchering operations. Moving low and fast through the dark forest, Walker shortly came across a skidder road less than a mile from the plane. The money-sucking bastards were everywhere, ripping the earth apart with their vicious, insensitive machinery. Untouched virgin forest was something you read about in history books. The corporate monster was the real Satan in the flesh, and nothing was sacred to it. Except money. Cops weren't paid to protect the average citizen, they were paid to protect the monster's money and to punish the offenders. The social order of the entire world—crime and punishment, war and peace—was playing out according to the monster's whims. Through incessant advertising propaganda the monster told you how to act and live, what to wear, what to smell like, what to eat. The monster grew fat on the helpless, mindless masses, bloated on money and power. The monster ate these great tracts of precious trees like a filthy vulture tearing and swallowing chunks of carrion. It was real crime. It was obscene.

He gave himself a few moments to let the debilitating rush of raw rage pass, then he reconnoitered his position. The logging trail looked like it skirted the ridges to the west, beyond which must lay the Allagash Wilderness. If he could reach the nearest high ridge, he would be in an advantageous position as far as detecting the approach of any enemy. The location also had all the earmarks of the type of place where a man might find a cave to hole up in for a while. Because once it snowed, the search would be over. But even if they did track him up there, which was likely, there were plenty of options for evasive action—if evasion happened to be on his mind at the time. Maybe he just might decide to declare war on the rotten motherfuckers.

Walker took a big drink from a bottle of fine whiskey, freshly liberated from the governor's decadent country palace. He drank not only for the warm, soothing effect of the alcohol but to ease the dull throbbing of his wounded arm. Yes, sir, maybe he just might make a profound social statement, he thought with a wry grin. He felt good. He felt free. He breathed deeply of the fresh, crisp, pine-scented night air. The rolling hills were right up there, directly before him. The high country. His home was out there somewhere. Somewhere out there was the quiet, peaceful place where Claudine could join him and share his freedom with him. So let the bastards come for him. They'd hear a social statement all right—a statement they wouldn't soon forget.

He stashed the bottle and moved out. He followed the logging road a few miles, then he slid down a game trail, which would have gone unnoticed except to the trained eye, and he headed for the deep woods that would take him to the ridge. He'd find a nest along the way for a few hours sleep and some grub. He'd need the rest, he figured, because tomorrow was liable to be a hectic day. They'd have the dogs out here for sure. So let 'em come. Walker had a few surprises of his own in mind. For one thing, he had a theory about tracking dogs . . . dead ones don't smell too good.

He glided through the woods for about half a mile before coming across the type of undergrowth that was suitable to his needs—a natural cave of intertwined alders, a kind of thicket used by deer both to elude predators and to scrape parasites off their backs. How fitting, Walker mused with a scowl.

He meant to leave no margin for error.

Utilizing both flashlight and moonlight, he shucked his weapons and rucksack and immediately went to work with the bayonet. Carefully choosing ground that sloped slightly downward so a man would be inclined to follow his forward motion, he dug a small trench about a foot deep and a couple of feet square. Quickly scrounging the surrounding area, he was finally rewarded with a short section of dried log. He split the wood with the heavy knife and whittled until he had two rough-hewn boards cut to size. He gouged and reamed the center of one of the boards, creating a hole through which he could press a tightly fitting buckshot shell. Then he removed a screw from the butt plate of his rifle and screwed it through the middle of the second board, until a section of metal protruded through the other side. Using the file, he blunted and shaped the screw tip until it resembled a firing pin. He placed this board, pin side up, in the bottom of the hole, securing the edges with tightly packed dirt. Using long, thin strips of wood from his whittling operation, he banked both ends of the trench only enough to support the weight of the board embedded with the shotgun shell and to insure direct downward movement. During this operation he carefully poised the cap end of the shell directly over the screw stub, leaving not much more than an inch before impact. Then he gathered a handful of the most brittle, fragile twigs he could find. He cross-laid these across his hole and covered them with light forest duff.

Squatting on his haunches, he allowed himself the luxury of a stiff drink and a cigarette while closely examining another segment of the trail. "Yeah," he muttered with a whiskey hiss, "dead ones don't smell too good." He capped the bottle, field-stripped his cigarette, and set to work once more.

Again employing the heavy blade, he chopped down a number of young maple saplings, always careful to keep his movements confined to the upward direction of his intended target area. He fashioned a square out of four of the poles, about three feet to a side, and securely lashed the ends together with wire taken from Fishhook's camp. He made a framework by cross-weaving a number of sapling poles within the square, which he also fastened with wire. Then he sat down to sharpen a handful of foot-and-a-half-long stakes, which he would lash into the crotches of his framework.

His mind drifted as he whittled the stakes to needlelike sharpness. Knife working rapidly, wood chips flying, he dwelled on Dudley. Anger gave the blade speed, but there was also an untouchable sadness in his work. Dudley. Dud for short. A smiling, moon-faced kid who couldn't even grow fuzz for whiskers, Dud was the team fuckup. Every company had one. The guy who could never do anything right. The guy who always had the drill sergeant shaking his head with disgust. The guy who could take ribbing from his fellow troops with great good humor, always a joke on his lips about his own incompetence. The team mascot. The very heart of the team morale. He was a thin, silver ray of sunshine in the dark and ugly world of covert murder and awful destruction. But he couldn't survive. He didn't have the black temperament necessary for stone-cold survival. So he didn't survive. There weren't enough cards left on the bottom of the deck to deal him. Maybe Dud, in his innocence, in his ignorance, never knew that nobody in this filthy game ever dealt from the top. He walked his last mission into denied territory as point man, as unconcerned about drawing enemy fire as he was about being out of step while marching around the compound. This time he was way out of step. This time he did the last thing wrong that he was ever going to do. This time he tripped the wire on an indigenous antipersonnel device.

Walker winced as he remembered Dud's uncoordinated young body dripping limply from the bamboo spikes that had suddenly punctured him through the guts.

The commando lashed his spiked gate to a pair of strategically located, sturdy young maple poles. He bent the poles to the ground, straining with exertion but careful not to stress the fibers of the green wood. He staked his gate down, secured it with wire, then ran the wire around a tree and across the trail, ankle-high. He set a wooden peg into a tree across the trail, attached the end of the wire, then unstaked the gate, slowly, carefully. Tension brought the trip wire taut. And now all that held the spiked gate cocked was a length of wire and a peg embedded in the farther tree trunk. And the slightest forward movement of the wire would dislocate the delicately placed peg. And Dud's short existence would not go unaccounted for.

Walker cleaned up his wood shavings and scattered leaves and forest debris around, careful to comouflage his work area. Then he pissed all around the traps, to insure that nocturnal woodland animals would steer clear. His surprise was not intended for wandering scavengers, and human scent would keep them away.

Then he put his gear back on and hauled ass up the trail. Motherfuckers, he kept thinking, helplessly angry that this thing should even be happening to him. He never asked for this. He hadn't even been bothering anyone. Why couldn't they have just left him alone? Why? Why did they have to drag him back into it? Rotten motherfuckers.

He didn't get a full klick, a thousand meters, up the ridge before a snarling black shape bursting from the dark-shadowed bushes struck him. Walker, thoroughly surprised by the suddenness of it, rocked backward with the ferocity of the attack. What the hell . . . his mind instantly questioned while priming himself for disaster. What wildlife acts this way? Bear? This ain't no fuckin' bear! Jesus! It's a sonofa-bitchin' big-ass cougar! Of all the fuckin' luck. . . .

The commando instinctively threw his left arm across his face in an effort to protect his throat from the hot, meat-smelling jaws that were going straight for his jugular. And his right hand locked onto the blade at his hip. The impact sent him sprawling, a thrashing, clawing bulk of fury on top of him. Then Walker screamed in unrestrained pain as frantic flesh-eating teeth tore into his wounded arm. And the white-hot pain triggered insane rage. This fucking thing was hurting him. This fucking thing meant to rip his guts out with raking hind claws!

Walker drove the blade upward into belly meat with such force that the cat was literally lifted. It let loose a bone-freezing screech, dripping poisonous saliva onto the downed commando's face, and then it redoubled its murderous efforts, slashing and gnawing and squirming. Walker stabbed again. And again. And again. Until the cat went limp, collapsing heavily on top of him.

He let himself breathe for a moment, let his jangling nerves settle. Then he pushed the black bulk off him. Painfully he struggled to his knees, aware that he was hurt bad. He had blood all over him, both his and the cat's. Pissed, he grabbed the dead cougar's throat and yanked the limp head upright. And that's when a heart-wrenching sadness numbed him, a pain deeper, greater than the wounds that hurt his body. He saw the festering quills in the animal's tortured mouth, its eyes rolled and glazed in death, its tongue lolling in an infected maw. He saw a strayed soldier, lost, wounded, hunted, drifting aimlessly through enemy territory, driven by fury, blinded by pain.

"God," the commando whispered hoarsely. He let the cougar's head down easy. "I wish you hadn't picked me, friend. You fucked us both. You fucked us good."

They didn't have much trouble finding the governor and his party. The first search plane of the early dawn spotted smoke from their fire. Within a few hours aircraft and four-wheel-drives loaded with armed men had converged on the skidder road near where the plane had gone down. Archer, miraculously the only one hurt in the crash, was immediately flown to the hospital. Brandon refused to leave. Displaying a fierce bitterness Collins had never seen in the man, the governor adamantly insisted on being part of every step it took to track the crazed commando down. It was his fervent desire to actually see that wild-eyed fugitive brought down from those mountains in shackles. For similar reasons of her own, Nancy also would not go, and no amount of persuasion could convince her to evacuate the area.

It was a cold, frosty morning, although the bright sun rising in a cloudless blue sky promised a pleasant autumn day. The men had built a big bonfire, and soup and coffee were on. There was a kind of festive air as the men sipped hot brew, warmed their hands over the fire, and speculated on the ridge where the commando was believed to be hiding. There was excitement and a sense of camaraderie as they discussed the eventual confrontation, most of them quite sure that blood would be shed before the day was over, if last night's terrible activities were any indication of what they were up against. Most of them had never been anywhere close to such violence. But they were secure in their numbers, and they felt a strong confidence with the governor and other VIPs among them, which lent the endeavor a greater than ordinary significance. The commando had to lose. Even still, they held a healthy respect for him, a certain awe. And if the naked truth was discussed, it would have been discovered that no one was eager to take the front line. But there was a silent agreement among them that speaking the naked truth was not in good taste.

Two light spotter planes and a surplus Huey chopper were doing a search of the distant ridges, dipping in and out of valleys. They received constant radio warnings to maintain altitude, the ground-base operators not wanting the pilots to forget what had happened to the Warden Service chopper last night. Finally the air search was temporarily called off. It was decided that it might not be wise to spook the fugitive any further. A silent ground search would be tried first.

Brandon, after having greeted everyone with cheerful bravado, and after assuring all, particularly the fussing medics and his security men, that he was perfectly fine, took conference with Collins, Mort Roderick, and Colonel Jarvis. Roderick dismissed his men to help with the search effort, as did Jarvis, leaving one of his men to look after the nervous Claudine, indicating that this was a private conversation.

"Before you start running me a line of excuses, I just want you to know that I'm not blaming you, Dick," the governor said, aware of Collins's discomfort. "Or you, either, Mort. I gave you the weekend off. You can't be blamed for that." Both the superintendent and the security man expressed visible signs of relief. They had both been expecting a thorough dressing-down. But the governor just being alive, unharmed, and free superseded all other feelings. For the time being, anyway.

"I met the man," Brandon said quietly, gazing to the shadowed hills, his boyish face wearing a strange expression. "By the good Christ, I guess I met him!" He swallowed a drink of his coffee, then he took a survey of the officials before him, evaluating each with a grim eye. "Walker is without question the most dangerous human being I have ever encountered, or expect to ever encounter again. He may be thoroughly deranged, but he's damned sure on top of the program. His efficiency will astound you. It did me. You'll not take him alive, that I can just about guarantee. And from what I've seen, ten to one says he's capable of taking half this party to hell with him." He looked straight at Collins. "What I don't understand, Dick, is how such a person could end up in medium security. What I don't understand is how any two-to-nine officer in his right mind could have let someone like that go anywhere without a heavily armed escort."

Collins groaned inwardly. He knew what the governor was saying. Someone had to be dragged through the mud, and Ralph Mendel, the two-to-nine officer responsible for inmate transports, had just been elected to take the dirty dive. After all, Brandon couldn't very well persecute his superintendent of corrections, which was an appointment that came from the governor himself. Such a move would insinuate a poor reflection on Brandon's discretion in making the appointment in the first place. Naturally, Collins would be given the job of ruining Mendel's career. It was worse than dog-eat-dog. But like it or not, someone had to be thrust into the face of public outrage. And such were Walker's atrocities that the unknowing two-to-nine officer would be all but trampled under the forthcoming waves of public outrage. He'd be lucky if he ever got a job cleaning shithouses. Another good man destroyed by that commando. That fucking commando. Walker had to die. And this goddamned Army spook, or whatever the hell he was, was just as guilty too. Smug as a fucking Nazi technician. Who the hell did they think they were, turning loose their kill-crazy psychopaths on decent society?

"Listen, John," Collins said. "Before we start dragging our officers through the shit, there's a few things about Walker that you should know." He looked toward Jarvis, and his expression held no warmth. "Colonel Jarvis is from Military Intelligence. At least that's what his papers say. I think he can explain the situation better than I can. He is, after all, more informed on Walker's military occupational specialty than any of the normal folks around here."

Brandon looked quizzically at Jarvis. "Ah, yes. I do remember the transfer request. Now I don't wonder why." He extended his hand, finding Jarvis's grip filled with strength. And the slight smile was not in keeping with the distantly evil eyes. "Indeed, I can see why the Army would be interested in that man. Good God, he thinks he's still fighting a war! There must be quite a bit you can tell us, Colonel."

Jarvis, lean, square-cut, rigid as a plank, laid it out without mincing words. Like Collins, the first thing Brandon thought of was a sinister robot. And like Collins, he was horrified at the unwelcome bit of information Jarvis imparted concerning the fugitive's profile.

"If what you're saying is true," the governor said, after long reflection over the colonel's information, "and having spent time with the man, I have no question that it's true, then there's not a man here qualified to go after him."

"That's quite right, Governor," the colonel stated simply.

Brandon flushed with exasperation. "Well, sir, what do you suggest we do? Am I sending those men over there to the slaughter or what?" He looked away in disgust. "Just what we need in this state—an expert fanatic. Why didn't you bring a few specialists along with you? Or is Walker top-of-the-line?"

Jarvis took out a cigarette, lit it, blended smoke with cool, steamy breath, conjuring images of a heat-breathing demon. His very presence, in his crisp war fatigues and cocked beret, had an ugly, unsettling quality, particularly among the generally peaceable men of Maine. Although Jarvis might be capable of emotion, it was not obvious to the casual observer. "Walker is top-of-the-line," he said. Then he muttered, "He's end of the line."

The colonel's steely eyes observed, recorded, computed the preparations of the search party. The Dogman was priming his pup's nose with an article of clothing taken from Walker's cell. Six men would accompany the Dogman. Another two dozen would go in different directions by twos and fours in an effort to surround the ridge. These men would draw first fire, and then forty backups, with more showing up every minute, would rush to the position once it was located. Nice plan theoretically, Jarvis thought. But it was obvious that none of them had ever been up against a high-tech jungle fighter. Walker not only thought like they did, but he did it better.

This initial flushing operation had to be done quietly, and only two men out of the whole misassorted bunch knew the first thing about quiet. Those two were the snipers, known only as Chip and Dale. The governor and his rinky-dink associates might be interested to know that Chip and Dale were a pair of international political assassins who had taken part in some of the most covertly underhanded coups in the world. The governor and his associates might be interested to know a lot of things. Jarvis, with his jaundiced view of the petty population in general, found such thoughts amusing. But this, he knew, would be the snipers' toughest gig.

Chip and Dale had their 7-mm modified Remington automatic rifles, they had their hand grenades, and for short arms they had Ingram M-10 submachine pistols. Walker would recognize them as pros immediately. And he would go for them. Many of the others were armed with a wide assortment of firearms. Among the more impressive were auto-loading shotguns, a few AR-15s, some M16s, and a couple of those rednecks even had some goddamned Uzi automatic assault rifles.

Jarvis sighed through clenched teeth as he gazed toward the cold blue morning sky. He alone knew that before this was over, Walker could possibly be the single most well-armed man alive. He'd take those weapons like a snarling bully snatching candy from a kid. If the commando wasn't killed in the first major encounter, then the shit could get even deeper than Jarvis cared to stand in. As it was, he wasn't giving odds on a respectable portion of those hillbillies going out there. And if by mischance Chip and Dale bought it on the first run, then the day could easily end up in a bloody massacre. It would all depend on the commando's mood. And this provocation was not calculated to make him very happy. Men with guns turned him weird. His rear-ranged brain cells, secretly programmed for deliberate dys-function, jammed him into a horrific hyper-exterminate phase, and he would remain in that altered state until he was blasted into oblivion. Utterly devastating. But this altered mood was all part of the master plan and was indeed counted upon. Jarvis was unwilling to enlighten the governor on any of the finer peculiarities of the setup just yet. Brandon and his lackeys knew too much already. And that was another problem that would have to be dealt with—once this was over. Right now that commando had to be wasted, even at the cost of every man here. Every man. Jarvis had his orders. And those orders came from way up.

"We've finally got him on the ground," the colonel said. "And I don't think he's any farther than that ridge out there. He'd want the advantage of surveillance for sure. He'll be thinking he can watch us and elude us at the same time. And he's right. He does have that ability. The best thing we can do right now is to go after him with everything we've got. I don't have to say that the sooner he's stopped, the better. I don't think anyone here wants to take the chance of letting him slip away. I doubt we'll be needing the National Guard, with all the men we've got out here now, but you might want to put the nearest unit on alert in case we do have trouble. And if we do have trouble, we've got his girlfriend. She might be able to lure him out yet."

Jarvis indicated the first search group with a thrust of his chin. "That's Chip and Dale over there. Crack shots, both of them, and they've had SWAT training. Best send them along with the dog so they'll be up there first. Get the ridge sur-rounded, then send in backups right away. When the shoot-ing starts—and you can bet your ass, boys, the shooting will start—it's best to be in a position to try to get Walker pinned down. I'm not going to give you false hope, because that may or may not be possible. He's a slippery little devil. Anyway, it's a major objective. We have to put the squeeze on him." He gazed again toward the hills, then added very quietly, "He has to be overrun, and when you overrun him, you will quite likely have to kill him. That's all, Governor. If it were my men, I'd be moving them out."

"Jesus!" exclaimed Brandon, followed by a nervous sigh. "It sounds like we're dealing with some kind of a Star Wars death machine instead of a human being."

"You got that right," agreed Collins, puffing deeply on his cigarette.

"My fucking word!" was all Roderick had to say.

The governor turned and strode off toward the radio truck, grumbling, "I don't believe this shit." Then he yelled, "Okay, Ray! Move 'em out!"

"Remember," Collins cautioned, "keep it quiet. Keep your radios on, but keep 'em turned down. And don't talk unless you have to. And don't take any chances. If he opens up on you, move the hell back to some good cover and just concentrate on keeping him pinned down."

A big lumberjack-looking fellow, in heavy boots and thick vest, patted the AR-15 assault rifle he was carrying. "Don't you worry, Mr. Collins. We'll keep him pinned down, all right. Permanently!" He laughed gruffly, and his friends chuckled with him. But it was a nervous kind of laughter.

Standing by the radio command truck, Brandon, Collins, Smith, Roderick, and Jarvis, all filled with a sick anxiety, with the exception perhaps of Jarvis, watched the first scraggly line of thirty men advance up the rough road. They would break up into teams once the trail was found. Twenty more men would shortly follow them, and another twenty behind them.

What an outrageous army of men, Brandon was thinking absently, just to collar a lone criminal. The taxpayers would surely go nuts over this one. In the pressure of the moment it never occurred to him to wonder where Nancy was. Which was a good thing. Because she was in the company of a group of men farther up the line, trying to wheedle a gun out of someone.

CHAPTER
TWELVE

The cougar had hurt him. But it was not as bad as it had appeared at first. His right leg had a long claw-gash in it, and his bullet wound had been opened afresh. He'd had neither the means nor the inclination to perform field surgery again, so he'd simply bound the wounds tightly, stanching the bleeding with gauze. Infection didn't seem so important anymore. He'd be permanently infected if he caught one between the eyes. The pain wouldn't slow him down, not with the help of the whiskey. He was intimately familiar with pain. He'd lived with pain much, much deeper than this for many years. He was involved in a long-standing, secret, silent brotherhood with pain.

The binoculars Walker had liberated from Archer's lodge were of excellent quality. From a protective stand of fir trees atop the ridge, he lay on his belly, studying the preparations for the manhunt below. He chuckled. What a pack of self-centered assholes. Bunch of buffoons living in a fantasy. What did they know about war? A motley collection of incompetents fiddling with their popguns, yapping in their radios, strutting around like a bunch of goddamned roosters. Yeah, stamp your foot and they'd squawk and run like chickens. The dumb bastards were no match for a commando. Not in this terrain. Not this time around. But that was a "tough-shit lesson" they'd have to learn the hard way.

Then his lens came to rest on Collins, and the strange rage that blinded him to all sense of logical reasoning consumed him. The commando's lip curled with insane venom, his eyes filmed over with that most eerie glaze, and there was an animal sound emitting from low in his throat. As suddenly as clicking channels on a television, his mind started screaming: You pig fucker! You filthy gook pig fucker! You! I will kill! Kill! Kill! "What's the spirit of the bayonet?" The giant drill instructor had roared those words, his voice mightier than God's, his heavy cheeks atremble, streaked with sweat, his snarling mouth spraying froth. And a dozen quivering-lipped, bald-headed boys resembling humanoid mutants filled the air with their response: "Kill! Kill! Kill!" And again. This time the DI was bigger than a giant, uglier than all the sins of hell, and the sweat beading in the pores of his cavernous face was streaked with red this time. This time he screeched so loud that straining veins in his bull neck threatened to burst, and surely he would tear the vocal cords out of his larynx. "I said, *what's the spirit of the bayonet!*" And this time the response was like a deafening electrical thunderclap: "*Kill! Kill! Kill!*" And Walker was sure the top of his head would blow off like a charge of C-4 plastique explosive.

Again like changing channels, reality came back as suddenly as it had left him. There were men around Collins, important-looking men, and Walker was amused that the governor was there too. But Collins stood out. Walker saw him like a crow sees a shiny object from afar. Collins shone. Collins was the jail keeper, the man with the key, lord of the squirming, groaning inmate mass. He was a power-drunk prick. He was a prissy, lard-ass wimp when stacked against a real man. He was prim, sharp, second-looey, fresh out of cadet school, and took delight in razzing the bedraggled, battle-wasted vet. He was the man with the plan. He was the insufferable jerk who had just enough rank to put good men in ridiculous, humiliating, and deadly situations. Like this one. And he was the stupid, asinine motherfucker who got the grenade rolled under his ass when no one was looking.

Collins had a pair of binoculars, too, and he was raking the ridge with them. The commando was confident that his secluded position could not be detected except by the most excruciating scrutiny, sophisticated equipment, and a veritable scientific knowledge of target identification. None of which that swaggering asshole down there had.

Walker watched Collins's fruitless lens search. You miserable motherfucker, he was thinking. I asked to talk with you, but I was so subhuman that you couldn't even spare me a note. Now, son of a bitch, look at me! Look at me because I'm looking at you! I'm looking at you because I'm going to grease you because I've killed fuckin' Cong who were better men than you will ever be!

He forced himself to look away, and he shifted his attention to the big band of men moving up the skidder trail, the bloodhound pulling them along like an engine hauling a train. Men began to break off in pairs and groups and disappear into the woods. An attempt, the commando correctly deduced, to encircle the ridge. Dumb. They would be a hell of a lot better off in one large, well-spaced unit, with another large unit air-dropped behind the ridge. Then they could march toward each other, catching the commando in a crossfire. But they were dumb. They were giving him all kinds of room to move. It was inconceivable that they could know what they were up against and still be so dumb. Unless they still regarded Walker as just another jerk con who'd run off and gotten lost in the woods. Surprise, surprise, assholes.

The dog, nose to the ground, tugging at his leash, unerringly led the hunters down the game trail Walker had taken last night, and they were lost from the commando's view. He lowered his binoculars. Now was the time to go, if he ever intended to. He had taken a reconnaissance of the enemy and knew their strength. He could go now. He could lose them forever, wander forever in these hills. Alone but free. But the snake in his belly, the twisting, hissing snake, slimy with hatred, would not let him leave. The snake was strangling on rage, its forked tongue flicking, its poisonous fangs dripping rage. They! They! They tried to kill him off in some stinking jungle. They stole the freedom he had ruined his mind for, lying in some shit-stinking, leech-infested paddy, hearing the sounds of midnight death all around. He was crying with his machine gun in his hands, sobbing, retching with indescribable fear and revulsion. The boy-soldier with the body-racking dry heaves, dysentery, foot rot, malaria. His pathetic weeping went unheard, unheeded amid the hellish racket of automatic gunfire and mortars and rockets, and the moans and screams of the wounded and dying. He was alone under a black moon, expectantly waiting for the next brightly streaking tracer round to rip his guts out or tear his face off. And now, now these rotten cocksuckers had the dirty gall, the incredible audacity to run him down like some kind of a deformed freak just so they could finish the job.

He brought the lens to his eyes one more time, and that's when he saw J, wandering with his stiff posture through a group of armed men. An utter and complete coldness crept through the commando's blood, and his jaw went tight. And then he saw Claudine, a soldier serving her coffee and sandwiches by the fire. And he thought his heart would explode through his throat. J! The bastard! The dirty, contemptible bastard! Had he grown so utterly ruthless that he could use the helpless women and the children and the unarmed civilians for war? Yes, J was a warrior, but had he turned into that kind of a monster? God, Claudine had no business out here. And then a sickness filled his belly. That she should even be here to watch him being run down like a rabid animal. That J should force her to participate in this filthy mess, because the commando was sure that J had coerced her with deceit.

Till death do us part, motherfucker!

He did not retreat back over the ridge, as had been his

original plan. Instead, like the snake inside him, he slithered forward, his glassy, unblinking eyes seeking warm meat . . . of the human kind.

The light morning wind made her skirt billow and her long hair dance as she stood on a mound overlooking the ridge, overlooking the manhunters—Lord have mercy, so many of them, all busy with their grim and deadly purpose. Manhunters. Why was she having so difficult a time realizing that it was her man they meant to hunt? She hoped and prayed to God Almighty that Colonel Jarvis was right. That Walker would want to talk to her. That he might surrender himself before the guns did the talking. Couldn't he see how futile his efforts were in the face of such a force as those armed men down there? Worse, did he even care? Was this an act of suicide? And then she found herself mistrusting the strange colonel, and somehow the thought made her stomach churn.

Her big eyes, now red and tired from lack of sleep, gazed to the cloudless sky. Such a beautiful day . . . such a terrible day with the scent of death and dying commingled among the fresh aroma of cool woods. The pain within her breast was almost more than she could bear. She could hardly comprehend the tragedy. She knew she could have made him better. She knew she could have made him happy. Given precious time she could have relieved his awful torment and shown him peace. Did she go wrong, or was it simply the fickle finger of fate? A sickness filled her belly. She covered her mouth with her hand. With all her hopes for a peaceful resolution, she could not stop herself from wondering who would tend to his bleeding body when they shot him down. Why was this nightmare invading her mind? Who would give him comfort? Would they let her hold him and rock him gently as he drew his last breath? Because she knew. Deep inside herself, she knew. And so she gazed toward the heavens, seeing both her shattered dreams and a young soldier lying motionless upon the vast plains of war. And then she fell to her knees, her body shuddering with the pathetic sobs that racked her body.

"This here bloodhound has sixty thousand times more smelling capacity than, say, a German shepherd," the rotund Dogman was saying as his beast hauled him along. Keeping a firm leash on the dog, he dodged branches and plowed through the brush. "You'll notice how Red, here, stays to one side of the trail or the other. That's because a man is continuously raining micro-droplets of perspiration, and that's what a hound picks up. The prevailing wind will determine how straight a line the dog will take to the actual trail the man made. Now see, here in these woods where there isn't any wind, Red is almost right on top of the trail."

Chip and Dale, wearing their perpetually surly expressions, and with rifles at port arms, were directly behind the Dogman. Behind them were two local law-enforcement officers and two corrections officers from Buckley Ridge. These latter four were all suffering from a severe case of the jitters, gawking around nervously and experiencing massive adrenaline rushes every time a timber creaked. The forest was permeated with a hushed, spooky aura that no one was happy with.

"That's all mighty interesting," Chip said to the Dogman. He spoke quietly, his lips pressed tightly against his teeth. "But seein's how ol' Red, there, is on the trail of an armed killer, why don't you just keep your goddamn mouth shut before the son of a bitch hears us comin' and sets up an ambush."

The Dogman, who'd tracked down more criminals than he cared to count, was undaunted. With a twinkle in his eye he gave the sniper a chuckle. "No need to get your balls in an uproar, sonny. Not yet, anyways. You'll be able to tell when we're close. Red'll give plenty of sign. He won't yap, which is a good trait among trained bloodhounds, but he'll kind of stop and kind of sway his head with his nose high. That's why we only use one dog at a time instead of a bunch of them like you see in the movies. Hell, they'd be getting all balled up and yowling and warning the fugitive. Only need one good nose, as far as that goes. Anyway, you'll be able to tell."

Chip hawked up a ball of phlegm and spat. "Yeah? Well, just kind of keep a lid on it, anyway, huh?"

The Dogman shrugged, made a barely audible comment about the difference between legal and illegal killers, and they went on in silence.

Seemingly loud silence.

Boots crunched over frozen ground. Frost-filled trees cracked alarmingly. Breath hung in thick clouds of condensation, and each man thought the other was panting too loud. Step by nerve-bending step they followed the dog deeper into the woods, expecting a burst of gunfire at any second. Whether they knew it or not, they were feeling the same naked fear that the commando had felt in the jungles of Southeast Asia. Their swallowing came hard, their breathing was labored, their heartbeats tripled, and they carried sick lumps in their bellies as they walked the borderline of panic. But their purpose drove them on. They were running down a crazed killer on behalf of the law. The law. And once they put the pressure on him, the con would surely break and crumble like they all did, crawling out of his hole, begging for mercy. Then, because he had a gun, because of what he did, because of what he was putting them through, they would kick his fucking face in and beat the living shit out of him. They would drag his bruised and bleeding pulp back and fling it at the feet of the law that demanded him. And then they would have their day of glory. The press would praise them before the cheers of an admiring public. The commando would either make them heroes . . . or, much as no one liked to think about it, he would make them dead.

The dog led them through a wet, boot-gushing cedar swamp. Then he led them into a tight, brushy corridor through a thick alder overgrowth made by grazing deer. And it was up this deer trail, within the confining thickets, that ol' Red, with his trusty and flawless nose, sixty thousand times better than the average dog, walked right into it.

Ol' Red, intent on his nosy work, snuffling around like he was trained to do, walked right across the thin wire that held the booby trap cocked, and slipped the peg. There was a snapping swish as the cleverly contrived latticework of sharpened hardwood stakes sprang forward with frightening velocity. With a sickeningly muffled slap, the dog caught four of the wicked spikes head-on. The animal was instantly impaled through the eye, neck, and chest, with an upper spike protruding bloodily from beneath its floppy ear. It yelped and thrashed horribly for a few seconds, then petered down to a guttural whine, then was still, its forequarters lifted from the ground. And frothy red foam ran in rivulets down its dangling tongue.

The Dogman exclaimed a horrified, "Holy Jesus!" He took a step forward, as though to save his grotesquely hanging animal, and his foot slid into a shallow depression. He did not immediately connect the abrupt explosion with something happening to himself. But when spraying blood, bone fragments, and boot remnants geysered past his face, he realized, on his nauseous journey into unconsciousness, that he had stepped on something awfully unkosher.

What he had stepped on was the buckshot shell Walker had embedded in the rough-hewn board, driving the cap end of the shell into the makeshift pin. Diabolically simple, the ignited 12-gauge shot effectively ripped apart the whole front half of the Dogman's foot, which would, if the shock didn't kill him, certainly take him out of action.

At the first snap of the improvised version of the Cong antipersonnel device, Chip and Dale instinctively leapt to opposite sides of the trail. They thrashed through the frustrating brush, pushing to forward point, then squatted and gawked around wildly, both feeling coldly conspicuous because of the lack of proper cover. Their rifle barrels followed their frantic eye movement as they scanned the woods for the faintest sign of the enemy. And then, when the Dogman stepped on the shell, it so startled them that they jerked around and came within a hair's breadth of blowing away the remainder of the search team, who were so momentarily stunned that they were incapable of movement. But then the terrible spell broke, and they all rushed to the aid of the stricken Dogman.

Chip yanked his radio out of its belt sheath and hit the transmit button. "Chip One to Base, get some fuckin' medics out here! On the double! Our Twenty is about a half mile due west from where we left the road. Now get me J-One on the line. Move it!"

The radio crackled with a "Ten four," then Colonel Jarvis came over the air. "Christ Almighty, Chip-One, what the hell's going on out there?" The colonel's deep, robotic voice held some semblance of emotion.

"The X-Two greased the dog with something like a Malayan Gate," the sniper replied coolly. He was still squatted, radio in one hand, rifle in the other, trying to look everywhere at once. "The handler stepped on a slug. You know how the gooks used to rig 'em in 'Nam? Blew his fuckin' foot right off!"

There was a short silence, then, matter-of-factly, "Want some more gunners with those medics?"

With an air of obvious superiority Chip looked down his nose at the overwrought men huddled around the handler. "Yeah, better send a few. These jokers are kind of rattled. But hold most of 'em on standby. If the X-Two decides to come down, he'll sure enough pick a firefight with one of those teams on the prowl. Once we get his position, have every man you can spare run up both ends of the ridge and meet at the middle—about mid-ridge up, I'd say. We'll at least have him inside a perimeter."

Suddenly the forest echoed with the heavy booms of a powerful rifle, far to the left, drifting up from a hollow. There was the chattering of automatics, then the big booms again. Then silence.

"That's it!" the sniper yelled over the radio. "You heard the position! Move those men out! Me and the Double-D are goin' after the shitbird! Jesus! You can bet your ass he's got himself a machine gun now. Movin' out. Over and out."

Unhesitatingly Chip and Dale crashed their way out of the

confining brush and got up into the line of trees where they could move. Rifles poked before them; they ran low and hard toward the sounds of the gunfight. They moved fast but with professional caution, covering each other . . . like commandos.

CHAPTER
THIRTEEN

On Colonel Jarvis's recommendation they had moved their base of operations up the skidder trail to the place where Walker had veered into the woods. A long line of jeeps, power wagons, and four-wheel-drives were strung out both ways from this center point, and group after group of armed men stood facing the dreaded ridge. None of these men were very happy about the radio reports concerning booby traps, or the distant sounds of gunfire. By now, everyone was aware of the unsettling fact that this fugitive was anything but ordinary. Most of the guys involved in the search effort had regular jobs on construction or in the lumber mills. Volunteer law enforcement was just a sideline to enhance meager wages. Weekend warriors. They were basically family men, and their idea of enforcing the law pertained mostly to running down drunken rowdies and collaring juvenile burglars. This commando shit was distinctly for the birds. The full birds, like that colonel.

Jarvis was giving emphatic instructions to a group of reluctant team leaders. "The idea," he was saying, "is to get

163

the top of that ridge cordoned off. You've got enough men here to make a substantial loop without losing sight of the next man. Keep spaced out, but keep visual contact from one to the other. Once you've got your circle completed, dig in and hold your position. I mean, stay put no matter what happens below you. It's extremely vital that Walker doesn't get through you. We'll handle him within the perimeter. Now move on out. And hurry! And for God's sake don't bunch up or have your men wandering around inside that perimeter, or he'll pick you off like fish in a barrel!" In his bush greens, bloused boots, and cocked beret, Jarvis fit perfectly the newsreel version of the military adviser standing importantly amid the ragtag, innocent-faced peon riflemen.

The spokesman for the team leaders was ill at ease, and he was flushed as though he had been drinking. "Sir," he said, clearing his throat, "don't you think this is a little out of our league? I mean, this guy acts like someone the Army ought to be taking care of. You know, the National Guard or something."

The team leader shrank under the Intelligence officer's positively glacial expression. "We've almost got the man's precise location," Jarvis coolly replied, his gaze so unrelenting that the cowed team leader had to look at the ground. "By now we must have over a hundred men. We'll shortly have him surrounded . . . as soon as you guys get your asses up that ridge. I hardly think we need the National Guard at this point. If a single man can kick the shit out of a hundred representatives of every law-enforcement agency in the state, then common sense says he can also be long gone before any Army unit ever got here. You can let him make fools out of you if you want, but from a tactical viewpoint he's more at a disadvantage right now than you're ever going to get him again. The only thing you need to do right now is set the fucker up. I can't believe you haven't already gone."

"Uh, yes, sir. Right, sir," the team leader mumbled. Then he and the others joined their respective groups. In a flurry of activity, with the help of Jarvis's men, they began the unsavory task of encircling the ridge.

Jarvis went back to the radio command truck where Collins, Brandon, and Roderick were waiting. Although the colonel's military efficiency was to be appreciated, there was something about his presence here that made Collins decidedly uncomfortable. Something was not on the up-and-up. Such as his cryptic radio conversations with those two snipers, Chip and Dale. J-One, Chip-One, Double-D, and the X-Two—as though they had their predetermined codes, and their operation was entirely separate from the main event. Collins tried to remember, in the hectic confusion of the previous night's long hours, exactly when the snipers had come on the scene. And he realized that they had just quietly happened along. They were suddenly just there, solemnly, unannounced, in the midst of things.

"Those two hit men out there—they're a couple more of your sick prototypes, aren't they?" Collins asked point-blank.

Jarvis flashed his thin-lipped Auschwitz-technician grin. "Number-one contenders."

"Why wasn't I informed of their status?"

"For what?" The colonel lifted his binoculars and trained them on the ridge, blatantly ignoring the corrections officer's rising rage.

"For what? I'll tell you for what! Until that killer out there is properly released to you, he's supposed to be in my custody. That makes him my responsibility. That means I'm in charge of all efforts to apprehend him, which means this is my operation, pal, and I want to know everything that's going on inside it. That's for what!"

"I'd say it was a minor technicality, Dick," Brandon interrupted. "After all, we can use all the help we can get. Personally I feel a little better knowing there're some guys out there in Walker's class. Who cares where they came from?"

Collins, his rugged face sagging under the prolonged strain, was livid with anger. "That's where you're wrong, John. It's not a minor technicality. It's major. If it wasn't major"—he viciously jerked a thumb at Jarvis—"then Dr. Doom wouldn't be here. You want to know what I think? I'll tell you what I think. I think this leering gargoyle, this messenger from hell, is using our troubles as a goddamn training exercise for his 'number-one contenders.'"

The implications behind this monstrous accusation brought on a most unnatural silence. Jarvis lowered his binoculars and turned his rigid body slowly. It was the quality of his movements, the distant apocalyptic threat of his alien features, that pervaded the atmosphere with a creepy, unreasonable sense of horror. If looks could kill, Collins would have been blown to rat shit. Brandon shivered, and it wasn't from the cold.

The radio crackled, and the spell was broken. The urgent call was from Chip-One to J-One, which caused Collins to snort disgustedly. It was obvious to him who had infiltrated control of the situation. And if his conjectures proved correct, it would become painfully obvious to everyone else, too, before this was over.

Mike in hand, the colonel leaned calmly against the truck. "J-One, read ya, Chip. What do you have?"

"Got a body count of two, sir," the impersonal voice in the receiver replied. "Sheriff's deputies. Personal clothing. ID says Reginald Patterson and Steffin Coleman. Recon indicates they were picked off at around two hundred meters. Long-range, high-power rifle, 30-06 shell casings. Top of Patterson's head's gone. Coleman's got guts all over the place. Real mess. Recon indicates they were both carrying automatic weapons. Uzi machine gun and GI-issue M16. Both missing. X-Two has abandoned shotgun. Conclude that X-Two is armed with Uzi, M16, and 30-06, with undetermined quantity of ammo. X-Two functioning at maximal capacity, position unknown. Chip-One and Double-D proceeding to recon of southeast slope. Watch your ass, motherfuckers! Over and out." And the radio went silent.

Governor Brandon stared slack-jawed at the radio. "What the hell are we up against . . . ?" Then, when he had recovered from the shock, "All right, that does it! We've played with this maniac long enough! I'm calling in the National Guard!"

He reached for the field phone on back of the truck, but suddenly Colonel Jarvis's hand shot forward and snapped like a steel vise around the governor's wrist. The colonel's unblinking, ice-blue eyes drilled Brandon like a pair of stilettos.

Uh-oh, thought Collins. This is it. This is where we find out who's who on the shit heap.

"I beg your pardon, sir!" the startled governor exclaimed, alternating a mixture of angry, but fearful, glances between the colonel's cold eyes and the grip on his arm.

"I'm afraid I must ask you not to do that just yet, Governor," Jarvis said calmly, releasing his hold.

Flustered, Brandon edged toward Roderick, who had his big jaw thrust forward in outrage, and he had his hand on the pistol beneath his jacket, should it become necessary to execute defensive measures.

"Just what the hell are you talking about?" The governor rubbed his wrist, which still had red finger marks on it.

Jarvis reached in his shirt and brought out a telegraph communication, which he handed to Brandon. He slowly went about taking out a cigarette and lighting it up as the governor read.

Brandon's eyes went wide as he examined the communication, then his face paled. "Good God, man, this is from the president himself! He's asking me to relinquish responsibility for Walker's capture to you. Why wasn't this given to me sooner?"

Jarvis blew out a stream of smoke. "I didn't think it would be necessary. Like you, I thought Walker would be apprehended by now. Anyway, you can verify the instructions through the Department of Defense if you wish. There's the phone. Just bear in mind that I am here by the authority of the United States government, and any indication of noncooperation in a matter this severe might not set very well with those guys."

But Brandon had been privy to enough federal intrigue to know that the colonel was not lying. And it was more than obvious that Walker fit into an other than ordinary category.

And Jarvis was also right in that the only thing the big shots would want to hear was that the commando was either in custody or dead. So let the army bastard have his way. Who cared, as long as that madman out there was taken care of. And if the operation turned into a failure, Jarvis would be in an excellent position to take the flak.

"Oh, I don't doubt it," Brandon fumed. "No telling what you goddamned spooks are up to these days. But what I don't understand is why you object to having the National Guard here."

"Because Walker is on the offensive right now," Jarvis answered. "He thinks he has an advantage. Bring in a bunch of soldiers and he's liable to retreat so far back into those woods that we'd never find him again." And somehow Collins thought he detected the fine edge of a lie.

Brandon harrumphed. "Well, go right to it, then, fella. Just don't be telling me that my word doesn't mean diddly-shit."

"That's not at all what I'm saying, Governor." The Intelligence man's voice was condescendingly smooth. "In fact, your word means quite a bit. That's why I would like for you to go down to the other end of the line and have a talk with those pressmen and curiosity seekers. Then, when you get rid of them, I think it would be best for you to take your wife, get on one of those planes, and get the hell out of here before you get your ass shot off."

"Oh, I'll have a word with the press, all right," Brandon replied hotly. "But I'll leave when I'm goddamned good and ready! And when this is over, you'd better be prepared to answer a few questions, mister. Such as, what's that freak of 'your people's' doing out of his cage in the first place? C'mon, Mort, let's go find Nancy and the boys. The air around here is getting kind of stuffy." He stomped away, his big security man following in an angry huff.

"So now all you have to do is get rid of me, huh?" Collins bitterly said.

Jarvis chuckled, finished his cigarette, and ground it under his heel. "Afraid not, Mr. Collins. You stay with me.

You have the distinction of being the most important man out here. Without you the commando might hightail it, and we wouldn't have a chance at him."

"What the hell do you mean?"

"I mean that Walker is coming down off that ridge. And he's coming down for at least one major reason. He's going to kill you, Mr. Collins. I intend to be ready for him when he gets here."

That flat statement hit Collins like a slap in the face. It was a chilly morning, but the cold was nothing like the ice-ball that suddenly had filled the pit of his belly. He subconsciously cast furtive glances around. His back was feeling like an open target, no matter which way he turned.

"What . . . what are you talking about? How do you know he's after me?"

Jarvis ignored the question. He reached in the door of the radio truck, brought out two M16s with loaded clips, and handed one to Collins. Collins took the weapon with unsteady hands. He stared at the light, vented rifle as though it were something unclean. He gulped. "Don't you have anything like . . . you know . . . like bulletproof vests or something? Besides, how do you know he's after me?" The question became almost frantic. "How do you know?"

Jarvis snapped the bolt on his weapon in order to chamber the leader round, and Collins jerked as though shot. "I listened to the radio," the colonel said. "You know, the conversation you had with him while he was holding the governor hostage. You should have acknowledged his request while he was in jail. Now you've done gone and gotten him mad. Well, heh, heh, you can see what happens when he gets mad. Which is why I'm here. I know how he thinks when he gets pissed off. Well, it's not exactly what you'd call thinking. More like a guided missile, to be more specific. You kind of have to blast it out of the sky before it hits the target. You can't reprogram it once it's in flight. I guess you could say that Walker is in flight. He's accidentally programmed himself, and he will stay in the kill mode until you're dead. Or he's dead. Whichever comes first. But if it's any consolation to you, I figure he aims to waste my ass too. We, as it were, are what he identifies as enemy, no different to him than a Cong in the bush."

The first of the medic teams was coming out of the woods. They were carrying a stretcher on which the Dogman lay, his face ashen, moaning sickly, deliriously calling for his mutt. The sheet covering his lower half was all bloody.

"Dear God," Collins groaned.

Nancy was in great fear. She had managed to get her hands on a gun, but she had not been able to find a team that was willing to let her tag along. So, successfully eluding her husband's security men, she tagged along, anyway, at what she thought was a prudent distance. But somewhere along the way, although she couldn't rightly recollect how it had happened, she lost sight of them. Now she was suddenly alone in a dark, gloomy spruce and fir thicket, with no clear idea of which way she ought to go. She was lost.

Her first impulse was to cry out for help, but she didn't dare. What if *he* showed up first and caught her with the gun. She shuddered at the thought. Panic gripped her, threatening to drive out reasonable thought. She had to force herself to remain calm. She made herself sit down and think it over. Why she was here. Finally her hatred for the commando brought her back into focus. She had come here for a shot at him, or to at least have the pleasure of watching him die. He had slapped her. He had humiliated her as no man had ever done before. She bit her lip in fury when she thought of his explosive entrance into the boat house, the utter mortification she had felt when he had paraded her naked in front of her husband, with Gorman the perfect caricature of a whipped dog. Her face was hard as she clutched the cold rifle.

The tall trees swayed, hissing softly as a light breeze swept through groping-fingered branches. The forest floor was thick with a carpet of conifer needles and spongy moss, giving off a damp, mulchy smell, the thickness lending a sense of awful quiet to the whispering air. Great, moss-covered boulders, carried by the glaciers eons ago, rose all through these woods, their bulk lurking like the shapes of hungry beasts on the hillside.

Nancy was cold. She hunkered into the down-filled camouflage jacket she had borrowed. She pulled the green knit cap she was wearing lower over her ears. She felt watched. She felt as though the big, dark rocks were glaring at her with hidden eyes. She was sure the trees, thick, all the same everywhere you looked, were chuckling with sinister delight at her uncomfortable predicament. Every nerve in her taut body sang out against the unseen malignancy surrounding her. *He* was here, somewhere, close by. For some reason she was sure of it.

She didn't know how right she was.

He was there, all right, not a hundred feet above her, lending malevolent eyes to an ancient mound of stone. He was not surprised to see her. Nothing surprised him anymore.

She was just another Cong bitch, no better than the hounds that fucked her. A raging pain swept through his head, momentarily clouding his vision. Then, with amazing, almost terrifying clarity, he saw the stupid, gangly country boy standing like a lost pup in the middle of a rutted, bomb-pitted road. Gawking. Gawking like a rubbernecked fool. Standing there twiddling with his M16 like it was a limp dick, gawking at a group of ARVN soldiers. The ARVN gooks had a skinny little Cong bitch in their midst. She was struggling furiously with them, panting, gasping, but not crying out. They were laughing, throwing her from man to man, ripping her black jungle pajamas off her. She was bony and had saggy little tits. The whole scene had a dirty, caveman texture which the gangly boy could hardly attempt to articulate. They pinned her down and took turns fucking her, fucking her in the mud like a bunch of goddamn grunting pigs. And the dumb country boy gawked. And the ARVNs laughed at him. And when they were done, they offered her to him like a piece of fucking monkey meat. But all he could do was gawk. And twiddle his M16 like a limp dick.

Nancy got up and nervously glanced around. When she moved, the commando moved. But then the commando froze, Uzi cocked, pushed before him. He remained as still as the stone that concealed him. Something was wrong. His heightened sensory perception was sending hot waves of alarm to his brain. Nothing tangible, nothing he could readily see. A feeling that only a jungle fighter could identify. Danger. Enemy presence screamed from the silence.

Suddenly, thunderously reverberating gunshots split the forest calm. Nancy was literally lifted off her feet, sections of her body blowing apart in red gushes of blood and gore. Caught in a crossfire, she was having a hard time falling. Her rifle flew out of her hands as the heavy slugs made her do a jerky, macabre ballet. But finally she did fall, a shapeless, riddled heap.

Her killers cautiously, tentatively emerged from the shadows among the trees, their powerful weapons smoking, ghosts of death in their dark fatigues.

"I reckon we got the motherfucker," Chip whispered harshly.

"Yeah? Well, let's just make sure," Dale snarled.

And the 7-mm's belched again. They emptied a clip each into the lifeless body, splattering already torn meat all over the place, the bullets slapping into wet, red flesh, making the bulk jerk electrically.

Chip chuckled. "I reckon that fried him." He automatically replaced his spent clip with a fresh one.

The snipers approached the body with more confidence this time. Dale knelt down to examine their handiwork. But when he rose, he was wearing an odd, baffled expression. "I reckon we fucked up," was about all he could say.

"Yeah, I reckon you sure did," Walker agreed sarcastically, rising from behind his rock. The black Uzi barrel was pointing like a finger of doom.

Chip and Dale were momentarily stunned. Soldiers of fortune, they instantly recognized the specter of their death. "Shit!" was the last thing Chip ever spat. Dropping into a low crouch, he swung his rifle to bear, knowing it was a futile effort.

The Uzi submachine gun chattered—an angry demon puking out crimson death, cutting the surprised snipers apart like a crazed butcher with a couple of desperate chickens. Walker wasted not a second. He ran toward the flailing bodies, firing steady bursts even as the men fell. Quickly, deftly, he searched the warm, still twitching corpses. He found what he wanted. Hand grenades. Two each.

He could hear excited voices, feet crashing through the brush, coming quickly. He yanked the pin from one of the grenades. Chip lay facedown, blood running from his nose and mouth, his eyes rolled in death. Walker slid the armed grenade under the sniper's belly, careful that the dead man's weight held the handle in place. Then, after a final glance around, he vanished into the woods as swiftly and silently as any wild animal.

CHAPTER
FOURTEEN

Colonel Jarvis paced back and forth beside the radio truck. He had a walkie-talkie in one hand, and with his other hand he kept dry-wiping his mouth. He tried not to listen to the distant rattling of gunfire, the frantic radio transmissions, men hollering and running every which way. Christ, he was getting too old for this shit. Too many wars. Too many bodies laid across the killing fields of this planet. No more. This was it. He'd hand in his resignation when this mission was over.

What was happening was utter disaster. Utter chaos. Jarvis wasn't particularly surprised that four men got their shit blown away by a grenade hidden under a dead body. The gooks were fond of that trick. But what really knocked the wind out of his sails was that Chip and Dale seemed to have bought the farm on a classic sucker play.

It was the grenade, though, that set off the pandemonium, as Walker no doubt figured it would. The boy had certainly learned his lessons well. A search team, bunched together like they weren't supposed to be, had hurried toward the sounds of the shooting in the hollow where the governor's wife had foolishly gotten herself killed. It wasn't immediately apparent to the manhunters what had happened, but they weren't long in identifying what was left of her. The bullet-riddled carnage left the team with a bad case of the jitters, and when they rolled Chip over, on the odd chance that he might still be alive, they were not prepared for what lay underneath. Just as the grenade went off, blowing four men to kingdom come, another team, approaching from the opposite direction, blundered onto the scene. The remainder of the first team was so unnerved by the explosion that when the second team came crashing through the brush, they opened fire on them. The second team, thinking they had encountered the commando, returned fire, and by the time the mistake was realized and sanity returned, only four out of twelve men were left standing. And of those four, not a one of them was fit for any further combat.

Colonel Jarvis kept pacing and dry-wiping his mouth. The incredible body count did not come as a major surprise to him. He'd seen worse under unusual circumstances of varying degrees. In fact, he'd expected a high kill. Those secretly indoctrinated killer commandos were absolutely phenomenal in combat situations. It was a pity that there was nothing you could do with them between actions. They had been so thoroughly immersed in the sights, sounds, and smells of war that whether they were aware of it or not, their bodies craved it like a junkie craves smack. The slightest tingle of danger rammed their modified nervous systems into a nearly orgasmic hyper-alert, and they functioned with terrifying accuracy, mindless, yet in complete control of razor-keen kill-savvy. They were bad news, and like bad news, they traveled light and fast. When you followed them through the jungle, you followed a dreadful trail of mayhem and destruction. Their objective, once oriented, was to annihilate their target by whatever means possible, and with disregard to themselves, like state-of-the-art kamikaze. They would maim, slaughter, destroy anything in their way. They would find and reach their target if they had to crawl, frothing at the mouth. And when they got there, the target would die, no matter what. Anything that came into their hands was a deadly weapon, and even their bare hands were deadly weapons. Whatever ordnance they had to destroy with would determine the extent of the havoc they wreaked. They might simply break a man's neck, or they might obliterate a village from the face of the earth. It simply depended on what kind of arsenal they got their murderous hands on. Either way, the target would die, and it made not a whit's difference to them whether or not ten, fifty, or even a hundred men went down with it. A little hole or a big bang, it didn't matter as long as the result was final. And the result was always final.

No, Jarvis was not particularly surprised about the body count. What made his blood run cold was that now Walker had hand grenades. It was terrible to think about what that one very special commando could do with them. Already he had these undisciplined, poorly trained dingbats shooting at each other. He was close to turning this whole thing into a complete rout. Up on the ridge they were still shooting at each other, or emptying magazines on shadows, scared shit-less. Worse, though, was that even with a heavy guard stationed around the radio truck, and the truck in the middle of the convoy, it was conceivable that Walker was still going to penetrate security and kill Dick Collins. Maybe even Jarvis too. What was to stop him? Employing savage, most damaging terror tactics, he had the whole operation confused and running in circles. And now the motherfucker's got some hand grenades!

Again and again, Jarvis dry-wiped his mouth.

Collins was not in a much better frame of mind. He was sitting on the running board of the truck, absently toying with the rifle he hardly knew how to use, staring vacantly at the ridge where an inmate of his was spreading more sense-less death than he ever would have imagined possible. If he were not here as a living witness, there was no way he ever would have believed that a single man could create so much bloody waste. That Walker was so elusive was absolutely remarkable. And Walker's lethal determination escaped the corrections officer's understanding. Of course, he would pick a thick evergreen forest to conceal his movements, Collins thought bitterly. But they were fortunate, he supposed, that the kill-crazy bastard didn't pick downtown Portland to live out his war fantasy. Better to have him isolated in the woods than running amok in the city. Collins had to admit to himself, though, that he was genuinely afraid of that . . . that thing out there.

The superintendent shifted his uncomfortable gaze from the ridge and directed it toward the pacing colonel. He couldn't help but feel that Jarvis was an intergral part of all this. Shrouded in the dark obscurity of some unnatural world of the cloak and dagger, this creepy-crawly military man was somehow inextricably linked to the deranged, blood-thirsty commando. It was all Collins could do to control his mixed emotions of loathing, a deep sense of tragedy, and the awful fear of dying.

"Do you think we should call in the National Guard now?" he asked cuttingly. He was swallowing hard, and he was tense to the point of trembling. "Or do you think we should wait until he kills everyone out here?"

Jarvis ceased his incessant pacing and went as rigid as a block of ice. He glared at the ground like an enraged bull and talked with his stiff back to the superintendent. "I should think by now that it would be obvious to you why I haven't called in the Guard."

Collins snorted in disgust. "Oh, of course. It's perfectly clear. That man is killing us off like a bunch of clowns, but there is no reason on earth why we should clobber him with a professional armed-forces unit."

The colonel wheeled sharply, and Collins started. For a brief second he thought the MI man was going to kill him, his glacial face was so contorted. However, Jarvis's voice was calm and restrained, although he spoke with a tight jaw.

"The Guard is nothing but a bunch of pansy-ass kids so far out of Walker's class that it's pathetic," he said. "They are no better than the men we already have out here, except they're probably more dangerous to themselves. The only difference between our men and the Guard is that the Guard is equipped with a shitload of mighty expensive toys. Toys that Walker could and most definitely would get his hands on. So instead of a couple of burp guns, he'd have a rocket launcher or two. Maybe he'd have an M-60 machine gun and a few mortar rounds and a claymore mine and an M-79 grenade launcher. Bring in the big shit so he can commandeer a tank or an armored personnel carrier and really flatten us. Believe me, turning the Guard loose on him would be just like handing him a walking supermarket. Or maybe I should send the aircraft back up so he can lob a round or two into their fuselage with that fuckin' elephant gun he's got.

"I want you to understand something, Mr. Collins. I want you to get a clear picture of this situation, because I'm not going to mince words with you. Listen to me . . . your life depends on it! Those two men, Chip and Dale, were the best I had to offer. Between the two of them they could outfox and outkill any Guard unit on this continent. Well, our man Walker fried them like a couple of clumsy jerks. That, my friend, scares the shit out of me. Not so much as a testament to his ability but because now he has hand grenades. Which, I don't need to tell you, greatly increases our vulnerability. You and me, I'm talking about. You are probably our best chance to kill him because he wants you and he wants you bad. And if he's seen me, he'll be coming for me too. But I'm staying right here beside you. We'll wait for him. Don't worry, he'll make a play. You can bet your life on it. So snap your ass out of the self-pity shit and brace yourself for a firefight. And start praying to whatever the hell it is you pray to that we get the drop on him first." J stared at the ridge with a strange expression, then added in almost a whisper, "He has to make a play. We have his girlfriend. And he knows me."

Not really understanding this last statement, Collins rubbed his tired face, then kneaded the stiff muscles at the back of his neck. "You're right." He sighed heavily. "But, Jesus, this is hard to take. Poor John. He must be in rough shape. Nancy . . . God! Maybe we should get him down here under the protection of our guards, although I wish to Christ he would leave before things get any worse."

"He won't leave," the colonel replied. "He's got too much of a personal stake in this thing. Anyway, he's better off up the line. There's plenty of men up there to watch after him. No need to bring him down here. Believe me, pal, this is where the heat's going to be. When the shit hits the fan, you might be surprised at how little protection we really have. I'm telling you, this guy in action is an awesome spectacle to behold . . . if you survive it." Then he chuckled and winked at Collins. "But he can die, buddy. He's not bullet-proof, he's not superhuman—just incredibly well trained. He can die just like you and me. All you have to do is hit him. That's the bottom line . . . and that's the rub!"

Suddenly multiple explosions shattered the morning air. Giant fireballs shot skyward, trailing thick smoke from the landing zone where the chopper and the two spotter planes had been standing by. Thunder rocked the ground, and the heavy, acrid stench of burning gas immediately wafted all around, filling the drifting breeze with the smell of hell.

Collins bolted upright as though jerked by a string from above. "Holy Jesus!" he exclaimed. "He's blown the air-craft!" He started forward, drawn magnetically to the running guards who were responding to urgent radio requests for assistance. The metallic voices on the receivers were positive that their enemy was close at hand, and they were issuing a general call to arms. But Collins was held back by a hand tightly grasping his arm. He suddenly became aware that the colonel was yelling at him.

"Stay here!" Jarvis shouted, yanking Collins's arm. "Stay here! There's no need to go down there. Walker is a long way away from that scene by now. He'll be here. After us. We've got to stay here and watch each other's back. Listen to me, goddammit!"

* * *

It was true. Walker was well on his way away from the scene.

There had been only two pilots lingering around the landing zone. Everybody else had joined one or another phase of the manhunt, believing the killer was still somewhere in the area where, it was being said, a bloody massacre had taken place. The pilots had been sitting under a wing of one of the spotters, drinking whiskey, wishing to hell they had been unavailable when the call had come for their services. Following the beep on a tagged moose was one thing, they agreed, but drawing ground to air fire from a homicidal maniac was quite another. Those planes might be small, but they went down with a big crash. Not many survived a crash in heavy woods like this. Crashing was the topic the pilots dwelled on as they drank. And they drank heavily.

The commando, a crawling, crablike, alien thing, making not a whisper of sound, crept up on them, coming at them from behind the landing gear. His bayonet, as though driven by the arm of some otherworldly demon, did the dirty work. He moved from one to the other so swiftly that the pilots' throats had been slashed before they were even aware that the enemy was upon them. They surely never had time to reflect on the fine art of dying.

Walker had quickly found a spare fuel can. He sloshed gas on and under all the craft and removed all the gas caps. Then he stepped back, pulled the pin from a grenade, and rolled it under the plane in the middle. In the four seconds that it took the grenade to explode, thus creating the chain of explosions, he was already back in the woods. And now he lay as still as death in a shallow depression, buried under a scraggly heap of dead leaves and rotted branches, as frantic men rushed past him.

He was amazed at what chaos a simple diversionary tactic could create among these blundering idiots. They had no business inside a war. Running rats. Rats running, squealing, screaming. What were they doing inside a war? Why? Walker's head screamed. Why couldn't he get this shit into some real perspective? His head thundered like it did when he took the injections. These fuckers didn't even look like gooks. Something god-awful wrong. His head. Rapid feet pounding frozen ground. Goblins drawn big-eyed to the flames. Jesus, his head hurt. Yelling voices invaded his aching mind. Gooks? Was it an ambush? What the fuck . . .

It was time to go. He crawled out of his hole, stood in a motionless crouch, his blackened face streaked with sweat, the white dripping in weird patterns with the black. His face looked like it was melting, a surrealistic rendition of the living dead. His eyes, squinting, unblinking, looked unholy, eerie, as though out of focus with this world. But they were in focus—acutely so. He took a careful recon before drifting apparitionlike through the woods, aiming himself toward the front of the convoy. Because Collins was up there somewhere. Somewhere. He could feel it. The injections made you *feel*. And there were many, many, many injections. Even now he could feel the medicinal taste on the end of his tongue. He could feel Collins's jangled nerves, filling the air with static electricity. Up there. Somewhere.

The commando moving through the woods was a form of high art. He was a spider crawling across the mossy floor. He was a sparrow flitting from tree to tree. He was a woodchuck dashing for its hole. He was shadow merging with shadow. He was a broken stump. He was a robot jerking inhumanly from rock to rock. He was rock. He was brush. He assimilated, digested, and gave off the forms of all those things surrounding him. He was animal, mineral, and vegetable. He was earth. He was a paradox of himself. Warm blood coursed, throbbed through living flesh, but his mind was a machine, a ticking time bomb, a heat-seeking missile, equipped with an ultra sophisticated directional device. He needed. And the need was wickedly possessive, insane, overwhelming. He needed . . . to *kill*!

He needed to kill Collins. Why? Haven't you done enough already? He needed to kill Collins as desperately as a

hurt man needs morphine. Why? Look at the mess you've
made. You probably don't even know how many men
you've killed. This isn't even war. Because it's war, motherfucker! Because a Bouncing Betty ripped Pete right in half.
Right in half. There were guts all over the place, man. All
over the place. You couldn't even pick him up without guts
dripping through your arms. Because Collins was the fairy-
assed, cocksuckin' second looey you fragged when no one
was looking. Because Collins wouldn't stoop to answer a
simple motherfuckin' request because the man making it was
worse than something you wiped your feet on—beneath the
welfare bums, lower than a sewer rat. Walker was just another incessantly bitching, semi-retarded inmate in a hidden
social order, all of them unfit to serve their miserable lives
among decent society.

And then he would get J. He would get J because of his
treachery. He would get J because J came back from the
jungle and stole him away from Claudine and dragged him
back to the war.

The need to kill hurt... but first he needed to somehow
find a way to extricate Claudine from the merciless clutches
of the monster.

He reached the front of the convoy without encountering
the enemy. No big surprise. They were too busy gagging
over their dead. They had important things to do—like
watching their aircraft burn. It was taboo to imagine that the
commando would have the effrontery, the impudence, the
audacity to wander among them when he was supposed to be
running scared. It was preposterous to imagine that he would
approach their sacred vehicles. Preposterous.

The first truck up the line was a power wagon with a
winch on front. There was no one around it. The whole line
of vehicles had the appearance of abandonment, except for a
few jeeps down, where two men seemed to be engaged in
conversation. Although closer scrutiny indicated that the
conversation was slightly one-sided. One man was seated on
a wooden crate, his hands on his knees, his staring eyes
possessing an utterly vacant expression. The other man was

big. He had bristly short hair and wore a rumpled suit. He kept gesturing frantically at the seated man, and he kept pointing down the line, as though trying to convince the seated man that they should leave. The big man had his back to Walker. Walker immediately recognized the seated man as Governor Brandon. Walker wanted to talk to Brandon, to tell him. Just . . . tell him. But he didn't want to talk to the big man.

The commando quietly rolled into the drainage ditch alongside the skidder road. He sneaked a cautious peek up over. The governor was still sitting on his box, and he was wearing the look of a dumb mute. The big man was still gesturing, talking rapidly, trying to get his boss to get up and move. The big man was less than fifty feet away.

Lying on his back in the freezing mud, the commando made sure his cross-slung weapons were secure, their barrels above the muck. Mud. Hot mud. Cold mud. Could it be true that he was more intimate with mud than he had ever been with a woman's soft body? Cold, cold mud. Maybe everyone was wrong. Maybe hell wasn't hot at all. Maybe hell was blistering white cold. He unsheathed his gore-spattered bayonet. Maybe hell was like the soul-freezing blasts of an Arctic blizzard. He eased in a long, slow breath and held it. Maybe hell was daggerlike icicles, perpetually dripping, suspended in a frozen tomb.

He scrambled. He sprang from the ditch as though shot out of a catapult. He measured the broad back of his target even as he streaked for it. He was an awesome blur of muddy earth. Even if Roderick had known that the commando was flying in to kill him, he still would not have been prepared for the incredible suddenness of it.

Walker stopped, his legs in a firm brace, just when it appeared he would slam into the back of the security man. His iron-muscled left arm snaked around Roderick's neck, dragging the target backward, off-balance, as his right rammed the bayonet with titanic force, the commando's sinewy body bunched mightily behind the driving stab. There was the feeling of a ripping crunch as the long knife ground upward through gristly ribs. The thick blade sliced in deep enough to puncture Roderick's heart. Roderick went stiff, gave a strangled gasp, sighed, then went limp. Maybe, thought Walker as he let the heavy man fall, hell is as cold as a cheating bitch's heart. When he yanked the bayonet free from the falling body, it trailed a red arc of viscera.

Brandon watched the barbaric murder of his chief security officer with deep fascination. His hands still rested on his knees. He hadn't even twitched. He just stared with that odd vacancy, as though he might have been engrossed by something particularly interesting on a television screen.

Walker squatted to wipe the knife on Roderick's jacket. He eyed the governor warily, knowing a madman's glaze when he saw one. Brandon was in shock.

"There's something I want to tell you," the commando said softly. His tone was casual, as though he might have been in the governor's sitting room having coffee.

A silly smile spread across Brandon's haggard face, making him look like an idiot. His brows lifted, and his glassy eyes locked on the commando, perhaps seeing him for the first time, the smeared, black, melting face. The mud, the leaves, the twigs stuck to his torn and bloody clothing, which had now taken on the texture of the earth.

"Yes?"

"I didn't kill your wife." The commando jerked his head toward the woods. "They did."

Brandon nodded. "Yes. Yes, they did." He was still smiling idiotically.

Walker nodded too. He rose, sheathed the bayonet, and unslung the M16. "I have to kill your superintendent of corrections," he simply stated. "I have to kill Collins."

Brandon nodded more vigorously. He chuckled, then laughed. He was understanding a profound secret, hearing the punch line to a long, complicated joke. "Yes. Yes, of course you do."

Walker gave a last, pitying look at the stunned head of the state. Then the commando drifted down the line, dodging between vehicles, the ditch, rocks, trees, wherever the course lay. He knew that he was closing in on his target. He could feel it. And now, this close, the fool who stepped in his way would buy a one-way ticket to hell. The fool who got in his way would take a burning burst on the fast train to hell.

CHAPTER
FIFTEEN

"Hailstorm to Holy Mary. Can you read me? Come on, Holy Mary. Over."

Colonel Jarvis stared at the radio command truck as though it were something out of a midnight horror show. Collins's jaw went slack, and the whites of his eyes showed big. Good God...

J's hand looked like it was moving in slow motion as he reached for the microphone. If ever his jaw was tight, now his cheek muscles bulged with ironlike tension. He picked up the mike. He stared at it. It might as well have been some squirmy, slimy thing. Collins, watching it, was utterly speechless. The superintendent was unconsciously clutching his belly, quite sure that he was on the verge of having his first nervous breakdown.

J pressed the transmit button. "Holy Mary. I read you, Hailstorm. Over."

There was a nerve-bending silence, then the commando said, "Wanna fight, Holy Mary? Over."

Jarvis took a deep breath and regained his rigid composure. "Yeah, Hailstorm. I wanna fight. Give me coordinates. Over."

"Back off the girl, Holy Mary. You walk into it this time, if you've got the hair. You and Collins. Over."

Jarvis's lips curled tight against his teeth. The son of a bitch knows. He hesitated, weighed his options, then said, "Okay, Hailstorm. She's out of it. I need coordinates. Over." He knew that if he was ever going to get him, he'd have to play it Walker's way. The commando was no doubt watching the whole operation through field glasses.

"Okay. Move on up, Holy Mary. You'll find me. By the way, asshole, I never forgot 'Nam Dinh. Watch your step, Holy Mary. Over and out."

J glared at the radio for a long time, knowing that now the real show was on. Then he turned abruptly and yelled, "Captain! Get that girl the hell out of here! Take her home. Now!"

And there, hiding on the ridge he had terrorized, with binoculars intently trained, Walker watched Claudine get into the car. A lump filled his throat and a sadness swept over him. "It wasn't your fault, darling," he choked in a whisper. "You must understand that I was on a mission. Please don't ever forget that I was on a mission." Then he angrily heaved the binoculars away. Then he moved out.

If Walker could sense his proximity to Collins, Jarvis could feel the approach of the commando as acutely as the onslaught of a migraine. The Intelligence man had been in the business of dirty deeds since God was a baby. He'd learned a lot of things about the pathetic human condition. But the most important thing he'd learned was that a man didn't stay in this underhanded trade long without getting good at it. You miss one trick, baby, and the jig is up. His refined and naturally suspicious nervous system could sound out the commando coming as surely as his ears could detect the whine of an incoming rocket.

Now he needed to make a decision. It was a good thing that he was so immune to common emotions that he could pass a lie detector test with brazen impunity. Because no matter what decision he came up with, it was not going to be good for Superintendent Collins. Too bad. But the corrections man had inadvertently stepped in what you'd call shit, and in this game the shit gets deep. It gets so deep that the suction might haul you in and you may never step out of it. Like that commando. What a goddamned tragedy. Jarvis actually liked Walker, understood his unique situation, had immense respect for his ability. Killing him would be like trashing a sleek race car simply because it was too damned fast. But he was the last of the line. He was the final piece of living evidence representing a project gone awry.

It was too bad Collins understood the diabolical monstrousness of the thing. It was too bad Collins had some description of a conscience, which meant merely that he couldn't be trusted to keep his mouth shut. Unlike the governor, Collins didn't have enough power to insure his survival even tentatively, but unfortunately he had just enough position to lend credence to any statements he might make. And he would no doubt make statements, shift the blame in order to cover his own ass. The governor could be dealt with in a different way at a later time. Any others who knew the real story were so far down the totem pole that anything they had to say could be shrugged off as the lunatic ravings of glory seekers. Maybe. Infallible instinct would tell Jarvis how to handle the situation when the time came.

The colonel's orders came from the top. Ruthlessly simple. Terminate the commando and cover his tracks by whatever means deemed necessary. He'd thought surely that this search effort would have been enough to at least set Walker up for the professional assassins. But Chip and Dale had been killed, and Walker's tracks had turned into a swath of destruction wide enough to raise questions even in the mind of an idiot. The whitewash job on this mess was apt to rack the brains of even the technicians. So now the colonel's tactics had to undergo serious strategical overhauling. The decision. Field expedience. How to best set Collins up for the slaughter while giving himself an open shot at the commando. Time was a factor now, because Jarvis's tingling nerves told him that the enemy was damnably close.

The colonel was squatted beside the radio truck, chewing the filter of his cigarette, his M16 lying across his knees. He absently watched nervous men straggle out of the woods and head for the burning aircraft, where noise and confusion ruled common sense. Collins, rifle slung, was standing on the hood of the truck, staring through his binoculars as though his life depended on it. Indeed his life did depend on it. Jarvis scootched around so he could get an eyeful of the corrections man. So he could evaluate the man's worth as live bait in a deadly game of Fuck the Nun. Fuck the Nun, a "company" joke. Collins was overweight, he was anything but a jungle fighter, he was soft and flabby from too many years in a leather-covered desk chair, and he didn't know the difference between a hollow-point and a dumdum. But he would have to do. He would have to do because he was the next card to be drawn in a stacked deck.

Jarvis rose and ambled to the front of the truck. "Hey! Mr. Collins."

Collins lowered the binoculars with deathlike slowness. Inside, somewhere in there where his soul was, he knew it was time to jump into the fire. The gates of hell stood open and the demon within beckoned. It was time.

"He's up the line," Jarvis said. Collins wore an expression of profound resignation. He gave no indication that he had heard, so Jarvis yelled, "He's up the fuckin' line!"

Collins gave the rigid MI man a withering look of loathing. Then he climbed down off the truck, nodded, and said, "I know."

"Okay," Jarvis said with what could have passed for sympathy. He lit another cigarette, as did Collins. Both men smoked hard, subconsciously enacting the ritual of taking the last big drag before stepping out in front of the firing squad. And as heavily armed as Walker was, indeed he could be considered a mighty impressive one-man firing squad.

"Okay, here's the scam," the colonel said. "We go alone. Just you and me. If we take a bunch of guys along, he'll just spook. He'll blow your shit away at long range and just scramble. Nobody will ever find him again. This way we might get a shot at him. I figure he's got something he wants to say to you. If we give him the opportunity, he'll say it. And while he's saying it, I aim to try to fry the fucker. But if he greases me first . . . well . . . you'll be holding a bag of awful hot doo-doo. You just better hope to hell that weapon of yours doesn't jam, or it'll be the last bummer you'll ever bitch about!"

Collins chuckled cynically. "You have such a pleasant way of putting things."

Jarvis shrugged. "Just stating facts, buddy."

"Yeah, facts," Collins repeated. "Okay. We go alone. Naturally. No witnesses."

"What the hell is that supposed to mean?" Jarvis snapped boldly, drilling the corrections officer with his wickedly cold eyes. Could it be possible that Collins understood the broad scheme of things? Well, even if he did, it was too late now. Collins would participate in this terminal phase of the operation even if Jarvis had to drag him out by the hair. Collins would have his final words with that X-Two. And that X-Two would have his belated meal. That X-Two would be fed what he should have been fed during the evacuations back in Vietnam ten years ago. He would be fed a gutful of hot NATO rounds—just like the rest of his deliberately demented contemporaries. The "company" liked to make sure their prized projects never went hungry.

Resignedly, tiredly, Collins took control of the radio from the operator, who had been monitoring the activity to the south. The superintendent advised all units to maintain their present positions, and that all movement was temporarily forbidden. Strictly forbidden. And that if they became aware of any activity to the northwest, they were not to respond unless specifically requested by radio to do so. And that any failure to abide by these instructions might result in more killings.

There was temporary radio silence as this odd information was incredulously digested. The the voice of Ray Smith came over the air. The pudgy game commissioner had been trying to reestablish some semblance of order around the inflamed landing zone. "What the hell's going on up there, Dick?" He was breathing heavily, as though he'd just been involved in some physical exertion.

"We may have a fix on our man," Collins replied. "The, uh, colonel and I are going out to investigate. We know he has a radio, so keep it quiet. Maintain radio silence until you hear from me again. And remember, nobody move! My and the colonel's lives may depend on you staying put. If Walker gets spooked by some jerk thrashing around . . . well . . . over."

"Sure hope you know what you're doing, Dick. Over." There was worry in Smith's voice.

"Yeah," Collins muttered. "So do I. Call you if I need you. Over and out." He handed the microphone back to the operator, who was wearing a Warden Service uniform. "Any chance you can patch me through to my wife?"

"That's enough!" Jarvis interrupted impatiently. "It's time to go!" He eased off the harsh tone. "Come on, Mr. Collins. It's time."

Collins looked with a sort of hesitant uncertainty at the operator, a warm symbol of ordered familiarity, then at the creepy, alien-featured colonel, whose very being oozed an essence of the Grim Reaper. The contrast was almost over-whelming. It was almost absurd even to imagine that such a thing actually could be happening.

The corrections man ran a tongue over his lips, retrieved his rifle, and stepped out of the truck. "You're right," he said. He took a deep breath. "Let's go get the son of a bitch."

There was confused speculation among the groups of men who watched Collins and Jarvis head up the road. No one really understood the military man's role in this affair, but he had the texture of someone you just didn't question. And Collins was head honcho. So obviously they knew what they were doing. Right? Sure. The man said stay put. All right. Fine. Beats the hell out of getting your ass blown off by a mad-dog killer.

Jarvis felt sure that the commando was making his approach on the down-ridge side of the vehicle line. Walker no doubt deduced the perimeter positions and probably knew it didn't extend far on the other side of the trucks. Besides, it was swampy down there. A jungle fighter must naturally be drawn to his familiar swamp. Jarvis just had that . . . feeling.

They took each step slowly and with caution, remembering the Dogman's mangled foot. They walked semi-crouched, about twenty feet apart, rifles leveled forward, Collins closer to the vehicles. A brush-choked drainage ditch separated them. The general idea was to dive into that ditch at the first indication of anything uncopacetic.

Collins was ready to dive into it right now. He was ready to bury himself in the cold, slimy muck, to become invisible in it, to drown himself in it, to come up for air only when the danger was past. He could control his trembling hands by his tight grip on his weapon, but there was nothing he could do about the shaky knee joints or the ice in his bladder, over which he had the sensation of having no control. The whole thing had, with an untouchably inexplicable strangeness, suddenly turned so monstrously big that it dwarfed any of his original perceptions. He felt puny in the face of it, microscopic, insignificant. And he felt acutely vulnerable. A feeling akin to what a frog must feel just before a giant foot squashes it. The sun was rising to noon in a sharp blue sky, raising the temperature to a springlike pleasantness. Although there was a cool breeze wafting through the trees, it did nothing to eliminate the sheen of sweat on Collins's pale, strained face. Walker was right, Collins thought bitterly, it was a fucking hot day in November.

"What if he doesn't want to talk?" Collins asked nervously. "What if he just opens fire?"

Jarvis moved liked a mountain cat hungry for meat, his entire being caught up in the intensity of the death stalk. His sharp, aquiline features perfectly fit his tight, forward profile as he crept along, his laser eyes piercing every rock, brush, and tree like twin jets of infrared radar. "If that happens," he replied, "then it's tough shit."

A sudden revelation swept over Collins, which filled him with a morbid hilarity. This stranger in the army suit, this mad-eyed, robotic military man who called himself Jarvis, was no stranger to the act of tracking down and killing human beings. But of course. It all fit into the macabre scheme of things. It was only natural that this Satan would be out here to claim his own. It was just the sensation of it being funny at a time like this that Collins found so odd.

It happened about eight vehicles from the front of the line. It was impossible to say precisely where it came from, except . . . just out of the swamp somewhere. The dark, egg-shaped object came floating in a high, lazy arc. Collins marveled at the little handle propelling away from the main object. If it weren't for the dark, oblong shape, it could have been a beautifully spinning high ball, hit out of Yankee Stadium. If it weren't for the dark, oblong shape, it wouldn't have looked so remarkably absurd drifting through so serene a sky.

Collins didn't know it yet, but a lightning-quick adrenaline rush had just jacked his body into overdrive. It was like someone had thrown the ditch at him face first. He suddenly found himself flailing in the muck and brush, his body, of its own accord, trying to bury itself deeper, ever deeper. With amazing clarity he heard the grenade slap into the mushy ground somewhere behind him. He wasn't entirely clear about the explosion, though. His pounding temples must have drowned out the sound of the sharply hollow *thwuump*! His mind must have refused to acknowledge the sound of sudden death. He was aware of flying mud and debris. And he was also aware of white-hot metal ripping a raw furrow across his shoulders. The bullwhip lash of pain and the realization that he had been hit with shrapnel came at the same instant. And from somewhere in the swamp he thought he heard maniacal laughter, then someone calling his name. A voice from the grave, surely. Because everything was black. Black. Suffocating, choking black. He couldn't breathe!

"A frag don't frag twice," he heard a robotic voice say. "Close but no cigar. You can come out now, Mr. Collins."

Embarrassed, frustrated, angrily ashamed, Collins eased his face up out of the mud. Jarvis's mocking smirk made him want to kill, but the colonel's bloody leg dispelled the impulse. The outside of the Intelligence man's upper right leg was a mess of minced flesh, entwined with fatigue material.

Jarvis chuckled at Collins's slack-jawed stare. "So you took a splinter, too, pal. But it didn't kill you, did it? Lighten up, buddy. He was just saying hello. Believe me, if he'd wanted to, he'd have sent that grenade up your ass." Another irritating chuckle. "Shit, you hit it like a pro. I thought you were trying to dig your way to China!"

"Jesus H. Christ!" Collins blustered in disbelief. "What kind of an insane fucking game are you guys playing, anyway?"

"The big one," Jarvis replied as he sneaked a cautious peek over the lip of the ditch. "Get on up here and turkey-call your man out. He's down in that swamp somewhere."

Wincing with pain, feeling his shirt stuck to his back with blood, Collins crawled up alongside the colonel. Carefully and with great fear, he peered out of the ditch, staring hard into the gloomy, forbidden swamp. This was decidedly outside his realm of both experience and existence. It was too vivid a contrast to his daily living, and in the face of it he felt like a foolish, ineffectual clown. There had never been a class at the Institute that taught you how to deal with . . . Christ . . . convicted commandos. But when you've got your duty to do . . .

"Walker!" he yelled. His voice echoed dully. "This is Dick Collins, and I'm the superintendent of corrections! Come on out of there and give yourself up! This is your last chance! We've got you and you know it! I'm ordering you to surrender!"

This authoritative ultimatum was met with mocking silence. Which made the colonel laugh. Which made Collins mad, since he was feeling self-conscious enough already.

"I thought you said he wanted to talk," Collins snapped angrily.

"Oh, he'll talk, all right," Jarvis replied. The weird, war-crazy grin he wore was enough to make Collins's skin crawl. "But first you have to raise him from the swamp. You have to know how to bring him out of the jungle."

Impervious to his painful-looking wound, the colonel bunched his legs up under him. He made sure his thirty-round banana clip was secure, and hitting the select-fire switch, he made sure that his piece was jacked to—hey, hey—rock and roll. Then he threw his head back and screamed. The shriek that tore out of his throat was so full of venom, so demonically inhuman, so emphatic, that spittle flew from his mouth. The single sentence, delivered as abruptly as a knife to the guts, left Collins paralyzed with icy horror:

"What's the spirit of the bayonet?"

Kill! Kill! Kill! His head blew apart from within. The pain came in a blinding white sheet, like it did when you took the injections, temporarily immobilizing him. *What's the spirit of the bayonet? Kill! Kill! Kill!* He clenched his teeth against his bursting brain, clenched his teeth against the freezing water he was lying in, a swampy depression, covered with moss, an Asian water buffalo lost in the Maine woods, freezing. Freezing because in truth hell was cold, not hot like they wanted you to believe.

They always wanted you to believe something. It always had to be awfully wrong. It always had to make no sense. Like this. It was a setup—every instinct told him so. Who knew how to set up a commando? Kill! Kill! Kill! It kept reverberating, pounding, pulsing through his brain. Who knew the program? Who knew the codes? And now there was a voice, a screaming voice flung from the bowels of a lost hell. A voice to go with the image of the man Walker had seen through the binoculars. J! Who else? The sinister familiarity that had made his stomach lurch, his head burst from within. Something about being ruthlessly torn away from lovely Claudine. Something about prisons and the technicians. Something about old scores to settle, promises made to dying men. Scattered memories in the dark cave of his consciousness flew about like flapping bats, frantic, startled by a sudden flare.

Get your shit together, boy! You can't lose it now!

Then his mind was a fast-moving freight train, clacking rapidly through a kaleidoscope of bloody, mangled images, shoot-outs on the borderlines of madness, gunfights in some of the slimiest hellholes of the universe. Torn limbs flew by, colorfully trailing whatever bits and strands that used to hold them to functional bodies, and nonfunctional bodies lying in row upon row upon row, stinking up the heavy, wet air with their obscene stillness.

Finally the barreling ghost train ground to a screeching halt in the middle of the jungle. North. Way north. And Walker, the conductor, the ticket-taker, the engineer, stepped outside of his mind. This was it. The drop and the rendezvous. Infiltration, exfiltration. Escape and evasion. "You have but one purpose, and that is to close with and destroy the enemy." The unmarked chopper made a hasty departure, leaving the six-man team to do whatever it was they did. And only the squad leader, the lieutenant with the coordinates, knew whatever it was they intended to do. And he would tell his men what to do whenever it came time for it to be done. That was the way of it.

They would go north. And from this point onward they would be neither recognized nor acknowledged by any government in existence. What they were going to do was . . . was a burden the lieutenant alone carried. So they went north, beating their way through the steamy, suffocating, triple-canopy jungle, using trails known to no man. It was the

most taxing, physically excruciating exertion ever set before
the humble human animal. Whatever meager energy they
had left at the end of a wet day's struggle was quickly
sucked up by the leeches and the mutant mosquitos.

And then, by an off-the-wall chance, they encountered a
roving band of Cong bandits. They easily wiped out the
Cong, but as fortune would have it, one of their own took a
bad belly wound. Even in the midst of so much murder and
mayhem this accident was a profound tragedy. They ban-
daged their man up as best they could. It was a grim, silent
ritual, because no one needed to tell him that a dust-off
chopper would not be coming to take him to medical aid. He
would have to make his own way back as best as he was
able, which, bigheartedly, he assured everyone he could do.
And if he couldn't, well, there was the ring. The Black
Widow. They all wore one. On the inside of the ring was a
small black capsule, and inside the capsule was a cleverly
contrived little needle. The capsule was loaded with a lethal
dose of cyanide. The wounded man could puncture himself
wherever his hand could reach, should it become necessary
for him to liberate his struggling soul from his tormented
body.

The remainder of the team went on but not far. It became
apparent to everyone that the wounded man was never going
to make it back. They were so deep in denied territory that
his chances were next to nothing. The Cong would get him.
Of that there could be little doubt. And when the Cong got
him, he would talk. It was nothing to be ashamed of. The
body was not designed to endure what the Cong did to it.
You talked, then you died. The ring could get him out of it.
But even in the face of extreme adversity a man is still reluctant to do what has to be done. Even dangling by the
heels over a pit of open coals, smelling the sickening aroma
of his own roasting flesh, a man is still hoping for the next
deal that will give him a chance at a straight run.

So someone had to go back and help convince the
wounded man to do the right thing. Men never get so hard
that they can't find something harder yet to do. It took an

ignorant country boy to go back. The kind of ignorant, gangly country boy who could stand in the middle of a bombed-out road and gawk walleyed at a bunch of gooks fucking a Cong bitch in a mud hole. Twiddling his rifle.

The team went on. The destination was an isolated pagoda. Unusual activity. Unmarked choppers coming and going, dropping off dignitaries and high-muck-a-mucks who dripped money on both sides of the dirty game. Familiar faces whose identities were to be immediately and forever erased from conscious memory. And there, hiding in their tiger stripes, glaring out from the dark, dripping jungle, lurked the team come to kill someone. They came to kill someone because that's what they did for a living. Assassins come to claim a debt.

But just before the final phase of Operation Aggravated Murder, a radio transmission came through, canceling the mission. The word came from high up. Way high up. Deals had been made, contracts honored. So they returned to rendezvous with only the lieutenant ever knowing whose life had been bought by a timely transfer of funds. Or land. Or position. So what happened up there did not happen at all.

What really happened, happened on the way back to rendezvous. In a jungle clearing, just before they reached the LZ, the top of the lieutenant's head blew apart like a rotten cantaloupe, his memory splattered all over the jungle floor. It was the result of a single crosshatched dumdum fired by a lone sniper. A hasty search failed to turn up the sniper, but they found a shell casing with markings that indicated it had been ejected from an M14.

Finally the chopper came. When they boarded, they were not especially surprised to find another man inside, fresh out of the jungle. He had sharp features chiseled out of lava rock. He had eyes as cold as the winds of hell. He had a robotic voice. And he had an M14 in his lap, with the elevation window raised and the windage recently set. No, nobody was surprised to see J.

Later, in the forward camps, rumors came and rumors went. Most notable among the many rumors concerned the nonexistent assassin team that didn't go north. Rumor had it that had the nonexistent team been successful at not doing what they weren't up there to do, then they all would have met with an unfortunate ambush long before they ever reached the LZ. And somewhere in the obscure mists of all these things that weren't happening, there was J, slithering, sliding, shadowlike. Yes, and there were his eyes of ice, always there to coldly calculate and take inventory of the wreckage of hidden incidents that never took place.

Again the voice of the damned came screaming through the swamp.

"What's the spirit of the bayonet?!"

This time a disc slipped in Walker's brain. Channels changed with a metallic, cordite-tasting click. *Kill! Kill! Kill!* went spinning out of his mind, went spinning out into the cosmos to make its circle around the universe, to return within a hair's breadth of a second, screaming . . . *J! J! J!*

The water was freezing cold, cold like hell, and he knew that if he lay in it much longer, hypothermia would numb him, and J would kill him. Yes, J would kill him. J would kill him because you never left the jungle. They brought your body back, and it was only a shell. Your mind, your soul still sweltered in the steaming jungle, sad because it could not join its body. You were already killed, and this was just a final hanging on in a ghost world that no longer knew you. Walker was a fool ever to have thought otherwise. He understood the width and the depth of the monster. Oh, God, how he understood.

He rose. He rose fast. The freezing water came cascading off him, and the dripping moss flew away from him like parts of a reptilian body torn free. His wet, smeared face was twisted in a death grin, the lips pulled as though by G-force back over his teeth.

"I've killed you, anyway, Collins!" he screamed weirdly. And his M16 bucked in his frozen hands like a thing alive, the sputtering, *ack-ack*ing shells seeking to cut a stitch through some shadowy gook who lived at the back of his mind.

And when his magazine clicked empty, and before he could bring the Uzi to line, there came J. J rose up out of the ditch like the mulchy stench of the jungle, come to claim the body and join it to the soul.

"Tough shit, motherfucker!" J snarled as spent casings came flying out of the rapidly working chamber, and 5.56-mm NATO rounds cut through the commando.

Walker jerked with every slug that hit him. He shook. He rocked. He teetered. Water splattered off him with the hammerlike force of the bullets hitting, and blood spewed in spraying fountains out the back of him. But when J's clip ran dry, he was still standing. A hollow, bubbling sound was working in his throat. Then it came out of the weirdly grinning mouth in a grotesque burp of blood.

"Fuck you!"

And slowly, and with what looked like intense relief, the commando sank back down into the swamp that was his forever.

CHAPTER
SIXTEEN

Collins was shaking so bad that getting his cigarette lit was a major endeavor. The sight of Walker bursting up out of that swamp like some prehistoric demon had rattled his cage. Worse, though, was the raw, brutal ferocity of the exchange of gunfire, which had unnerved every civilized fiber in him. Barbarians! Jesus, these guys were nothing more than ancient, savage barbarians, equipped with the latest in modern technology! Mutant barbarians. Where the hell did they come from? Who made them?

Well, thank God it was over. This shit had no place in twentieth-century American life. Imagine something like that come screaming through your living room right in the middle of the evening news! Collins meant to make sure that no other prisoner of his ever stepped over the deep end like that again. By God, there would be some serious changes in security! He'd learned his lesson. No telling if any one of those seething punks might be capable of the same thing. The only way to make sure was to make sure every one of the bastards toed the line.

He pulled the radio out of his belt sheath and was about to press the transmit button when he suddenly became aware of a hot barrel pressing gently against his ribs. His face went white with horror. Horror because he instantly knew what the next play in this military man's vicious game was. He could tell by the absolute lack of expression on Colonel Jarvis's face.

"W-what's the meaning of this?" the superintendent of corrections asked desperately. God, he didn't want to get blown away in some dirty ditch like a . . . a common grunt! "I mean, we got our man. What are you doing?"

"In this funny little circle of ours," Jarvis replied softly, "you have to understand that things . . . well . . . they go round and round." With the slightest twist of his lips he pressed the trigger, putting a burst of automatic gunfire through Collins's heart.

And then there was J. And J's mind clacked away like an alien computer. Who else? Who else had been privy to the conversations concerning X-Two's profile? Input. Digest. Readout: Roderick. Brandon. Progress status to phase . . . *terminal!*

He wobbled up out of the ditch, limped, dragging his bloody leg, oddly glazed eyes fixed forward, twin chips of cold ice. And he was breathing hard, nostrils flared, inhaling deeply the singular intoxication of fresh carnage. Front of the line, his mind kept clicking. Front of the line. Roderick. Brandon.

Brandon was still sitting on the wooden box, never suspecting that his security men had been searching frantically for both him and Roderick. But they'd been looking in the secure zones, not up the line, and they'd been afraid that maybe the governor had been taken hostage again. But Brandon's stupid grin had not left him. So lost was he in dark fascination with Roderick's dead body that he hardly acknowledged J's dragging approach. Dragging. Dragging his worthless leg like a machine flapping along with a flat tire. The engine hummed perfectly, but one of the exterior parts was malfunctioning, giving it awkward, out-of-balance motion.

J absorbed the scene like a dry sponge soaks up liquid. A crimson stain radiated out from a small black slit in the back of Roderick's crumpled jacket. He was dead. That was dark heart blood, which told J what had happened as surely as if he'd been there to witness it. The commando had made a clean and flawless kill. But he had left Brandon. Why? Because in the commando's distorted visions of right and wrong Brandon was already dead, therefore unfit to be killed by a man of war.

J, fortunately, did not hold such distorted visions. He assimilated the extent of the governor's shock and concluded that he might possibly snap out of it. But he would never be the same again. And if he would never be the same again, then it only followed that he could never be trusted again. Not that he was ever trusted in the first place. But that wasn't the issue at hand. It never was. For anybody.

"We might have been able to find you a seat in the Senate," J said. His voice was tinted with cynical regret.

"Yes." Brandon grinned dumbly.

"It's unfortunate that that is now impossible."

"Yes." Brandon grinned dumbly.

J machine-gunned him at point-black range, blasting him off the box and wrecking his whole upper torso as though it had been plowed through with a meat grinder. The chopper effect of the M16's ballistics was something that only a Pentagon death technician could appreciate.

"Holy God Almighty!" a horrified voice yelled from somewhere down the line. "He's murdered the governor! Did you see that? Jesus Christ, did you see that? He's murdered the governor!"

It was Ray Smith. Hearing the sounds of war up here somewhere, the game commissioner had gotten worried and had come creeping up with his main force, believing that Walker might have been forced into a final showdown, at best pinned down. Believing that Colonel Jarvis and Collins might be in need of help, regardless of radio instructions. He didn't know that the commando had been shot to shit down in the swamp. He didn't know that Collins lay in a dirty ditch, blown away like a common grunt. He had come upon the scene just in time to see that strange army guy kill the governor in cold blood.

"Get him!" the commissioner hollered hysterically. "Get him! Hurry! Jesus, he's murdered the governor!"

With the spell of stealth broken, men came charging out of everywhere, most of them not knowing what they were going for but rushing, anyway. Some thought it was the commando, others didn't think at all.

J wheeled in fury, hissing like a trapped animal. Swinging the M16 around, he let loose a burst, hitting a few, sending the rest diving for cover among the trucks and the trees, thus giving himself a chance for a break. "Dumb shits!" he kept muttering as he hopped madly for the woods. He hopped. He hobbled. He staggered with grim purpose. Into the jungle. "Dumb-shit motherfuckers!" he kept muttering. What did they know about it? What in Christ could they possibly know about it? None of the ignorant scumbags had ever been out of their own backyards. What did they know about it?

And then, on the far side of the skidder trail, just before he reached the woods, just before he stepped into his jungle, Jarvis stopped and turned. He saw hollering men running everywhere, dragging their wounded to the rear, while others surged forward, hot on the trail of the killer. Then he saw the remnants of the team, blown apart man by man. Then he saw Walker sinking into the swamp. Then he saw his daughter's body, mutilated, raped, lifeless in a ditch. Then he saw the vengeance he'd exacted in thirty years across three continents. His war against humanity. The bodies he had put in their graves. The souls he had lain to waste. And would it ever stop? No, it would never stop.

Yes, it would stop. Because, standing on the edge of his jungle, he took a hobbling step back toward all those men who had guns aimed at him. Some melt came out of the ice in his eyes. Some sag came into the hard marble his face was carved in. He laid the barrel of his assault weapon up against his head. He looked at all those miserable humans crouched down there in fear. He could clearly see their lack of understanding. "Mission accomplished," he said softly.

Then, sure he was aimed in the right direction, he let loose a burst.

EPILOGUE

A red scum lay on the stagnant pool. Then the pool trembled ever so slightly and clumps of moss bobbed. Then the dark water gave way with a sucking sound, and a splotched thing came crawling up out of it. It gasped harshly, wheezed, choked, belched out a curious spray of water, blood, and mud mixed together. It shuddered, heaved, trembled horribly, its teeth clenched, then clacking, then clenched against the awful cold. The freezing cold of hell.

The commando began to crawl, a picture of mighty agony. He was numb with pain. He was numb with cold. But his smeared, blackened, streaked face wore an unearthly determination. Because he knew that somewhere out there, somewhere over the distant ridges, there was a warm place where the sun would shine on him all day long. He could feel the warmth of it washing over him with a deep, glowing serenity.

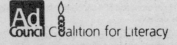